Panther Mountain: Lydia's Story

By Christy Perry Tuohey

Edited by Vicki Entreken
Cover design: Sheree Wentz/Rare Hare Creative
Author photo: Josh Wells/K&W Photography

Table of Contents

For Patrick and Dana

Prologue

I can't believe she's gone. She was just here, visiting, reading to the children.

It has fallen on me to write a memory of her. Not a flowery eulogy, but a true, fair accounting of who she was. I asked my sister to read back to me what I had written. Maude's voice was soft and clear.

"Mother's life was full of extraordinary challenges, but she also enjoyed material wealth, the love of her family and one particular lifelong friendship which, though born out of the violence of civil war, grew in love and grace over time.

"She and Edgar truly had a bond, didn't they?" Maude said, looking up at his photo on our mantel. I nodded. She looked back down at the paper.

"She faced disappointment, especially toward the end. Her family changed in ways she could not have expected or controlled, but she always held on to her faith. She was a strong woman, brave and kind. I am blessed to have had her as my mother and, indeed, a role model."

--Blanche Malcolm Coleman

Part One: War

LATEST NEWS

THE WAR HAS BEGUN!!!

FORT SUMTER ATTACKED

YESTERDAY MORNING!

Bombardment All Day

Yesterday.

By our telegraphic dispatches it will be seen that the ball has been opened and the dance of death has begun.

--Cleveland Morning Leader,
April 13, 1861

Early yesterday morning people began to collect on the Square and on Superior Street to witness the departure of the gallant Seventh Regiment. At about 8 ½ [8:30 a.m.] the sound of music was heard up Euclid Street, and they were seen approaching, headed by Leland's Band. Both sides of the street were lined with people, and the number grew larger momentarily, while yards, doorways and windows were filled with spectators, a large proportion of them women, and waving handkerchiefs or tearful eyes bore witness to the sympathy which was felt for those young men who were going forth to do battle in behalf of that which is equally dear to all of us.

At the depots and along the track there were gathered from five to eight thousand people, among whom were many of our most respectable citizens and several Ministers of the Gospel. An unusually large proportion of the crowd were women, nearly all of whom appeared to have husbands, brothers or lovers among the soldiers, and many of whom were weeping bitterly.

The soldiers were cheerful and endeavored to console those whom they were leaving, with promises of a safe and speedy return.

--"**Departure of the Seventh,**"*Cleveland Morning Leader*, **Monday, May 6, 1861**

Chapter One

Panther Mountain, Nicholas County, Virginia, late May 1861

Logan's green eyes glinted in the sun, his face flushed with challenge.

"Race you around yonder tree and back!!" he called out, as we cantered the horses in the pasture. Grinning, he looked tall in the saddle.

"You're on," I called back, scanning the field before us. "Maysie, count us down, okay?" We circled around to a stump as our starting point.

My friend nodded her head, brunette curls bobbing. She put a foot on the stump and shouted.

"On your marks. Get set. Go!"

I sat up in the saddle, shortened Blackie's reins and was off, galloping even with Logan and Miss Lou. "Hyah!" he urged her.

My sleeves flapped and hair whipped into my eyes. We circled a tree and then Miss Lou surged past, hoofs kicking up grass chunks. Barney chased us, barking, fur flying.

"Well, looks like I'm the winner," Logan announced as he sailed past the stump. "Better luck next time, Liddy!" I couldn't be upset. One look at that dimpled grin, that sandy hair, those eyes. Those eyes.

Logan jumped off of Miss Lou and Maysie sidled up next to him. "My, my, Logan, you sure are fast," she said, fingers twirling her bonnet ribbons. A shy smile crossed his face.

"Aw, it was nothin'," he replied, reaching down to pat Miss Lou's auburn neck.

"Next time, Stephenson, next time," I said.

I'd known Logan for all my seventeen years. We grew up on Panther Mountain. He lived with his sister Becky and her husband, my uncle Billy Grose, on account of Logan's and Becky's parents being dead. He was a

11

little older than me. We went to school together, played together, went to church together.

I dismounted Blackie, opened the gate and she wandered over to the trough where Barney joined her. Maysie said she needed to get back down the mountain and help her mama with supper. "Logan, I don't suppose you could walk with me down the hill?" she asked

"Sure, Maysie," Logan agreed.

Maysie looked up at him. *You sure are helpless for a country girl, Maysie,* I thought. *I've never known you to need an escort home.*

"All right, thanks for the race, Logan," I called out. "See you at church, Maysie." I stepped up onto the porch, then paused and turned to watch them walk off down the road together.

Inside, Mama stood with her hands on her hips, towel over her shoulder. She shook her head.

"I declare, Liddy Jane, if you keep riding that horse in your good dresses they'll soon be too dirty and ragged to wear."

"Don't worry, Mama," I said. "I'm careful as can be. 'Sides, this is my work dress, not a Sunday one."

Mama picked a rubber band off the kitchen doorknob and tied my thick, straggly hair into a ponytail. "You are a beauty, you," she said, standing on her tiptoes, and kissing my cheek. Me? A beauty? She's just saying that. She thinks all of her children are beautiful and handsome. I had straight blonde hair, skinned back. Freckles dotted my nose and cheeks. Were my eyes pretty? My lashes as long as Maysie's? Did Logan think I was a beauty?

****

"Brothers and sisters, in Jeremiah 12, verse five, we read that the prophet was complaining to God...imagine! Complaining to God! But Jeremiah had his persecutors, those who were trying to stop his efforts to spread God's message. Oh yes! Just as we have, today, those who would stop us from spreading the Gospel, who would criticize us for our beliefs. Just as we have those nowadays who are working to tear our land apart. Oh, it has been peaceful here for quite a while. We have had our quiet lives, our farms, our

12

homes, living and working hard, and resting well at day's end. We have had mostly contentment. Security.

"But God warns Jeremiah: 'If thou hast run with the footmen, and they have wearied thee, then how canst thou contend with horses? And if in the land of peace, wherein thou trustest, they wearied thee, then how wilt thou do in the swelling of Jordan?'

Pastor Phelps' scripture reading about fast horses reminded me of Logan rushing past me in our race.

"God asks the great prophet that if he has trouble contending with only the smallest of life's annoyances, how will he handle the big crisis? If running with footmen wears Jeremiah out, God asks, how will he keep up with the fast horses? If he grew weary in times of peace, what would he do when war came?"

After the service ended, I climbed over the back of the bench and scooted over to Maysie who was in the row behind me. Mama gave me a stare over her spectacles, a look that told me she wished I would stop climbing over church benches in my Sunday dress. Daddy had always called me a tomboy but Mama kept after me to be a bit more ladylike. I would be 18 in a few months and would have to think about becoming a real lady then.

Maysie tied her bonnet strings under her chin and looked up, smiling. "Hey, Liddy. How are you?"

"Alright, I guess," I said. Logan walked over to us and sat down. He punched me in the arm. "How ya doing, Lids? Uh, nice dress, Maysie."

I rubbed my arm. "Good. Goin' fishin' later?" We had a favorite spot on Laurel Creek.

"Nah, not today. Maysie asked me to give her some riding lessons this afternoon."

Maysie looked down, pretending to be all shy and coy.

"Well, you are a good one to learn from," I said with a catch in my throat. "Maybe you could teach me sometime, too, Logan?"

He snorted. "You could teach *me* a thing or two!" He turned back to Maysie. "See you after lunch?"

A feeling came over me when he said that. Like cold water in my face. I realized that Maysie's behavior the other day wasn't so much strange as lovestruck.

After Logan got up and walked away, she tilted her head and looked at me. "Oh, you don't mind, do you? I mean, I thought you and Logan were just friends. Isn't that right?" she asked.

"Uh, yes. Yes, that's right," I stammered. "Just friends. Neighbors." I didn't know what else to say.

Maysie pursed her lips. "Well, that's what I thought. I knew you wouldn't mind." She grinned and squeezed my hand.

I slipped my hand away, stood up and said, "Well, I must be getting along now."

I took my little sister's hand, we called her Little Peg, and shuffled behind the others walking out of church. I squinted in the sunlight. Squeaky wagon wheels rumbled up the road. Ben Dorsey, dark-haired and hazel-eyed, cut quite a fine figure in his Sunday vest and string tie. He held the reins as his kin rode in the wagon, bobbing and chatting.

Ben tipped his hat. "Mornin'," he called out to the bunch of us before they headed toward their farm at the back side of the mountain. He and Logan were friends, but I didn't know him that well. His family went to the Bethel Methodist Church, South. Ours was the Bethel Methodist Church, North. There used to be only one church up until the split over slavery, the year I was born.

****

Uncle Frank waved and shouted, "Hello, ladies!" Little Adam burst through the screen door, shouting, "Who's comin', Papa?"

"Why it's your Aunt Peggy and Cousin Liddy and Cousin Mary Ann," he answered, scooping the little towhead into his arms. Adam was scrawny for a five-year-old. He waved at us. "Come on in and see our Lucy!"

"All right, Adam Clark, here we come!" Mama chuckled. "Where's your brother?"

Out back. We've been playin' soldiers."

Just then I heard sobbing coming from behind a bush. Out came three-year-old Billy Backus, red-faced, tears streaming down his chubby little cheeks.

"What's wrong, Billy?" I asked, stooping down to get a better look.

"Adam won't be the Reb." His little chin trembled. "I wanna be a Yank!"

"Aw, I'm sorry, Billy," I said and opened my arms. He ran into my hug. "Right now, I need your help. I need you to show me where Baby Lucy and your Mama are."

He sniffled and then pointed to the front door. "Thatta way."

He held my hand and we walked in, met with a nice breeze from the back door. Mama and Mary Ann were already in the bedroom with Aunt Caroline.

"Come on in, Liddy," Aunt Caroline called out to me. "I'm just feeding Lucy." My lovely aunt was propped up on bed pillows, her dark, braided ponytail falling across her nightgown sleeve as she nursed her baby.

The little bundle in her arms was wrapped up snug in a white cotton blanket. Lucy's skin was rosy, not reddish like some babies. Wisps of light brown hair stuck up around her tiny head. It was good to have a new baby, so tiny and calm.

"Peggy, I wish I could have gone to church today. Who was there? What did the pastor preach on?" My mother sat next to her sister's bedside and told her about the sermon, the songs we sang and the folks who had come out that sunny May morning to worship together.

Aunt Caroline asked Mary Ann if she'd like to hold Lucy. "Sure," she answered, her voice ever so slightly wobbly. She looked at me and I imagined what was going through her mind. *Do you think she knows? Does she want me to practice holding a baby?*

I felt a tug at my skirt. Adam looked up at me with big blue eyes and asked if I would play pick-up sticks with him. He pulled me out of the room and toward the porch.

Uncle Frank was rocking Billy, who had fallen asleep. Mr. Hendrickson from next door was leaning up against the porch rail, chatting away. I sat cross-legged with my sister and cousin, picked up a bunch of wheat straws and dropped them onto the warm wood floor.

"Mason says he saw bags tossed in the ash can," Mr. Hendrickson said. "The secesh may have looked at our ballots and then throwed them out."

On Election Day, Daddy voted at the court clerk's office while Will and I waited in the wagon. Our family and most of our neighbors were for the Union and did not want Virginia to break away from the rest of the United States. There had been a flurry of shouts, curses, and name-calling. The secessionists stood near the door of the rough frame building, hands on their rifles and revolvers, trying to cow the men they suspected were going to vote to stay with the Union.

"Well," Uncle Frank started, lowering his voice, "I guess we can't know for sure. I heard the same story. We all need to be on our guard."

"I for one do not want to become part of that mess Jeff Davis is stirring up," Mr. Hendrickson said. "I want Virginia to stay right where we are. But I don't say that too loud these days."

"No, neither do I," Frank said.

Daddy had told us that it was worth facing the barrel of a gun to vote against secession and slavery, which was against our Christian principles. But listening to the men talk, I had a feeling his vote didn't count. I snapped a straw in my hand.

Chapter Two

Renick home, Panther Mountain

I shared an open loft, divided by sheets tacked onto the rafters, with my sisters. Mary Ann was closest to my age at 15, Caroline was eleven, Little Peg was eight and Lizzie was just old enough to climb up the ladder since turning four. I was changing out of my Sunday dress when I heard sniffing in the far corner.

"Mary Ann? Are you alright?" I peeled back the sheet and saw her sitting on the edge of her small bed, her back to me. She nodded. "What is it? What's got you upset?" I sat down next to her and saw the tears rolling down her cheeks.

"I…I know I should be happy. But I'm also scared. And…and…ashamed."

"Ashamed?"

She put her right hand on her stomach.

I touched my fingers to my lips and squinted. Mary Ann and Jon Pierson had been sweet on each other since last summer's camp meeting. He was older. His family's farm was near Bethel.

"You will have to tell Mama and Daddy, the sooner the better."

"I know," she nodded, wiping her nose on her dress sleeve.

I grabbed her hand and squeezed it. "Don't you cry now. God has blessed you with a child."

"Will He forgive me? For not waiting until my wedding night?"

"Sister, he forgives everyone who asks," I answered. "But that doesn't mean you can't also give thanks to Him for your baby." She hugged my neck hard. I felt so bad for her. She wasn't the youngest bride I'd known but being pregnant while most girls her age were still carefree would be hard for her. Goodness, what will Mama and Daddy think?

Later that afternoon, I was watching the little ones play in the sun. It was so hot, I went inside to fetch some lemonade for them. As I walked toward the kitchen, I heard my mother's voice. "What? How could you let that happen?"

"I thought we raised you better than that, young lady." Daddy's voice sounded sharp as a scythe cutting through weeds as I stood behind the kitchen door, listening.

"I...I'm sorry..." Mary Ann answered them in between sobs. "I know I have sinned."

Somebody slammed a hand on the table. "It's a lady's duty to refuse a young man's passions," Mama said.

There was a long pause where no one said anything. Mary Ann's sniffing was the only sound.

Then Daddy's voice softened a little. "Mary Ann, you know we are fond of Jonathan. And I guess that's a good thing, seeing as how he'll now be our son-in-law...."

"You'll need to call on Pastor, James," Mama said matter-of-factly. "We need to have a wedding and quick."

****

I stood next to Mary Ann after Daddy walked her down the aisle. She wore her blue Sunday dress and a crown of larkspur and violets. Jon, hair slicked back, wearing his best coat, beamed at his bride. I was happy for them, but also felt a little pang of something. Jealousy? Sadness because my sister was moving out of the house? I wasn't sure.

Virginia Ordinance of Secession, 1861

Now, therefore, we, the people of Virginia, do declare and ordain, That the ordinance adopted by the people of this State in convention on the twenty-fifth day of June, in the year of our Lord one thousand seven hundred and eighty-eight, whereby the Constitution of the United States of America was ratified, and all acts of the General Assembly of this State ratifying and adopting amendments to said Constitution, are hereby repealed and abrogated; that the union between the State of Virginia and the other States under the Constitution aforesaid is hereby dissolved, and that the State of Virginia is in the full possession and exercise of all the rights of sovereignty which belong and appertain to a free and independent State.

And they do further declare, that said Constitution of the United States of America is no longer binding on any of the citizens of this State.

Chapter Three

Panther Mountain, Nicholas County, Virginia, early June, 1861

Crickets chirped as the sun slowly picked its way down through the clouds. Mama and my younger sisters and I snapped peas into pots on the front lawn. The air was still warm but in that early June way, not the muggy hot of July or August.

Barney sat up and barked. I felt the thuds of galloping hooves vibrate through the ground beneath me. Logan rode Miss Lou up to our front gate. "Did you hear the news?" he called out.

"What news?" I asked, shading my eyes against the setting sun behind his head.

"The governor ordered all Virginia troops to serve under Jeff Davis. Home guards, everybody. There are notices tacked on trees all around Summersville."

"Oh dear," Mama said, bringing a hand up to her chest. "I suppose we should have expected it, but it is all happening so fast."

Logan tied Miss Lou to the post. He walked over and sat down with us on the grass. His hands and wrists were red from washing troughs.

"Who's Jeff Davis?" Lizzie asked.

"He's the president of the southern states," Logan explained gently, popping a pea into his mouth.

Sister Caroline piped up. "I thought Abraham Lincoln was our president. What happened to him?"

"Well, he is still our *real* President. It's just that most of the folks in the eastern part of our state voted to leave the United States and join a new, made-up country." *Logan is so good at talking to children*, I thought.

"Could I give Miss Lou some pea pods?" Little Peg asked.

Logan grinned at her. "Sure. Just a few, okay?"

She nodded, brown strands of hair gently floating in the evening breeze. Mama stood up and picked up her pot of shelled peas. "I reckon it'll be dark soon, girls. You can stay out here and talk with Logan a bit longer, but come in when the lightning bugs commence to flickering."

Lizzie yawned and followed Mama inside. Caroline snapped her peas while Peg fed Miss Lou.

"How are those riding lessons going?" I asked Logan.

He let out a puff of air and chuckled. "Maysie's not much of a rider," he answered. "Not like you." I felt proud to hear those words. *Yes, I am good. Glad he recognized that.*

Maybe it'll just take her some time," I replied, looking down at the grass. I suddenly felt shy around my neighbor, my friend, my horse race challenger. "What were you doing in town today?"

"Picked up some supplies at Hardman's," he answered. "Oh, that reminds me, Mrs. Hardman asked me to tell you your book has come in."

"Good! I've been waiting a long time for that one."

"What is it?" he asked.

"The Marble Faun."

"About a deer?"

I looked up at him and smiled. "No, silly. It's about one of those Greek myth critters. A statue, I think. Mr. Backus told me I might like it."

Logan and I usually sat next to each other in Mr. Backus' home school, near the big open fireplace in the kitchen during the colder months. We attended classes until the time when Logan was needed on the farm and I was needed at home to help with the cooking, cleaning, and children.

"We got some good education from Mr. Backus," he said, nodding. "You sure love all that readin' and writin'."

"I do. But we're all right lucky you're as good at making saddles as you are."

"Did you hear about Ben?"

"No, what about him?"

"He signed up," he said, chewing on a pea pod. "Confederate, as you might imagine. Said he thought it was the right thing to do. Makes me think maybe I should sign up too. But, you know, with the Union."

"That's an awful dangerous business," I said, watching lightning bugs slowly rise like sparks from a fire.

"Billy says he needs me around the farm," he continued, "But I can't think of not doing my duty."

"Well, I...we...would certainly worry about you if you did go off to war." Off to war. The words echoed in my head. When would we see each other after he was off to war?

"Liddy, time to come in," Mama called from the door. She held up a lantern and in the light I could see the gold-green flecks in Logan's eyes.

"Coming!" I called back. "Do you think...well, maybe I could write you letters. If you think that would be alright."

He smiled so wide that both dimples showed up. "Well of course, silly! And I would write back to you if you did!" He patted my forearm.

I exhaled. "Well, I guess I'd better be gettin' inside." We both stood up and, for a moment, I thought about kissing him on the cheek. Instead, I picked up my pea pot.

"G'night, Lydia," he said.

"Here, take a pine torch with you." I grabbed one from the pile next to the door, lit it with the lantern flame and handed it to him. "G'night, Logan."

As he rode away, I watched his light fade into the night.

****

22

War report, Grafton, Va., June 25, 1861

General George McClellan, then in charge of the U.S. Army's Department of the Ohio, sat at his field desk, dipped his pen in a government-issue inkwell and wrote these lines, in hopes that when his men heard them from their commanding officers, their instincts to take revenge on fellow citizens might be quelled.

> *"You are here to support the Government of your country and to protect the lives and liberties of your brethren, threatened by a rebellious and traitorous foe. No higher and nobler duty could devolve upon you, and I expect you to bring to its performance the highest and noblest qualities of soldiers—discipline, courage and mercy. Bear in mind that you are in the country of friends, not enemies; that you are here to protect, not to destroy. Take nothing, destroy nothing, unless you are ordered to do so by your general officers. Remember that I have pledged my word to the people of Western Virginia that their rights in person and property shall be respected. I ask every one of you to make good this promise in its broadest sense."*

Barely a week after the ink on McClellan's proclamation had dried, the Restored Government of Virginia—secession opponents all—formed a legislative body in Wheeling, Virginia. Provisional Governor Francis Pierpont presented to lawmakers an official U.S. government document that confirmed Washington, D.C.'s recognition of the new state.

Wheeling, Va., July 3, 1861

"I have just learned that there were many of the Union men with their families driven into Ohio from Jackson County—from Ravenswood and that vicinity. It is also stated—for the truth of which I cannot vouch, that a regiment from Ohio passed into Virginia at Point Pleasant."

--Letter from Francis H. Pierpont, Governor, Restored Government of Virginia, to General George B. McClellan

Chapter Four

Along the Gauley-Bridge-Summersville-Sutton and Weston Turnpike, early July, 1861

As we rolled through town, we passed house after house of people loading up covered wagons with furniture, pots and pans, quilts and spinning wheels. Children filled jugs at pumps, grandparents packed food, pigs squealed in their pens.

Before the war, 250 residents lived in Summersville. The foundation for the new courthouse was partially laid before fighting broke out in Nicholas County, leaving an unfinished brick frame on the town green. "The exodus has begun," Daddy said. "I don't know where they'll all go but away from here."

Summersville buzzed with activity. Men tacked recruitment signs to trees and store posts. Boys stood in line on the town green, waiting to sign up for Captain Newman's Confederate regiment. Seated at a table, writing names into a book, was Private Ben Dorsey, dark hair parted to one side and falling over his right eye.

I caught a whiff of coffee as I opened the front door of Hardman's General Store. Floorboards creaked and popped from the heat. Daddy sat on a pickle barrel, waving his hands as he talked to a group of men.

"Good afternoon, Lydia," Mrs. Hardman called from behind the counter. "I have your package right here. Let me see now, where did I put it? Oh, here it is. There you go." She handed me the brown paper parcel, adjusted her spectacles, and wrapped the wire temples behind her ears.

"Much obliged, Mrs. Hardman," I said, dropping coins into her cupped hand. "I'm looking forward to sitting down in the shade to read it."

"Oh my, you'd have to get under a shade tree on a day like today. The heat is hard to bear."

"Yes ma'am," I replied.

"Well, Lydia, we appreciate your business. Only the Lord knows how we will stay open with all these folks leaving." The deep creases between her eyebrows showed her worry.

Just then my brother sprinted over to the counter. There was a shout out in the street, then another. Men's voices rose in a confusing chorus.

"Some Union men just got into town," Will said, his words rushing so fast he could barely get them out. "I heard him say they were ambushed and Clyde Brown was killed by a bunch of Rebs!"

"What!? Oh no!" Mrs. Hardman gasped, "Oh poor Annie and the children!"

The Brown family was big already, and Annie Brown was pregnant with her 8th. Losing her husband would surely devastate her. A tear rolled down Mrs. Hardman's cheek. The men sitting at checker boards stood up, one by one, and walked over to the store's front windows. We could see the sheriff through the glass.

A scuffle broke out on the green. Union supporters hurled rocks at the Confederate recruits and they, in turn, were charging after their attackers.

My heart thumped. Where was Daddy? I looked around the store but couldn't find him. I ran out onto the store's porch and clung to one of the posts to steady myself. Daddy was on the ground, prying a man's hands off of Ben's neck and ducking a brick as he did so. Captain Newman yelled for them to stop. Doctor Rader flew out of his office and sprinted across the road to help.

The captain fired a warning shot into the sky. Heads snapped and soldiers quickly formed a line, separating the angry mob from those who had been hit. I found myself walking toward the green, toward Daddy and Ben. "Liddy!" Will shouted behind me. "It's alright, brother," I said, panting. "Come along, let's get over to Daddy."

There were red finger marks on Ben's throat. Daddy helped him up from the grass. Ben coughed and sucked in a breath. "Thank you, Mr. Renick. You may have saved my life."

"Not at all, Ben. You would have done the same for me," Daddy replied. "Be sure to have Doc take a look at your neck."

26

The rock-throwers slowly backed away from the scene and walked, some in clusters, back to the shops and tavern. "Liddy and Will, let's head on home," Daddy said, wiping his brow, and motioning toward the wagon.

On the ride back, I sat up front. "Daddy, you helped Ben even though he's joined the Rebs," I said. "He's not on our side."

"No, he's not," Daddy answered. "But he is our neighbor and our Christian brother. We help each other because it's what God wants us to do

Blackie clopped over the rutted road, the wagon tottering side to side as it groaned up the mountain. I looked up through the thick green leaves as we passed under the trees. Dear *God*, I prayed in my head, *it is hard to understand why you allow fighting and war. Why?*

****

War report, western Virginia, late July 1861

One night, as raindrops tapped on a tent pitched about 35 miles north of Summersville, a young soldier who had signed up with his college classmates to fight for the Union wrote to his mother, a widow struggling to feed his younger siblings in upstate New York.

Salt Lick Bridge (Braxton County), Va.
July 27th, '61
Mrs. Elisabeth A. Hanson

    "Dear Mother,

    I, now amidst bustle & confusion in my tent in a camp of 3,000 soldiers, take my pen in hand to inform you that I as usual am enjoying health, a blessing much to be valued. Our regiment the 7th Ohio has now been in this state Virginia a month. As yet no engagements have occurred between us and the enemy, but it has undergone a few forced marches severe in the extreme in order to rescue Union men in Western Va. from destruction by the secessionists.

    When I look upon the people living in towns through which we pass, some talented, others not so much so, who might be ornaments in society were the opportunities of education to them accessible. I feel if necessary my life is going as a sacrifice to this cause."

    --Private Joseph Collins, Company C, Seventh Ohio Volunteer Infantry

Chapter Five

Panther Mountain, August 1, 1861

I woke up sweaty and wiped my face on the sheet. Summer heat and moisture swelled and filled the air around me. Coffee was brewing. I washed my face at the basin and tugged on a short-sleeved blouse and light cotton skirt.

Mama and Sis were standing at the stove, Daddy was perched in his chair at the kitchen table. Strips of bacon crackled in the skillet.

"G'morning, baby," Daddy said, his eyes puffy. He smoothed his ginger hair back. "How did you sleep?"

"Alright, I suppose," I said while yawning. "Come on over here, Sis." I sat down at the table and pulled my two-year-old sister up onto my lap.

"I reckon it was hot upstairs," Mama said as she cracked eggs on the edge of a bowl.

"Yes'm," I nodded and pinched off a piece of biscuit for Sis. We called her Sis because no one could think of a proper name for her. We had tried several names—Harriet, for my aunt Harriet Jane, was one idea that didn't stick.

Daddy sipped coffee as he read the Bible. "Here's a passage for our times," he said, putting his finger on a page.

He read to us:

> *"Finally, my brethren, be strong in the Lord, and in the power of his might.*
>
> *Put on the whole armour of God, that ye may be able to stand against the wiles of the devil.*
>
> *For we wrestle not against flesh and blood, but against principalities, against powers, against the rulers of the darkness of this world, against spiritual wickedness in high places.*

Wherefore take unto you the whole armour of God, that ye may be able to withstand in the evil day, and having done all, to stand.

Stand therefore, having your loins girt about with truth, and having on the breastplate of righteousness;

And your feet shod with the preparation of the gospel of peace;

Above all, taking the shield of faith, wherewith ye shall be able to quench all the fiery darts of the wicked.

And take the helmet of salvation, and the sword of the Spirit, which is the word of God:

Praying always with all prayer and supplication in the Spirit, and watching thereunto with all perseverance and supplication for all saints."

"Ephesians Six."

"What does 'supplication' mean?" Caroline asked.

Mama brought a heaping plate of eggs and bacon to the table and sat down. We bowed our heads, blessed the food, and dug in. "Supplication is a fancy word for prayer, I suppose," she answered gently. "A way of asking God for something you want very badly, that you ask very humbly of Him."

"It is no accident that God gave the apostle Paul the idea of God's armor," Daddy continued. "But instead of teaching us to pick up real guns and swords, he is telling us that God's truth and Spirit and salvation are the better weapons."

"Daddy, how can we...I...*believe* that faith and truth are enough to protect us? We've got soldiers all around the mountain, totin' guns, fixin' to fight each other and maybe us. How do we stay safe?"

"Well, darlin', we must be as wise as serpents but innocent as doves. That's what the Scripture tells us. We must be careful, and always on our toes about who is for us and who is against us. These are tough times, but we mustn't turn against each other, even those who want to break away and tear Virginia apart. We can't let them divide us."

Mama put her warm hand on mine. "Liddy Jane, be careful but don't be scared. We must be brave until this war is over. Pray God it will be soon." She half-smiled in a way that showed she was a little worried herself.

****

The church doors were opened wide when we got there. We took our mud-caked shoes off outside before walking into the sanctuary. Inside, benches were broken, the iron stove pushed onto its side, coal spewed across the floor. Pastor Phelps was picking torn pages from the pulpit Bible off the floor near the altar. He pushed a thick, dark swath of hair from his forehead. Hot moist air hung heavy in the room.

Our sacred place. Our safe place.

"Golly day! What a mess!" exclaimed my Uncle Covington as he walked in. Uncle A.J. shook his head and whistled low. "This cursed war...." he began, his voice shaking.

Pastor cleared his throat. "Gentlemen, we are in the presence of the Lord, even amid the ruins here. Let us temper our words out of reverence for the Almighty."

"Of course," Uncle A.J. nodded and blushed. "Please forgive my outburst."

I stepped up onto the chancel, rolled up my sleeves, and wiped sweat from my face as I plucked up crumpled pulpit cloths, the scarlet ones that Mama and Aunt Caroline had sewn for Pentecost. *The secesh did this! They knew how the men in my family voted and they were out to scare all of us into supporting the Confederates.* I flung the cloths into a basket.

There was no way Pastor could hold church that week. It wouldn't even be safe for us to come. This was where we always gathered, for every important occasion, more than just a room where we heard the word and prayed. Panther Mountain's Northern Methodists had been warned, dared to return to our most sacred place under threat of violence.

"I know you all have prayed on this for quite a while," Pastor said. "And we hate to lose you from the community," Pastor said. "Covington, you say your brother-in-law knows the land in that part of Ohio?"

"Yes," my uncle replied. His dark, honest eyes and bushy eyebrows reminded me of Grandpa's. "Henry worked at an orchard in southern Ohio. He knows the lay of the land there."

This isn't fair! I thought. *Why should we be the ones who have to pack up and leave? Just because some Virginians are afraid of losing their slaves, they've ruined everything for the rest of us. The United States is our country! Virginia is our state! It is our home!*

****

Alien Enemies Act, passed August 8, 1861, by Congress of the Confederate States of America

Now, therefore, I, JEFFERSON DAVIS, President of the Confederate States of America, do issue this, my proclamation; and I do hereby warn and require every male citizen of the United States, of the age of fourteen years and upwards, now within the Confederate States, and adhering to the Government of the United States, and acknowledging the authority of the same, and not being a citizen of the Confederate States, to depart from the Confederate States within forty days from the date of this proclamation. And I do warn all persons above described, who shall remain within the Confederate States after the expiration of said period of forty days, that they will be treated as alien enemies.

****

Matthew 5: 33-34

Again, ye have heard that it hath been said by them of old time, Thou shalt not forswear thyself, but shalt perform unto the Lord thine oaths:

But I say unto you, Swear not at all; neither by heaven; for it is God's throne:

Chapter Six

Panther Mountain, mid-August, 1861

They swept across the mountain, going door to door, pushing papers into every able male's hands. Those who refused to sign had to leave Virginia or be jailed.

There wasn't much my daddy could do when a gray-capped crowd came to the door toting rifles and demanding that he join them. They shoved enlistment papers at him, spat tobacco juice on our porch and threatened him if he didn't sign. We are Virginians, they said. We are Confederates now. Show your loyalty, James.

Daddy did not sign the oath. Nor did Uncle Covington or Uncle A.J. or Mary Ann's Jon. Would they force Logan to sign? The thought of him being roughed up by rebels made my heart pound fast.

****

Journal entry—Cross Lanes, Nicholas County, western Virginia

Friday, Aug. 16, 1861
This morning I spent the time before breakfast in writing. Helped clean up between tents: went out to drill with the men under [Sargent] Parmenter then went out to wash myself and clothes and to practice the flute. Did not get back in time for dinner, had to eat cold mush and beans.

--Private Daniel S. Judson, Company C, Seventh Ohio Volunteer Infantry

****

Friday, Aug. 16th, 1861
Cross Lanes, Va.
Mrs. Elisabeth A. Hanson

"Dear Mother,

I now hold my pen in hand to inform that I with the exception of a bad cold am well as usual and my honorable petition is that these lines might find you enjoying no worse state of health. We the Seventh Reg't as yet have been in no engagement with the enemy but, at present, there is fair prospect of our being in one before the war terminates. Much of the time all that appears necessary to conflict my happiness is the prospect of an immediate engagement with the enemy. When I say thus, I am not to convey the idea that I am blood-thirsty from revenge, far be it from that. Indeed, not once to my knowlidge [sic] since engaging in this struggle has anger toward our southern Brethren wrankled [sic] within my breast. On the contrary I at times pity them when I think of their condition the powers of both heaven & earth are against them. They cannot stand."

--Pvt. Joseph Collins, Company C, Seventh Ohio Volunteer Infantry

****

Renick home, Panther Mountain, mid-August 1861

General Floyd's soldiers stood watch on the road that ran past our house. During their breaks, they came into our yard, cranked buckets up from our well, put their dusty lips on our ladle and drank their fill. They helped themselves to our garden and begged for bread at the back door. One day a scruffy boy soldier walked right into our kitchen and grabbed a loaf from the table. I scared him away, swiping at his head with a skillet.

Flour puffed up as I kneaded and flopped a lump of dough on the wood board. The kitchen air was honey thick. Late summer rains beat down nearly every day and the dampness had seeped into the log walls.

I pulled the sticky dough into two knots, shaped and rolled them in oiled pans, ready for the oven heat to swell them. Sweat poured down my face and strands of hair stuck to my cheeks. I leaned against the kitchen table, wiping my forehead with the back of my dusty hand. Syrup was dribbled across the white tablecloth, crumbs scattered around a half-eaten biscuit.

Through the kitchen window, I saw Will coming out of the woods with a bucket full of blackberries. He stopped on the back porch, scraped mud off his shoes, and pointed to a grey kepi hanging from a backdoor hook. He shook his head. "They been helpin' themselves again?"

I nodded. "Like foxes in the henhouse. Soon we'll have nothin' left." I burned inside. My father had fled that cap. Its wet wool stank like the sheep in the puddle-filled pen.

My parents decided that we would follow once Daddy found a place for us to live. He told me to be brave the evening he, my uncles, Mary Ann, and Jonathan left for Ohio. "Don't let the Rebs cow you, Liddy Jane," he said, hands on my shoulders. Looking me straight in the eye, he added, "I've never seen you back down to anybody or anything, and I don't expect you will now."

"I won't let you down, Daddy," I told him, as I gripped the door jamb, hoping he couldn't see my hands shaking.

Mama held her arm tight around my waist as we watched them ride off in the dark, guided by a silver moon. The travelers had greased the wagons' axles and scattered sawdust along the road to quiet the horses' hoofs so as not to alert the sleeping soldiers at the opposite end of the road. Tears rolled down my face as we watched them close the front gate and set off.

"I miss Daddy," Little Peg said, bowing her head, tears streaming down her cheeks. Barney nuzzled her hand.

"We will see him again soon," my mother said, squeezing her shoulder.

****

Beat! beat! drums!—blow! bugles! blow!

Through the windows—through doors—burst like a ruthless force,

Into the solemn church, and scatter the congregation,

Into the school where the scholar is studying,

Leave not the bridegroom quiet—no happiness must he have now with his bride,

Nor the peaceful farmer any peace, ploughing his field or gathering his grain,

So fierce you whirr and pound you drums—so shrill you bugles blow.

--from "Beat! Beat! Drums! by Walt Whitman

Journal entry—Aug. 20, 1861, Cross Lanes, Virginia

This morning was quite clear, mud dry underfoot. I had no particular trouble in getting breakfast. Had some little time to myself during the forenoon. Hope Rap will come back soon as I had rather soldier than cook. For supper I got up some pancakes made out of crackers. The "boys" paid them a good tribute. Just after taps and we had quietly laid ourselves down to sleep, two messengers came in with the intelligence that the Capt. of Co. K with five of his privates had been shot by the rebels. A messenger from Gen. Cox came in, too. We were ordered to pack up immediately for a march. We got this order about ten and at eleven we were on the march, going in the direction of Gauley Bridge. We went very fast straight through mud holes and mountain streams which found their way across the road without the aid of sluices or bridges. Over in going a distance of about forty rods the stream crossed the road four times and in one place the road followed the bed of the brook for some distance. It was without exception the worst march I have had to make. The moon shone very brightly thus rendering our way much more passable to us.

--Pvt. Daniel S. Judson, Company C, Seventh Ohio Volunteer Infantry

Chapter Seven

Panther Mountain, August 24, 1861

As the noonday sun turned mud puddles steamy, we all walked over to Grandma and Grandpa Grose's house. Aunt Caroline and Uncle Frank were there with the boys, who were very excited to play with Frankie and Lizzie and Little Peg. I picked up Sis and went into the parlor, where Uncle Frank was telling Grandpa about his guard duty shift.

"A few days back, the Ohio soldiers—Seventh Regiment—got orders to march from Cross Lanes to Twenty-Mile. The road along the creek was mostly flooded and full of holes," Uncle Frank said. He whistled low and shook his head. "Never seen such a miserable, muddy bunch of Yankees."

Grandpa leaned forward in his chair, elbows on his knees, hands clasped. "Wonder why they got orders to go to Twenty Mile?"

"From what I hear, they got bad information about Wise's troops being ready to attack Cox's headquarters at Gauley Bridge," Uncle Frank answered, scratching his sandy beard.

Hearing those words, I felt the weight of war bearing down on us. Those Ohio troops had been marching to and fro right down at the foot of our mountain. What if the Rebs standing picket guard on our road went out and fired at them? How would we keep the children safe? Our neighbors had been hiding their animals in caves, to keep them safe from Rebs and bushwhackers. We had a cave under a cliff that jutted out over the far edge of our property. Logan and I used to explore it when we were younger. I wondered if we could hide everyone there if soldiers fought nearby.

Feeling agitated, I stood up. Sis was playing with quilt patches on the floor so I left her there with Uncle Frank and Grandpa, and walked into the kitchen where Mama, Aunt Caroline and Grandma sat around the table.

Aunt Caroline cradled Lucy in a soft cotton sling strapped around her shoulder and waist. "Lydia, could you hold the baby while I take my leave?" I was happy to oblige and she reached into the sling, gently scooping my little cousin out and into my arms.

"I love that baby head smell, yes, I do," I cooed at peachy-cheeked Lucy.

"It is the best smell in the world," Grandma agreed as she stripped off potato skin peels with a paring knife, her hands bony but strong. "Nothing like a new baby to bring joy into the home." Her hands had fed and clothed and washed and warmed many a baby, including my own mother and me.

My Grandma Grose was my only grandmother. Daddy didn't have a mama, at least not one he could remember. He was raised by his stepfather who never spoke of a first wife. I reckoned something bad had happened and Willis, my step-granddad, did not want to talk about it.

"I got a letter from James yesterday," Mama said when Aunt Caroline came back into the kitchen. "He believes he's found a home we can rent in Ohio. In Gallipolis."

"Gallipolis." Aunt Caroline's voice trailed off. "It sounds like a faraway land."

"Actually, it's not far from the orchard where Henry apprenticed, the next county over," Mama said, talking about Uncle Henry Backus. The orchard on his and Aunt Mary Ann's farm was shady and cool, the apples we picked there sweet and crisp.

I looked down at Lucy. How I would miss her. And Aunt Caroline. And Grandma and Grandpa. Uncle Frank was a home guard and they stayed behind so he could help protect the mountain. Grandpa was too old to be forced to sign the oath. I worried about how they would do back here with the war raging all around them.

"When will you leave?" Grandma asked. Mama was her oldest daughter, her first girl.

"In a few weeks, I suppose," Mama replied. "Depending on how soon we can pack up and how safe it will be to travel."

"We will be praying for you all, Sister. God will guide you, I am sure of it," Aunt Caroline said, reaching over to squeeze Mama's hand. Mama smiled a wary little smile.

****

It was Saturday, time to prepare for Sunday dinner. Mama baked cornbread. A pot of brown beans bubbled on the stove. I plucked jars of pickled okra off the pantry shelf and lined them up on the counter.

40

Will walked in, screen door slamming behind him. He had been at Uncle Billy's farm, helping to pick crops. "Did you take off your boots?" Mama yelled. He padded down the corridor in his sock feet. "Yes'm."

"Here," he said, handing me a folded piece of paper. "Logan asked me to give you this."

"May I be excused, Mama?"

Mama said yes and I slipped out the back door, walked over to the black oaks, and slumped against a tree trunk.

"*Miss Lydia Renick*" was written in cramped script on the paper square. I unfolded it.

> "*Dear Lydia,*
>
> *I am writing this to tell you that I will probably not see you again anytime soon. I was forced to sign the oath and the Confederate marshal sent me to Captain Newman. He told me it was my duty to Virginia to sign up and fight for the CSA. As you know, I did not want this to happen. But I have no choice. It makes me sick to think that I must put on the gray uniform and fight against the Union.*
> *Word will spread soon enough that I am gone. I know I can trust you and that you know my real heart and mind. I will write to you as soon as I can. Please write to me too, even after you get to Ohio.*
> > *Your friend,*
> > *Logan*"

No. This cannot be true. I sobbed and bit into my palm. Everyone I loved was leaving. *Please God, do not let this happen. Please protect Logan.* I hoped the rush of river water down below would drown out my cries.

****

Sunday, August 25th, 1861—Seventh OVI Camp, at the foot of Panther Mountain

I was awakened quite early and was soon to work at breakfast. Gave Wallace some coffee to buy milk and corn with. We had a good breakfast and I enjoyed it very much. I worked hard all the morning and had just got the things ready to go into the wagon when "Company C, fall in!" sounded in my ears.

--Pvt. Daniel Judson, Company C, Seventh Ohio Volunteer Infantry

Chapter Eight

Renick home, Sunday, August 25th, 1861

Mama and I woke at the crack of dawn, as we usually did, but on that Sunday morning we were cooking up extra food for the Union soldiers camped at the base of our mountain. I cut yesterday's cornbread out of the pan and sliced a hunk of ham. Mama bundled the food into a basket, which we dropped off at Aunt Mary Ann's house on the way to church. She and Aunt Caroline and Aunt Jerusha packed the food into saddlebags.

We passed the camp on our way to church. The wagon swayed and bumped over the dirt road, wood joints squeaking, wheels splashing through watery ruts. I saw rows of dingy tents in a clearing. A fire was burning in front of one larger tent, which I guessed served as their mess. There were other, smaller fires scattered here and there. One soldier was roasting green coffee beans in an iron skillet and I caught a rich whiff. Another sat on a tree stump, shucking corn. A cook stirred beans in a large black pot.

Across from the tents, men in ink-blue uniforms practiced drills, lined up in precise rows, shifting their rifles from shoulder to shoulder. Little Peg, Lizzie, and Frankie, eyes wide, gripped the side of the wagon like birds perched on a clothesline.

Sister Caroline sighed. "They look so fine in their uniforms."

"Welcome to Panther Mountain!" Mama shouted to a cluster of men polishing their boots.

"Thank you kindly, Ma'am!" one shouted back.

"Well, God bless you all, thank *you*!" she replied, waving.

Maysie sat with her family on a bench near the front of the sanctuary. We looked at each other after I sat down. "Logan's not here," she mouthed. Her big blue eyes looked sore and tired.

I nodded and held up my index finger. Wait, I signaled. We stood to sing Song number 12:

It is a melancholy road,
Both dark and lonely unto me;
And I have heard them say, there are lions in the way,
And they lurk in the mountain Calvary.

"Let's talk outside," I said to Maysie after the service ended.

We stood under a birch tree. Maysie pulled out a lacy handkerchief, dabbed at the corners of her watery eyes, gripped my wrist and asked, "What do you know? Where has he gone?"

"I don't know *where* he is," I said slowly, "but I do know he was forced to sign the oath and join up with the Rebs."

"Oh, no!" she cried out. Heads in the crowd turned toward us. "That can't be! He isn't…"

"Shh…I know," I whispered, "but we don't want anyone to hear us talk about that, now do we?" I lifted my chin and tilted my head at her. I wanted to cry, too, but forced myself to stick to the facts and not the feelings.

"My heart is breaking," she sniffed quietly, head down, dark curls spilling out of the bottom of her bonnet.

"I understand. I do. But we must be strong and we must keep quiet about his whereabouts if we should happen to learn of them. He is our friend. We don't want to do or say anything that would put him in harm's way." I heard my Mama's calm voice coming out of my own throat.

Maysie nodded and loosened her grip on my arm. "You are right, Liddy."

"Alright now. I will let you know if I hear any other news. You do the same, you hear?"

Maysie nodded again, looking at the ground. She raised her hand, and I wasn't sure if she was holding it up as if swear an oath or wave goodbye.

As we rolled up to the mountain after church, I saw that the Ohio camp tents had been taken down, some canvases flattened across the grass. A cook was pouring a kettle-full of corn water over a sizzling fire. The soldiers were on the march again. The supply crew were cleaning up, folding tents, packing up the wagons. I smelled wet, charred wood and worried.

****

War Report, Kesslers Cross Lanes, Monday morning, August 26, 1861

Suddenly, as Ohio Seventh soldiers munched on their breakfast of crackers and meat, shots rang out. Thousands of whooping Confederate soldiers charged across the fields at them, trapping them between hail of bullets and the thick forest of Panther Mountain. The Union men had no choice but to run, fleeing up mountain paths and jumping over thickets. Not everyone got away.

****

Chapter Nine

Around the walls stand the Antinous, the Amazon, the Lycian Apollo, the Juno; all famous productions of antique sculpture, and still shining in the undiminished majesty and beauty of their ideal life, although the marble that embodies them is yellow with time, and perhaps corroded by the damp earth in which they lay buried for centuries. Here, likewise, is seen a symbol (as apt at this moment as it was two thousand years ago) of the Human Soul, with its choice of Innocence or Evil close at hand, in the pretty figure of a child, clasping a dove to her bosom, but assaulted by a snake.

--from _The Marble Faun,_ by Nathaniel Hawthorne

****

Panther Mountain, Monday morning, August 26, 1861

Daylight. A familiar sound sliced through the loft window. I stopped washing, hands dripping. I heard it again. _Crack! Crack! Crack!_ Only bullets made that noise.

I pulled on my dress and climbed down the loft ladder. There was a knock at the door. Mama opened it just a wee bit, Sis clinging to her skirt.

"Good morning, ma'am," a deep voice said. I picked Sis up and saw a light-haired soldier tip his gray cap at my mother. "I am sorry to bother you at such an early hour. We are going house to house to inform people on the mountain that there's been a firefight at Cross Lanes. Many Yankees were captured, but others escaped into the woods and are likely hiding nearby. If you see anyone, please be very careful and report to us immediately."

"Thank you for the information, sir," my mother replied. A vein popped up on her forehead, her mouth pressed into a thin line. "We are always on our guard. Good day to you."

The soldier again tipped his cap, turned, and walked toward the hitching post where his horse snorted and chomped at the bit.

Mama closed the door and locked the bolt with a loud clunk. She exhaled. "I'd like to tell those mongrels to kiss my…foot!" she said, her hand pressed to her face. "Thank you, darlin' for taking the baby."

I shifted Sis onto my other hip and patted Mama's arm. "Don't blame you for being upset," I said.

The sounds of war faded mid-morning, replaced by dog barks echoing through the woods. We all busied ourselves as best we could the rest of the day. I fed the little ones while Mama and Will took to the field under clouds dark as bruises. We were nearly out of corn and the flour barrel would soon be scooped clean. Tomatoes cracked and burst in the garden, the overwatered leaves curled from all the rain. I thought my chores would keep my mind busy enough, but I was wrong. So many bullets flying out there, I could not stop thinking that Logan might get shot. The thought of him lying on the ground, bleeding, played over and over in my mind.

****

Some of our boys were down. We gained the hill, and facing about in good order, began to load and fire. This we kept up for twenty minutes or so, when the enemy's advance was checked; but it soon developed that Company C and parts of Companies A and K were cut off from the balance of the regiment. Cross, Orton, Jeakins and Collins were badly wounded and fell into the hands of the Confederates.

--Battle of Cross Lanes Report, Private Martin M. Andrews, Company C, 7th Ohio Volunteer Infantry

****

Application for U.S. Army Pension

Elizabeth A. Hanson, Saratoga County, NY, mother
Joseph W. Collins, Private, Co. "C" 7 Ohio Vols
Killed at Cross Lanes, Va
Aug. 27, 1861

****

Somewhere on Panther Mountain, August 26th, 1861

Immediately following the battle, Company C hurriedly left the field, taking to the near-by woods, in a more or less demoralized condition. However, our real confusion and flight followed several hours later, when we suddenly found ourselves almost entirely surrounded by [Confederate] Colonel Tompkins's regiment. The first we knew of their presence was their demand for our surrender. This happened at a time when most of the company were sitting on the ground resting, while the Captain and some of the sergeants had begun a conference as to the direction we should take.

In a sorrowful tone of voice Captain Shurtleff gave the order, "Fall in, boys, I shall have to give you up." The company was somewhat "strung out," and while those nearest the Captain began forming for surrender the larger part of the company ran pell mell into a laurel thicket which, providentially, was only about three jumps away. There was some shooting and much yelling "Surrender!" behind me. Reaching the channel of a small stream, I took to that, and spying a ledge of rock, reaching far out over the bank, I crawled back to its farthest recess and lay there for several hours.

--Private Edgar Condit, Company C, Seventh Ohio Volunteer Infantry

****

Renick home, Panther Mountain, late afternoon, August 26, 1861

Dit, dit, dit! A woodpecker worked on a stump. *Thud, thud, thud, thud.* I punched the pole into the churn as hard and fast as I could. *Crack! Crack!* I stopped churning. The blazing guns were closer now, in the woods past the field. I rushed to the front of the house and saw Mama clutching her skirt, high-stepping it toward the front gate, pinching wheat sheaves in the crook of her free arm.

"Where's Will?" I shouted. She tipped her head sideways motioning toward the barn. He was putting the horses in.

"Is everyone inside?" Mama called out. "Yes," I answered, but stopped myself, realizing that my little sister and brother had been out back picking berries while I churned. "I think!"

I rushed to the kitchen and smacked the back screen open. "Frankie! Little Peg! Are you still out there?"

Crack! Crack! The shots sounded closer. Two of the soldiers from our road whizzed through the thickets just yards behind our house in a gray blur, chasing, crunching through the brambles and bushes.
"Yes..." A tiny, trembly voice answered. It was my little brother. "We are here, Liddy. Can you get us out?"

I followed the voice to a bunch of laurel bushes. A bucket of blackberries was overturned on the ground nearby. Beneath the bright green leaves, I saw two little pairs of shoes. I reached into the bush and grabbed their hands, pulling them out. "Come on, now," I whispered. "Try not to get scratched. We must run fast back to the house."

Will held the back door open as we clambered in.

Mama let out a breath. "Alright now," she said to us, "you are all to stay in the house for the rest of the day. It is too dangerous out there right now." She wiped sweat from her neck. "And don't anybody let anybody in, y'hear? That's an order."

She sank down onto the rocking chair. Sis crawled into her lap, wailing, fresh up from her nap, cheeks flushed, strawberry wisps sticking up all over her head. "Shh, shh, now baby, shh..."

Keeping the little ones busy inside the locked house was a chore. Caroline, Frankie, Little Peg and Lizzie tried to play hide and go seek, finding spots to hide behind the pie safe and in the pantry, but Sis couldn't seem to find them and kept yelling "Not fair! Not fair!" I suggested playing dolls but the boys thought that was too sissy. I read Andersen's Fairy Tales to them until my throat was dry.

When bedtime finally came, I caught my breath and sat at the kitchen table. Will plunked down next to me.

"The woods are crawling with Yankees," he said. "I saw a couple hiding while I was picking corn."

"I hope they beat the tar out of the Rebs."

"Me too."

"I mean…except for Logan…."

Will nodded.

****

Renick home, August 27, 1861

We were eating breakfast in the muggy kitchen the morning after the battle when Aunt Mary Ann knocked on the front door.

"Peggy? It's me and Henry."

Mama invited them in and motioned them toward the kitchen.

"We worry about you now that James is gone," my aunt said, putting her hand on Mama's arm. "I reckon we would worry even if he was here, with all this fighting around us."

Mama nodded. "Well, we had a bit of a scare yesterday when Floyd's men chased Yankees through the woods. The bullets were flying and I nearly got caught in the crossfire."

"Oh dear," Uncle Henry said. "I heard them. I should have come over."

"It's alright, Henry," Mama smiled. "We know we can count on you to help. We just barred the doors and holed up in the house."

"Our big news this morning is that a gaggle of Ohio soldiers showed up at Mama and Papa's house after dark," Mary Ann said. Her eyes opened wider as she told the story. "They climbed the mountain after the fight. Caroline and the boys were there, too, on account of Frank being on duty. Nancy and Sarah came over to help. There were more than a dozen and they fed them all and let them rest before they headed back to Gauley Bridge before dawn."

"I'll declare," Mama said, eyebrows raised. "And they didn't get caught?"

"Not so far as we know, from what Papa told us. He helped them find the trail to the river."

"That is something," I said. "Will said he saw a pair hiding in a thicket and a hollow tree trunk yesterday, just beyond the cornfield."

"If any of them find us, we will help however we can," Mama said. "But I doubt they will be able to get past the pickets down the road."
Uncle Henry wiped biscuit crumbs from his beard. "It's hard to say. The bulk of 'em are from Ohio and that's flat land compared to what we've got here. Not sure they know how to wend their way through these mountains."

****

> Wearily pulling ourselves up the side of mountains, sometimes crossing deep ravines, always keeping within hearing of the roaring Gauley, we continued our wanderings until almost nightfall...
>
> **--Post-battle account of Pvt. Edgar Condit, Company C, Seventh Ohio Volunteer Infantry**

****

That evening, Barney nipped at cow hoofs as Mama and I got them into the barn. Will clanked the sheep gate shut. I could hear the Secesh pickets down the road, hooting and singing.

> "*Wait for the wag-u-u-n,*
> *Wait for the wag-u-u-n,*
> *Wait for the wag-u-u-n,*
> *And you'll all take a ride!*"

"My land, how noisy they are tonight!" Mama exclaimed as she bolted the barn door.

"I suspect they're good and lickered up," I replied. "Mr. McClung came up the road earlier today with some moonshine. Said he wanted to join them in a toast to General Floyd for sending the Yankees packing."

Mama shook her head. "No good can come from the bottom of a moonshine jar."

Fat raindrops suddenly spattered the path. I blew out the porch lantern and shut the door behind me.

****

I sat at the foot of my bed braiding my hair, staring at the flickering candlelight, when Barney began howling. The dog must have startled Sis; I heard her cry out downstairs. One of the boys hissed "SHH!" Even Caroline, the deep sleeper, stirred in her bed over on her side of the loft.

I imagined our dog was howling along with the drunken soldiers but had not actually heard a peep from them in a while.

There was a knock at the front door. *What now?*

I stuck my head through the hanging sheets. Mama grabbed the shotgun from over the hearth. She went to the door. "Who's there?" she yelled.

"United States Army, ma'am!" a muffled voice replied. "Permission to come in, please?"

Mama unbolted the door and waved them in. I scrambled down the ladder. There in the entry way stood three bedraggled Union men, muddy and covered with leaves and briars. Each one removed his cap.

"Begging your pardon, ma'am," said the tallest one, breathing hard. "We are... sorry to intrude upon you and your family, but...we have come from the battlefield and are in need of shelter and perhaps a bite of food, if you could spare some. We are much relieved to find we have happened upon a household of Union supporters. *Much* relieved."

They were so mannerly, despite their rumpled appearance. "Here now, give me your rifles," Mama ordered, in the same way she ordered us children to put away our toys. "I promise you may have them back whenever you need them." The soldiers carefully pointed their bayonets away from her as they handed over their guns. By this time, every Renick child was awake, standing and staring at the three soggy strangers.

"Lydia, would you and Will please direct these gentlemen to the pantry? That will be a good place for them to eat without being seen from outside of the house." Mama said in a nervous, low voice. "Caroline, I will count on you to get the children back to sleep. Oh, but children, first you must promise Mama that you will be nice and quiet. We don't want to raise any ruckus that would cause the pickets to come around. These men are our friends, they are fighting to protect our country, so do not be afraid." She smiled at the wide-eyed little ones. "Nighty-night"

Will and I dragged three kitchen chairs into the narrow back pantry. It had no windows, which made it a safer hiding place than other parts of the house. Mama pulled quilts out of the chest at the foot of her bed and stowed the soldiers' guns there.

"Much obliged, Miss," the tallest one said. His voice was deep and pleasant. I looked up at him. His face was sweaty and muddy, but his brown eyes were friendly. I was stuck in his stare for a moment.

"Oh, pardon me," he continued. "My name is Edgar. My companions here are George and Fred." The two others nodded their heads at me. "Nice to meet you, ma'am," Fred said quietly.

"My name is Lydia, and this is my brother Will," I answered.

Mama came into the kitchen and set a frying pan on the stove. "Liddy, we'll need honey and flour, some butter and eggs."

Will offered to fetch a ham from the cellar. "Good idea, darlin', I'll make up some red eye gravy with it."

"Excuse me, please," I said as I reached between Edgar and George to pluck some eggs from a pantry basket.

"We saw a fire a few hundred yards down your road," George said after gulping down a cup of water. "Figured it was Rebel troops."

"Yes," Mama answered, sighing. "They've been watching our every move for quite a while now."

"Helping themselves to our crops, too," I added over my shoulder. "I worry that we'll run out before we have to leave."

"Oh, you're leaving?" Edgar asked. I turned to him and nodded. "Where are you headed?" His eyebrows went up.

"Our Daddy escaped to Ohio after the secesh told him to sign the oath or get out," Will chimed in. "He found us a place to live and we'll travel soon to join him."

Fred nodded. "Ohio is a fine place to live," he said, "Lived there all my life. Good soil, good neighbors."

"But that is a long journey to make with so many children, ma'am," Edgar continued.

"Yes," Mama agreed, turning away from the stove to look at the three big men crowded into that very small space. She forced a smile. "But we are strong people. The Lord will see us through."

We dished up biscuits, ham and gravy and watched the hungry soldiers wolf it all down. "We are mighty grateful to you for this food," Fred said between mouthfuls. "After months of nothing but hard tack and sowbelly, this is truly a banquet!"

"I will go up and strip the beds and put on clean sheets for our visitors. Lydia, would you please fetch some of Daddy's nightshirts from the chest of drawers?"

I hurried into Mama and Daddy's room and pulled out the night clothes. Handing them to the soldiers, I said "I hope you will be comfortable in our beds."

Edgar smiled widely and the other two looked at him, nodding. "Ma'am, last night we were sleeping under the stars with only our cartridge boxes for pillows. Your beds will be the ultimate luxury for these weary bones. Thank you for giving them up for us." His eyes fairly twinkled as he looked at me. My cheeks flushed. I certainly had never had a man sleep in my bed and even the thought embarrassed me.

The girls and I huddled in Mama's bed. Will and Frankie took the floor. The soldiers' snores rattled the rafters. Mama spread their wet, dirty uniforms across a quilt rack in front of the fireplace to help them dry, but she didn't dare start a fire for fear of drawing attention. I thought about the men putting on Daddy's nightshirts. I wondered what Edgar's broad shoulders looked like beneath the flannel.

The mantel clock struck three times. I must have fallen asleep though it didn't seem like it. There was a rustling. Mama scurried up the loft ladder and whispered to the men. They needed to get dressed and leave before the break of dawn. It was too dangerous for us to keep them in the house. The Rebs would burn our house and crops if they found them here. Will would guide them to a spot in the woods where a giant tree had fallen last year. There was a deep crater there, big enough to hide three men for the time being.

I got up and stuffed food into the soldiers' haversacks. The three, wearing their stiff, damp uniforms, took their guns. "You can trust Will," Mama said to them. "He knows the land around here better than any of us. We will check on you as soon as we can see our way clear. God bless you and keep you safe."

"We are much obliged, ma'am. I apologize but I have not yet asked you your name," Edgar said softly.

"Mrs. James Renick," Mama answered. "You may call me Peggy."

We watched through the kitchen window as their figures disappeared into the woods, Will leading the way with a pine torch. The Rebs probably wouldn't suspect much. We always took torches with us when one of us needed to visit the johnny house in the dark of night.

****

That morning as I was fixing breakfast, one of the pickets stepped up onto the back porch and knocked. I opened the door a crack and saw his scruffy face, wet shirt stuck to his skin.

"Good morning, little lady," he said. "Any chance you could spare us some bread and coffee? We are mighty hungry. With the rain a-pouring down all night, we could scarce keep the fire burning for cookin'."

I clenched my jaw so hard my head hurt. *You take our food, take our state, take us out of our country. You stink like a wet dog. You'd just as soon shoot us as look at us.*

"You alright, Liddy?" Will asked from behind me. "Is there something this man wants?"

"Ah, young sir, good morning," said the Reb. "I was jes' explaining to the little lady here that the rain done doused our cook fire and we are in need of a bite for breakfast."
Will let out a loud sigh. "Stay right there," he said to the man. He wrapped a loaf of bread in a cloth and told him to hand him his canteen. He poured coffee into it.

"Much obliged, folks," said the picket, grinning wide to show a missing upper tooth. "Oh, and just a friendly reminder to report to us if you see any Yankees crawling about the mountain."

I got a chill when he said that. Did he know we had taken in the soldiers last night? "Uh, yes...yes, of course," I blurted.

When he was gone off down the road, I turned to Will. "Do you think he knows?"

"Nah," said Will, shaking his head. "He would'a said something."

"I don't know. Something about the way he looked at me when he said it. What do you think they'll do to us if they find out we're hiding Yankees?"

"Won't come to that, I don't think," my brother said. "We'll be extra careful." There was a look in Will's eyes, as if he were not sure of the words he was saying.

Chapter Ten

Panther Mountain, August 29, 1861

The rain kept coming and so did the Confederates, pestering us for food and dry firewood. The pickets moved up the road to the front of our house. I watched them through the window as they cleaned their rifles and chit-chatted amongst themselves. Guarded by soldiers of a foreign country, we were prisoners in our own home.

I fretted about the Yankees huddled in their dugout, that they would be found and captured or worse. We couldn't take food to them because the Rebel troops outside our gate were watching us, hawk-like. They must have been starving and probably swimming in the rainwater that pooled in their hidey hole. Hungry, wet, freezing at night.

The sun burned through the clouds the second morning after they had left our house. Dragonflies skittered across steaming puddles in the road. I could not stand being cooped up in the house any longer and asked the older girls to watch the little ones while I went outside.

One of the four soldiers tipped his cap as I came up the walk. "Morning, ma'am," he called. "Had enough of this rain yet?" The soaking wet crew was not wearing official Confederate uniforms but had cobbled together dress coats and bandanas and work pants, topped off with Sunday hats and caps.

"I should ask you the same thing, since you've been out in it," I called back. I walked over to the gate and lifted the latch. I needed to show them that I was not afraid, that I had nothing to hide. I stood right in front of them

"So what are y'all anyway? Soldiers? Bushwhackers? Rangers?"

The one missing the upper tooth laughed and cocked his head back as if surprised or amused by my frankness. "Well, we are soldiers of the Confederacy, y'see? We are waiting on our official uniforms and weapons. We're militia men. We represent the Confederate States of America."

"Any of you know a Rebel soldier named Logan? Logan Stephenson?" I asked.

A young one who looked about my age rubbed his chin. "Hm. I think I heard tell of him."

"He's from our mountain," I continued, turning the words over in my head before they came out of my mouth. "Haven't seen him in a while."

"Don't know which regiment he's with," the young man replied. His coat sleeves hung down to his knuckles, a belt cinching his oversized pants. "If I meet him, I'll tell him you were askin' after him." He grinned a little at me and I gave him a nod.

"What's your name?" I asked him. Fear drained from my muscles.

"John Williams," he answered, cocking his head a bit. "What's yours?"

"Lydia," I told him.

"Lydia," he repeated. "That's real pretty." Brown hair stuck out around his ears beneath his hat. He had one brown eye and one blue.

"Thanks." I felt I had a friendly audience in John. I would keep that in mind as I figured out how to keep our Yanks hidden.

Chapter Eleven

Panther Mountain, around dusk, August 29, 1861

All along the river between Panther Mountain and Gauley Bridge the woods were crawling with Confederate scouts and bushwhackers, lying in wait for Yankees to capture.

As the sun was setting, Will and I made our move. John Williams and the others had been relieved of duty and a new batch of pickets stood guard down the road and over the hill from our house. I carried a pail of food, a pot of coffee and three tin cups, trailing behind Will to the hiding place.

We reached the spot and found the men fairly floating in the water-filled hole. Mosquitos swarmed over their heads. Will gave the men a hand up out of their pool. He stood guard while I passed out the roasting ears and coffee.

Edgar smiled, shivering. "God has sent us an angel! Boys, if there were a preacher nearby, I would fight you both to take her to the altar," he pronounced, triggering their laughter.

"I am just sorry we couldn't reach you sooner," I said. "The Johnnies were all around our property. Please come back to the house this evening. You will surely catch your death of cold if you don't get out of those wet uniforms."

"What about the pickets around your house?' George asked.

"A new group came in and moved down over the hill for now. I'll go ahead and make sure all's clear. Will can lead you back."

"That's a great risk for you to take," Edgar said looking straight at me.

"It is worth the risk to help you," I answered, looking right back at him. "There is a cluster of berry bushes at the back of the yard, near the well. Once you get that far, duck down and hide there while I check around the house."

I slipped through the thickets as quickly as I could in the moon-lit woods, my blouse and skirt dampened by dripping leaves. When I reached the back yard, I sensed something was wrong. I walked around the left side of the

60

house and saw that the barn door was wide open. Mama paced around the barnyard clutching a lantern. From a few yards distant, she glowed like a lightning bug.

"Mama, what happened?" I asked as I hurried to her.

"They took the horses," she spat out. "There was nothing I could do. They had me outnumbered and outgunned." She sighed and kicked a slat of the sheep pen, rifle in the crook of her left arm.

"Just now?"

"Just after you and Will took off," she said. "They waited until the sun was setting. Took all of them."

My stomach tightened, fists clenched. Heat rose up through my body and I was breathing hard. My Blackie was gone. "Which way did they go?" I growled.

"Back down over the hill. What about the Yanks?"

"They're with Will. I told them I'd scout around the house.

"It should be safe for them to come in through the back door," Mama said. She walked with me toward the house and handed me the lantern, in the light of which her eyes looked tired. I walked around past the well and swung the lantern as a signal.

Will and the three soldiers sprinted quietly, bent over, through the grass and into the house. I followed them into the stifling hot kitchen. Mama was putting logs in the fireplace.

"Phew!" Will said. "I know it gets cold of an evening, but why build a fire?" Will asked.

"Got to clean and dry these muddy uniforms," Mama said pointing at the three standing in the pantry. "Gentlemen, if you'll take those off, I'll give you those nightshirts back."

Edgar fiddled with the brass buttons on his mud-caked jacket. I stared. *Steady there, Liddy.*

Mama turned to me. "Please fetch the scrub brushes, darlin'. Will, if you'll fill the tub with water we'll rinse off their clothes and hang them in front of the fire."

After everyone was in their nightshirts, we sat with them for a spell in the kitchen.

"I am so sorry to hear about the horse thieves," Edgar said. "When we rejoin our regiment, we will report them to Captain Crook at headquarters."

"Thank you kindly," Mama replied. "We surely do need to get our horses back, to pull our wagon to Ohio. But from what I hear, the scouts are thick out there. It's not safe yet for you to get to Gauley Bridge."

The men looked at each other. "Ma'am, we can't let you risk hiding us here in your house," George began.

"Please, call me Peggy," Mama said.

"Alright, Peggy, but I still say we are putting you in danger by staying here."

"Well, you can't rightly go back to that swimming hole." She paused, then said, "We have a cave on our property that might be a suitable hiding place for now. Why don't you all get some rest and we'll get you up and over there before the sun comes up?"

Edgar spoke up. "Gentlemen, I believe Peggy's plan is sound. And your offer of another rest in a comfortable feather bed is too good to turn down." He nodded at Mama and turned to me, smiling. "Lydia, you and your sisters will surely receive stars in your crowns in Heaven for sacrificing your comfort for ours."

I looked down and smiled. "It is a small sacrifice compared to the ones you are making for us and our country," I replied.

"Coffee anyone?" Mama asked, picking up the pot. The soldiers held out their cups.

I heard a tiny hiccup and turned to see Sis peeking at us from behind the kitchen door. "Hey, Sis, what are doing out of bed?" I asked.

Sis looked at me and then looked at Edgar. She toddled right over to him. "Well hello there," he said. "Would you like to sit with me?"

Sis nodded, her blonde curls bobbing, and held up her arms for him to pick her up.

"She surely likes you!" Will said, laughing.

"It's his friendly brown eyes," I added, grinning.

He looked at me and smiled, then turned Sis around so that they were face to face. "What's your name, young lady?"

"Sis," she said in a tiny voice.

"Is that your full name?"

She nodded. Mama explained how Sis hadn't yet been given a proper name.

"Well, I think Sis is a fine name," he said to her. She nodded again, cheeks pinked by the heat and eyelids drooping.

"Come on, sweetie, I'll put you back to bed now," I said as I got up from my chair. Edgar handed her to me and she clung to my neck. I could hear them all chuckling about how Sis had been drawn straight to him as I took her into the next room.

"I'll sing you a song," I said as I rocked her.

> *May God save the Union! The Red, White and Blue,*
> *Our States keep united the dreary day through;*
> *Let the stars tell the tale of the glorious past,*
> *And bind us in Union forever to last.*

Chapter Twelve

Mama and I were up through the night, scrubbing and rinsing the Yanks' uniforms, drying them near the crackling flames. It was sweaty work, but around midnight the air cooled and made us more comfortable. We kept a pot of coffee going, thanks to the beans Edgar had saved and shared with us from his Army rations. The hot cups helped keep my eyelids open.

"It's nearly six," Mama said. "Sun'll be up soon. Time to wake the boys up and get them to the cave."

I shook Will in his bed. It was like shaking a stone. Then I climbed up to the loft, one hand on the ladder and the other gripping a bayonet with a candle stuck on it. I whispered to Edgar. "Rise and shine."

He rolled over and looked up at me, candlelight shining in his eyes. "My angel has come back again," he said with a sort of half-cocked smile. "Good morning."

"I'll wake the others," I whispered, and pulled back the sheet walls to roust George and Fred.

Will and the Yanks set off for the cave under the full moon, laden with food and water. It would be up to my brother and me to keep them supplied as long as they stayed on our property. It might be for a few more hours or a few more days. But as soon as it was safe, they would head back to Camp Gauley.

****

The only good thing about the wet weather was that it made garden work easier. I pulled sopping weed clumps from between the rows of squash and cucumbers.

I looked up to see John Williams walking toward me. He was toting a bucket.

"Howdy, ma'am," he called out. He wore a rumpled brown coat and a red ribbon tie, knotted. He walked over to me and kneeled down, setting the bucket on the ground. Splashing fish flopped and gasped.

"I am might sorry about your –"

"Darn right y'all should be sorry!" I snapped. "How are we supposed to run our farm without our horses?"

He closed his eyes and nodded. "As I said, I am sorry. There was nothing I could do to stop the others from takin' 'em. I figger your family is probably scraping for food, and that's why I brought you these. I just caught 'em," he said, gesturing toward the bucket with his open hand. "They are for you."

I stuck out my lower lip and blew a puff of air up at strings of hair on my forehead. "We can't go anywhere, you know! Not even to the mill to grind what's left of our wheat!

"You asked me the other day about a fella named Stephenson," he continued. "I saw his regiment."

"You saw them? Where? Is he alright?"

"I don't know, Miss Lydia. The troops was camped near Fayetteville. Saw them on one of our night scouts."

I wiped my muddy hands on my apron and stood up. "Thank you kindly for the information, John. I will pass it on to his family."

"Again, I wish I could bring your horses back...." he said, head hanging down.

"Hmph." I watched him walk away.

Logan *must* be alive. But how could he put up with living among those weasel Rebs? Did they make him steal horses and set fire to houses too? In his heart he was on our side, and the thought of that burned inside me.

****

We were piloted to a small cave—a sort of chamber in the rocks along a creek bank, some eighty rods distant from the home. We had to cross the road, but the rest of our way was through a woods and laurel thicket. Here, in the dry, we made our home...while the daughter kept us provisioned as opportunity occurred. Every day or two came a large pail full of bread, meat, honey, boiled "roasting ears" and ripe peaches. Often she came to us soaking wet to her shoulders from the dripping laurel brush, for it still rained much of the time. She kept us posted on what the Confeds were doing about the premises.

--Private Edgar Condit, Company C, Seventh OVI

****

Chapter Thirteen

Panther Mountain, September 2nd, 1861

I stole away to the cave every chance I got. The rain had stopped the evening before, and on that particular Monday morning, I left the house with a pail and book and it would appear to anyone who might be watching from behind the trees that I was taking advantage of the drier weather to go read in the shady grove near the cave, taking a bite to eat for myself.

I drew back a thick curtain of honeysuckle that spilled over the opening of the cave. Edgar, George, and Fred were sitting in the cool dark on chunks of rock, shirts unbuttoned, faces soaped up, passing a mirror to each other, shaving. Candles stuck into rock cracks flickered.

"Good morning, gentlemen," I said as cheerily as I could. "I am happy to report that the rain has stopped, at least for now, and I have brought you some breakfast."

"Ah!" Edgar exhaled, rubbing his hands together. "Your kindness is so much appreciated, Lydia! Boys, finish up with your razors so we can eat!"

I laid out the food on a broad, flat rock. "I trust you got some sleep last night?"

"Although these accommodations are not nearly as cozy as the Renick family feather beds, we are managing to rest," Edgar said with a smile.

"I must say, the rushing river below provides us with a suitable lullaby through the night," Fred said as he wiped his face with a towel. "And the hum of the crickets does as well."

I poured coffee into a mug and handed it to Edgar. I felt his fingers as he took it. They were ice cold.

"I worry that with the dampness and cold night air, you may become sick," I said.

"It is certainly chilly through the night," he agreed. "But that is the price of cave living, isn't it?"

I smiled. "Is the land like this in Ohio?"

"Oh, in some places it is quite hilly," Edgar said, taking a sip. "But in northern Ohio, where I was living and going to school when the war broke out, the land is flat in comparison to these mighty mountains."

"Where are... where were you going to school?"

"Oberlin College. I was close to completing my second year there when President Lincoln sent out the call for volunteers. Many, if not most, of the members of my company are Oberlin classmates and faculty. Hoffman and Evans are with Company A, I am with Company C. We met under a cliff after the battle scattered us all."

The other two nodded as they ate. "It served as shelter long enough to let us catch our breath and reconnoiter," George added.

"We were making our way back in what we thought was the right direction to Camp Gauley when we heard your dog barking and saw light through your front window," Fred said. "Edgar here convinced us to make a break for it. "

"We were glad to see Yankee uniforms in the doorway," I replied. "It is hard to know lately who might be at the door, friend or foe."

"I only wish we could have arrived sooner, under better circumstances," he said. "Perhaps we could have done something to help, to see that your father did not have to flee the country." He smiled a little and tilted his head a bit toward me.

I nodded, not able to say anything else at that moment. I felt sad and yet warmed by his words. I got up and gathered the dishes from the rock.

As the days rolled by, Edgar and I talked about many things. When I came to the cave after dark, we would sit outside on a log under the stars or, when it rained, we would sit near the cave mouth, inches below the honeysuckle branches. He told me about his Ohio childhood, and how his family moved to an Iowa farm when he was sixteen. I told him about growing up on the mountain and learning to ride horses and the books I was reading.

He was just three years older than I was, but seemed so much more mature, more sophisticated. He had gone to college, lived in two different states, trained with the U.S. Army, and come to western Virginia to protect us. Yet there he was, stuck in a cave on a farm talking to a mountain girl whose only education came from classes held in a country kitchen.

****

> After we had shared such hospitality for eight days, we were chafing under not only our confinement in this cave, but the appalling fact began to stare us in the face that we were really eating the last bread of this mother and her children.

--Private Edgar Condit, 7th OVI

****

Renick farm, Panther Mountain, September 5, 1861

I was stuck in place, so to speak, by a passing wagon in service of General Floyd. The soldiers had stopped at our farm to pluck as many apples from our orchard as they could. They left only rotting fruit on the ground. There would be no trip to the cave for the time being.

I scraped the last bit of flour out of the bin. Mama sat at the kitchen table, rubbing her eyes. "What are we to do?" she asked. "Flour is gone, apples are gone, cellar almost empty."

Gripping the rolling pin, I flattened biscuit dough.

Don't let the Rebs cow you, Liddy Jane. Daddy's words came to my mind. *I've never seen you back down to anybody or anything, and I don't expect you will now.*

"I know what to do," I said, standing up from the table.

"Where are you going?" Mama asked.

"I'm going to the mill," I answered.

From the front porch, I held up the flour scoop and yelled, "Look here!" Soldiers were loading bushels of our apples onto the wagon bed. "We are going to starve if we don't get more flour."

I walked up and stood in the road in front of them, arms crossed over my chest. "Seems to me it's only right that you should take me and the last bushels of our wheat to the mill. It wouldn't look very good to your captain if he found out you've been stealing crops from a poor defenseless family without a Paw here to protect them."

One of the soldiers snorted and wiped his nose on his gray sleeve. "Oh yeah? Don't tell me the blue-belly Yanks haven't done the same to loyal Virginians around here."

"Yeah, but to my knowledge, they haven't been guzzlin' McClung's moonshine while on duty," I shot back, my face hot.

The soldier's eyes got big. He looked like I'd slapped him.

"We're headed past the mill," said a dark-haired private who looked to be about my age. "Get your bushels and you can ride along."

Will and my sisters helped me haul grist to the Rebel wagon. I hopped on board and we were off down the road to Likens Mill. I sat between the bushel baskets behind the driver, guarding our precious grain.

The water wheel at the mill creaked and groaned. Mr. Likens poured our grist into bins and peppered the soldiers with questions. He'd heard there was a firefight at Hawk's Nest. Was it true that Generals Wise and Floyd were at each other's throats? Had they found any more Yankees on the mountain? Rumor had it that not all of them had returned to camp.

I strained to hear their chatter over the conk-a-chonk of wooden gears turning grindstones. One of the privates claimed that Union soldiers were rounding up suspected Confederate citizens and sending them up to Camp Chase in Columbus.

I sat on our flour bags all the way back up Panther Mountain. What stories I had for Edgar and the boys next time I could get to them.

Chapter Fourteen

Renick farm cave, Panther Mountain, September 5, 1861

"The mountains are still crawling with Confederates," I told the men. The troops who took me to the mill told the miller they knew that not everyone from your regiment had made it back to camp and they were hunting for the stragglers. And they said a good number of your fellow soldiers had been taken prisoner and were being marched to Richmond."

Edgar's eyebrows pinched together.

"We still need to try to get back, boys," George said.

"Yes," Edgar began, exhaling slowly before explaining. "It has become painfully obvious to us that we three are consuming your family's dwindling supply of food. Your hospitality and generosity have been lifesaving."

"Have been?" I asked.

"We...believe it is best at this point if we take our chances and make our way back to headquarters."

"We know it's a risk," Fred said, "but we have decided to try."

"Well, we have been *honored* to help you..." I began.

Edgar stood up. "Let me walk you out, Lydia. You had best be getting back. You are taking such a risk even being here." He cupped his hand under my elbow.

"You are truly fearless," he said as we stood at the cave's mouth. "What a brave thing you did, commandeering that Rebel wagon to the mill. You are selfless in caring for your family. And for us, who have devoured your biscuits all these days."

And so it went. I felt pressure on my chest as I said goodbye. I returned to the house and told Mama of their plan.

"It's too dangerous," she said, shaking her head vigorously.

Convinced of their resolve to leave, though, my mother scared up a scrap of paper and roughed out a map with directions from Panther Mountain to Gauley Bridge, which was about 20 miles distant. At around dusk, Will took the map and a few light provisions to the cave. I tucked a note for Edgar into the bucket.

September 6, 1861

"Dear Edgar,

"I have enjoyed our conversations and just wanted to thank you for awakening in me a curiosity about the world. I hope to travel someday, to the places I've read about and that you have described. I hope we might someday meet again after this dreadful war is over."

Your friend,
Lydia"

Chapter Fifteen

Summersville, VA, Friday, September 6, 1861

It was kind of Uncle Frank to drive us to town in his wagon, and also necessary to have an armed scout along. Never mind the fact that we had no horses of our own to get us there. We'd heard stories about bushwhackers stopping folks on the way to market, threatening them, stealing their horses and leaving them defenseless, stranded on desolate roads. A trip to town had become very dangerous.

"Whoa...whoa..." Uncle Frank's voice bounced off the front doors of Main Street, doors of homes, hotels and stores now locked. Only Hardman's was still open for business.

Mama, my uncle, and I walked through empty aisles, past bare shelves. Mrs. Hardman was behind the counter, as always, stacking boxes. She smiled at us, but her eyes looked sad.

"Good morning, Peggy. Lydia, Frank. Good to see you again."

"Good morning, Belle, how are you?" Mama asked.

"To say business is slow would be an understatement, I reckon," she replied, sounding tired. "We are trying to keep the store open for as long as we can, especially so folks can get their mail. Which reminds me, I do believe I have some for each of you."

"Any for me, Mrs. Hardman?" *Maybe Edgar had written to let us know he and the boys got back to Camp Gauley. Maybe Logan...*

The shopkeeper went into the mail room behind the counter and came back with several letters. She laid them on the counter and I saw that one was addressed to "Miss Lydia Renick, Panther Mountain."

My hands trembled as I picked up the envelope. "Confederate States of America" was printed on it, and it was postmarked Fayette Court House, Virginia. There was a water stain beneath my name and address.

"Excuse me please," I said to Mrs. Hardman and my mother. I found a chair next to the cold pot belly stove and sat down, my head swimming.

"Dear Liddy Jane,

I am writing to you from where we are camped but I cannot tell you where that is. They read our mail to make sure we don't give away our location. I am with Company D of the 22nd Kanawha, Virginia Infantry. I have thought about you most every day since I left the mountain. I hope you are well and that you are still reading those books about make-believe beasts. I cannot imagine how hard it must be for you and your family, with your Paw over in Ohio and the dangers all around the mountain. I am glad you have your kin close by. Please call on my sister and brother if you need anything. They would be glad to help. I hope that you can ride Miss Lou while I am gone.

It has rained a lot in the past few days and the nights are mighty cold when a man is soaking wet. Some in my company have come down with measles and typhoid. I am fine for now and trying to keep my strength up.

Please write to me as soon as you can. I am starving for news from home and eagerly await your letter. I will pray for you and your family and please do the same for me.

Fondly,
Logan"

I folded the letter back up and a wave of guilt washed over me. I was so enamored of Edgar that I hadn't even thought of Logan waiting for word from me. Poor, sweet Logan. What must he think of me? I missed him so much but had been distracted by the soldier from Ohio.

Before we left Hardmans, I purchased a pen and paper and quickly scribbled a letter to the boy with the golden-green flecks in his eyes.

****

We had just finished supper and I was clearing dishes from the table when we heard a rap at the front door. What now? I thought. More begging Rebs? A bushwhacker? A hobo?

"I'll get it," I called out.

"Ask who's there first!" Mama called back.

"Yes, yes," I answered, a little irritated that she didn't think I knew to do that.

"Who's there?" I yelled, my head leaning against the door.

"Edgar!" a husky male voice answered.

I swung the door wide open, felt my jaw drop, and, sure enough, there stood Edgar, handsome as ever, with George and Fred behind him. "What...how...?" I stammered. "Come in, come in!"

The men removed their caps and shuffled inside. Mama came running out of the bedroom and clapped her hands with delight.

"We were forced back by Rebel scouts," Edgar said, bending over and out of breath.

"Come, sit down, all of you," I said, waving them back to the pantry. My eyes welled with tears. God had brought them back, I thought. It was God's will that Edgar came back.

Chapter Sixteen

Panther Mountain, September 7, 1861

A cool breeze flowed across my hot cheeks as Edgar and I sat next to each other on a patch of crunchy leaves near the cave. The sun was setting. He picked apart a milkweed pod as we talked. Silky white stars poured out and flew on the air like tiny fairies.

"Did you miss me?" he asked, joking.

"Why yes, I did," I answered, seriously.

He looked at me and the cut of his jaw sent a tingle through me. "Really?" he asked.

I looked down at the ground. "Of course. A girl can get mighty used to visiting caves where dashing soldiers are hiding."

"Dashing, you say? I am blushing." His voice was warm, like a cozy blanket on a cold night.

"Oh well, sir, it is true," I said. "Quite dashing." I looked up at him and knew I wanted him to kiss me. Then he did, his hand cupping my cheek.

He pulled back and looked down. "Forgive me..." he began.

"No, don't be sorry," I said, putting a hand on his forearm. I looked around to see if his cave comrades were nearby.

"You are so lovely," he said, running a cool knuckle down my cheek. "And I wish somehow that I didn't have to leave again. But I must."

I nodded. I couldn't think of anything to say. I stood up and picked up his cup and plate from the ground. "I guess I should get back to the house."

"Thank you, once again, for taking such good care of us all these days," Edgar said, watching me gather up pail and cloth.

"I thank you for the sacrifice you have made, to leave school, join the United States Army, travel here to Virginia to defend us," I said looking into his eyes.

"I was raised to believe that helping others is our Christian duty, he responded. "I was influenced at Oberlin to work for the rights of others, to do what I can to help free people from slavery. How could I do otherwise?"

I nodded and stood up, walked a few steps, and then stopped and turned toward him. "Come back to the house tomorrow. Will can fetch you. We will give you and the boys a proper send-off."

****

General Rosecrans was drawing his lines around Carnifex Ferry. This caused Floyd to draw in all his outposts, and though we were wholly ignorant at the time of what was going on, it opened the way to our escape. Scarcely any Southern soldiers were now passing the house or stopping to visit the family.

--Private Edgar Condit

Chapter Seventeen

Panther Mountain, Sunday morning, September 8, 1861

My little cousins placed hymn books on the benches in Grandma and Grandpa Grose's parlor. Since Bethel had been ransacked and travel was so treacherous, Pastor Phelps had stopped riding the circuit and held services whenever he could safely travel at my grandparents' home. As many as could came. Some families with elderly parents or young children were leery of going too far from home, especially since the battle at Cross Lanes. It was understood that God would forgive them for not attending services and that they were allowed to pray and have Bible study on their own at home.

Aunt Jerusha dusted off the top of the piano, straightened her sheet music and sat down, ready to play. There was special music planned that morning. Maysie and her brothers and sister, talented singers all, stood next to the piano and lifted their voices unto the Lord.

>*Nearer, my God, to Thee,*
>*Nearer to Thee!*
>*E'en tho' it be a cross*
>*That raiseth me;*
>*Still all my song shall be---*
>*Nearer, my God, to Thee,*
>*Nearer, my God, to Thee,*
>*Nearer to Thee! Nearer, my God, to Thee,*
>*Nearer to Thee!*

I slid my hand into my dress pocket and rubbed the folded paper of Logan's letter. I had read it again and again, as if going back over the words might give me some clue as to where he was.

Grandpa led us in prayer and then preached for a spell. He was well-known in the community for being an inspiring teacher. As soon as he ended the lesson and gave us the benediction, Maysie scooted across the bench to me.

"Good singing, Mays," I told her.

"Thank you, Liddy," she said, smiling. "I heard you were in town yesterday."

"Yes, we did some shopping and picked up mail," I confirmed. "Actually, I got a letter from Logan."

"You did?!" Her eyes popped wide open. "What did he say? Where is he?"

I gave her some of the details, but kept the more personal parts to myself. Then she asked me what his regiment was so that she could write him a letter. I paused for a moment.

I knew that Maysie was sweet on Logan. The thought of her writing him letters didn't sit well with me somehow.

"Ah, I'll have to go back and look at the letter to see what he said."

Her eyes narrowed and she stuck out her chin. "Well, seems like you might remember something like that," she said with an edge in her voice. "Please do let me know at church meeting next Sunday, would you?" Maysie stood up from the bench, crinoline swishing, and sashayed away.

****

The women of my family were bustling around the house, placing plates and silver, stirring pots on the stove, carving meats, slicing bread. Our farewell party for the three Ohio soldiers would leave them well-fed for their journey, no doubt about it.

"Liddy Jane, I can't wait to taste that apple cake you made." Aunt Caroline wrapped her arm around my shoulders. She looked beautiful, as usual, her glossy dark hair in a knot, fair cheeks tinged a healthy pink. She wore a red dress that beautifully complemented her features.

"I hope it tastes good," I said. I was nervous and she knew it. I had talked to her about Edgar and she was the only one who knew how I really felt about his leaving.

For the first time since they came to our front door in the dark of night a couple of weeks before, Edgar, Fred, and George walked up to our back door in broad daylight. We hadn't seen Floyd's pickets in days. Uncle Frank told us that they were all gathering elsewhere for the next fight with the Yankees.

One look at Edgar, haversack slung over his shoulder as he stepped into the kitchen, made me sad. It was final. This was really the end of our time together. They would not get lost wandering around the mountain again. As their guide, I would see to that.

"Boys, come on in," my mother urged, waving them into the front room. "Take a seat. Let's get you some coffee."

Grandma sat down next to Edgar and took his hand in hers. "Thank you so much," I heard her say through the din in the room. My aunts and cousins were practically swarming the soldiers, wanting to meet them and express their gratitude for their service. I left the room to check on my cake.

As I pulled the pan out of the oven, I saw Sis out of the corner of my eye, pinching off a piece of cornbread from a plate. "Hey now, Sis! You get away from that. That's for company!"

She looked straight at me and stuffed the piece into her mouth, looking like the cat who caught the mouse, chewing slowly. I took her by the hand and gently guided her toward Mama. But when Sis saw Grandma talking to Edgar, she ran and jumped into Grandma's lap.

"Well hello, Sis!" Edgar said with a wide grin. "So nice to see you again, young lady."

Mama smiled and walked over.

"Edgar, it really is high time we gave Sis a proper name. Would you do us the honor of giving her a fine Yankee name?"

Edgar's eyes went wide and his head jerked back. "Me, madam? Why me?"

"Because Sis has taken such a shine to you. Wouldn't you agree, Liddy?"

"Yes, yes indeed. I believe you are the perfect person to give our Sis a name," I said.

"Well, let us see now....hm....I am thinking. Maybe I should think of the names of some ladies I have courted." Everyone chuckled. Aunt Jerusha murmured to Aunt Harriet, "I'll bet that's a long list of names!" Harriet giggled, nodding.

Edgar put a hand on Sis's little shoulder and said, "How about Leonora? She could be Nora, for short?"

Everyone aahed and cooed and there was some light applause. "Let's hear it for Nora!" Fred called out. Sis was now Nora, and Edgar's place in our family cemented.

Over the chatter, I heard Barney barking outside, in the furious way he sounded when he saw deer.

"Shh!" Mama hissed sharply. The chatter in the room died down.

Horse hooves pummeled the road. Aunt Caroline peeked around a curtain and cried, "Rebs!"

The next thing I knew, Edgar, Fred and George had dropped to their hands and knees and were crawling beneath the window. "Quickly!" Mama said, "Climb up into the loft!" They shuffled off and clambered up the ladder just as a half-dozen Confederate soldiers dismounted and made a beeline for the front walk.

Aunts Mary Ann and Becky stood side by side on the front door threshold, their plump shoulders and full skirts blocking the men from peeking in. "Good afternoon, ladies, how are you today?" The cavalry captain craned his neck. "Looks like you have got a real party going on here this fine Sunday."

Aunt Mary Ann spoke. "Yes, we are enjoying my sister's hospitality this afternoon. And what brings you here?"

"Ma'am, we are going door to door on the mountain to check on whether anyone has seen anymore Yankee soldiers since Cross Lanes. Have you seen any?"

"No, we have not," Mary Ann lied. "Anyone else here seen any Union men?"

No, no, voices called out.

"There you have your answer, sir," Becky said, arms folded across her chest.

82

"Much obliged, ladies," said the soldier, tipping his kepi at them. "Enjoy your gathering."

My aunt closed the door and bolted it. Sighs of relief puffed out across the crowd. "I believe God will forgive us for this one white lie," Grandma said, with a wink.

****

> As darkness closed down, we took another farewell of all the family, with an audible "God bless you!" and struck out, the second time, to reach Gauley Bridge. The daughter, who had already risked so much for us piloted us some two miles down the Gauley River to an uncle of hers….

--Private Edgar Condit

****

I led them through the woods by lantern to the foot of the mountain, down a path lined with dripping trees. I had made a plan with Aunt Becky to bring the three soldiers to her farm. Uncle Billy would take them from there on toward Gauley Bridge.

Billy waved at us. "Ya'll had best get inside," I said to Edgar, George and Fred. We got to the front door and said our goodbyes.

"Boys, I will follow you in a moment. I would just like to have a private word with Lydia."

The other two soldiers smiled at each other. In the lantern light near the Grose's front door, Edgar took my hands in his.

"Lydia, I will never forget you," he said, squeezing my hands gently. "I am grateful to God that we poor, sodden chaps happened upon the Renick farm two weeks ago. Please give my best again to your mother and all of the children." Then he kissed my forehead.

My eyes filled with tears. Smiling as best I could, I thanked him, said that I would miss him and wished God's mercies on their journey back to headquarters. I turned, and without looking back, I whispered, "Farewell."

I shook as I climbed the wooded mountain path back home.

For we do not wrestle against flesh and blood, but against the rulers, against the authorities, against the cosmic powers over this present darkness, against the spiritual forces of evil in the heavenly places.

--Ephesians 6:12

Chapter Eighteen

Panther Mountain, Tuesday, September 10, 1861

After I finished my chores, I walked down to Billy and Becky's. The sun was out for a change. Miss Lou was out in her pen. I stepped onto a fence rail and stuck out a carrot. She clopped over to me. I stroked her velvety nose while she nibbled.

Hoof beats pounded up the road. I turned to see Uncle Frank, Uncle Henry and the Masons galloping past, rifles slung across their backs. Uncle Frank saw us and slowed down long enough to yell "Carnifex!"

Uncle Billy walked out from the barn, hand shading his eyes. "I reckon the fighting's begun," he said. "We heard tell that Floyd's men are holding the hills around the ferry. I guess the Yankees decided to go after 'em."

Becky walked out onto their front porch, wiping her hands on her apron.

"Do you think Logan's regiment is involved?" she asked, a deep furrow in her fair forehead.

"Hard to tell, sweetheart," Billy said. He walked up the porch steps and put his arm around her shoulder.

She put her hand to her mouth and tears spilled down her cheeks. I chewed on my thumbnail.

A trot with Miss Lou will clear my head, I thought. Blanket and saddle, harness and bit in place, I mounted the russet mare.

Riding wasn't the same without Logan. I loved watching him put Lou through her gaits in the barnyard, listening to the cling and clang of her tack as he walked her out after a ride, helping him hang her saddle and blanket over the planks of the stall, inhaling the sweet smell of clean shavings and hay. How I wished he were there with me right then. I prayed he wasn't at the fight.

BOOM! I jerked back in the saddle at the sound and accidentally squeezed my legs tight around Miss Lou. Off she galloped, as I struggled to steady her, tightening the reins.

"Liddy! Come back!" Becky was waving me in from the porch.

I managed to slow the horse down and trotted her back. I dismounted, shaking, and hustled her into the barn.

On the porch, Becky put a shawl across my shoulders and patted my arm. "Thank you for riding Miss Lou," she said. "Logan surely would appreciate it."

"I'll walk you up and make sure you get home safe," Billy said, and we trudged up the muddy hill. The longer we walked, the heavier I breathed and the madder I got.

"You're awful quiet," he said, looking at me sidewise. "Is everything alright?"

"No, it is not," I answered, my voice quivering. "I am just so sick and tired of this fighting, tired of being afraid, tired of worrying!"

I saw him nodding out of the corner of my eye. "Times are bad lately," he said. "Makes me mad, too. Sometimes I ask God why it's all happening."

I shook my head. "Doesn't make any sense."

We reached the top of the hill and I could see Mama through the kitchen window.

"Thank you for walking me," I said to my uncle. "I can take it from here. But I have to ask, do you know if Logan *is* there fighting?"

He breathed out a long sigh. "Truth is, he probably is. His unit is the Nicholas Blues. They're part of Floyd's troops. I'll have to tell Becky when I get back."

My eyes filled with tears and I pulled the shawl tighter around me. "I appreciate your telling me," I said.

Chapter Nineteen

War Reports, Carnifex Ferry, September 1861

Shortly after daylight, on Tuesday, September 10th, 1861, a runaway slave scouting for the Union reported to General William Rosecrans of the 23rd Ohio that the enemy had crossed the Gauley during the night, having used a ferry boat to build a bridge. By one o'clock p.m., bullets and cannonballs were flying.

A Confederate sniper using a Whitworth .45 caliber percussion rifle shot Union General William Lytle in the left calf, severely wounding him. Soon after, Confederate General John Floyd was shot in the arm and fell off his horse, knocking him out of the battle.

Union troops who were engaged in the fighting on Henry Patterson's farm had marched 17 miles before reaching Floyd's well-fortified position on the north bank of the Gauley River. Reports vary widely on how many soldiers each side fielded that day. Floyd estimated that between eight and nine thousand Yankees were engaged, while his troops numbered only two-thousand.

A Baptist minister who witnessed the skirmish reported to a Virginia newspaper that the Southern regiments had only eight wounded, while he counted five hundred Northern troops killed and a thousand wounded. Those were wildly inflated figures; by a Union Second Lieutenant's count, only two Union soldiers were killed and six wounded.

A Confederate surgeon present at the battle came up with an even different number of Union wounded:

> *"The hours was full of ball & shell. I was in the midst & came off without "one bone being broken," we being loose one man, the enemy' loss 413. We fell back in the night else we would have been totally annihilated the next morning. We lost some horses & prisoners. I lost my tent & fine blanket"*

> **--Dr. Samuel Crockett Gleaves, Surgeon, 45th Virginia Infantry, C.S.A.**

Chapter Twenty

Renick home, Panther Mountain, Wednesday, September 11, 1861

Mama pushed boxes and bottles around on pantry shelves. "Blackberry tea leaves," she murmured. "Where did I put the blackberry tea leaves?"

"Right here, Mama," I said handing her the wooden box from the shelf right in front of her.

"Well I'll declare, I ought to have my eyes examined," she said, shaking her head. She pulled out a basket and began filling it with supplies.

"Your aunts and I are going to the ferry," she said. "I'll need you to stay and watch the young'uns."

"Can't Will and Caroline?"

"No, I need you to stay here. You bar the door and don't open it for anyone, y'hear?"

"Yes, Mama." I wanted to go with them, to help tend to the wounded soldiers, to see if there was anyone there I knew.

Through the front room window, I watched Mama and Aunt Caroline pack up the Backus' wagon and head down the road. Little Peg and Lizzie came in and sat down on the rug.

"Liddy, will there be daisies in Ohio?" Lizzie asked, chewing on a swatch of her long brown hair.

I leaned over and covered her small hand with mine. "Why yes, I am sure there are daisies in Ohio," I answered.

"And corn?" Little Peg asked.

"Oh my, yes. *Lots* of corn."

"Is it a long ride in the wagon to get there?"

"Well, it will take a while, but before you know it, we'll be seeing Daddy. And he'll be waving and smiling at us, standing in front of our brand-new house near the river."

"The river?" Her eyes opened wide. "We're going to live near the river?"

I laughed at her expression. "Yes indeed, a big river, bigger than the Gauley. Daddy has found us a house in a town near where the Ohio River flows. And it will be a bigger house than this, and we'll fish in the river."

"Oh, I like that!" Peg said, a smile cracking across her face.

"Who said we were going to live on a river?" Sister Caroline called out from the kitchen. She walked into the front room holding a potato in one hand, a paring knife in the other. "I read a book about a girl who lived on a houseboat," Caroline said, her voice getting higher. "Are we going to live on a houseboat?"

I smiled and shook my head. "No, silly, not a houseboat, a house close to the river. And maybe we'll plant peas in the garden and you can dig for worms and Daddy will take us fishing. Would you like that?"

She nodded her head. "Yes!"

Frankie walked in, rubbing his eyes. He sniffled. "What's wrong, Frankie?" I asked.

"I miss Daddy," he said, hiccupping sobs. "I was scared when I heard the thunder last night. But it wasn't raining."

"When it thunders, Daddy makes us feel better by singing 'My Bonny,'" Little Peg said.

"Come here, Frankie," I said, arms outstretched. I sat down in the rocking chair and he climbed up on my lap. "That wasn't thunder. But don't worry, it's all over now."

"What was it?" he asked, his blue eyes peering into mine.

"Well, our Yankee soldiers gave the Rebs a good fight up at the ferry," I explained. "And they chased them away with their cannonballs."

He laid his head on my chest. "I don't like the fightin'. I don't like the Rebs."

"Me neither!" Peg cried out.

"Me neither too!" Caroline joined in.

Will walked in carrying Sis. "Hey now, what's all the yellin'?"

"Was Logan there, Liddy?" Little Peg asked.

"I...I...don't know," I stuttered.

"He's a Reb but he don't want to be," Frankie said.

"Yes, that's right," I said, smoothing his sandy hair. "Logan does not want to fight with the Rebs. We must remember to pray for him, every night, and ask God to protect him."

"What about Edgar?" Will asked. "Do you think he's back to soldierin' and fightin'?"

I shook my head, my jaw tight. I put my head back and looked at the ceiling. "I wish I knew," I said.

The creaky rocker accompanied me as I sang:

> *My Bonny lies over the ocean*
> *My Bonny lies over the sea*
> *My Bonny lies over the ocean*
> *Oh bring back my Bonny to me.*

Chapter Twenty-One

Since I have been writing, another of "our boys" has come in from the brush where he has been fed by Union women.

--Pvt. Daniel Judson, Company C, 7th OVI, Camp Gauley, Sept. 12, 1861

****

Renick home, Panther Mountain, Sept. 15, 1861

My heart pounded as Uncle Frank laid out the mail from town on the table. I sifted through the envelopes and found one addressed to me, in Logan's handwriting. I clutched it to my heart and ran out of the room, climbed up the ladder and jumped onto my bed, carefully peeling open the gummed flap.

"Dear Lydia,

How are you? I am sorry I haven't written more often, but I have been laid up in camp with a nasty case of the measles. I will not see action anytime soon."

He wasn't there! He couldn't have been at Carnifex, because he's been sick!

"A lot of the boys in my unit have come down with them, too. I heard tell that more Rebs are getting sick up in these mountains than the Yankees are. Small wonder, with all the rain and chilly nights. They're not used to the cold. The food they give us is awful also.

I hope you and your family are safe. I know your Uncle Frank is helping guard the mountain. When will you be leaving for Ohio? Please let me know your address after you get there. God willing, this war will end soon and we can all get back home and live our normal lives.

Please write to me when you have time, you can use the address on this envelope.

Your friend,
Logan"

I let out a big breath and laid back on my pillow.

"Liddy?" Uncle Frank called up to the loft. "You ran out of here so fast, you didn't see the other mail you got!"

"*Other* mail?" I asked. "What other mail?"

"You got a package. Return address is Camp Gauley."

Camp Gauley? I scampered down the ladder and took the brown paper parcel from Uncle Frank. He grinned at me, no doubt amused by my red face.

"Miss Lydia Renick, Panther Mountain," I read out loud. Sure enough, the return address up in the left corner was Camp Gauley, Virginia. "Well, I'll be. I wonder what this is?"

I sat down at the kitchen table and cut the string with a paring knife. I unwrapped the paper and found a dress pattern. A beautiful pattern for a silk dress with capped sleeves and a sash. "What in the world?" I whispered. There was a note with the pattern:

"Dear Lydia,

The boys and I returned to camp thanks to the sure-footed scouting of your Uncle Billy. Being that we have not yet received our first payment in the service, I borrowed from my erstwhile bunkmates in order to buy you this pattern at a shop on the Gauley Bridge pier. I hope this small gift will convey to you my appreciation for all that you have done to help us. I suspect we would have fallen into Confederate hands without your assistance and for that, I am eternally grateful to you and your dear mother. I hope you and she might find just the right shade of fabric for this to complement your lovely hazel eyes.

I do not know how long I will be stationed here. I expect we will eventually ship off to Charleston. I will keep you apprised of my whereabouts.

When that dress is finished and you have an opportunity, please send me a photo of yourself wearing it. I would like to carry it with me.
                                          Yours,
                                          Edgar M. Condit"

Had Doc Rader checked my heart at that moment with his cold stethoscope, he would have heard quite a commotion. Mama came to the kitchen door.

"From Edgar," I said, still not quite believing that he thought I should have a beautiful silk dress. I held up the pattern and showed her.

She smiled and took it from me, looking at the drawing on the front and then the instructions on the back. "Well now, here's a dress you surely won't wear for horse riding," she said with a chuckle. "Let's put this somewhere for safekeeping. We are more likely to find some fine silk in the shops of Gallipolis than on the Gauley pier. We will be there before you know it."

"I believe our Yank is sweet on you, sugar," she added, winking at me. "And you're blushing, so there must be some tender feelings on your part too."

****

Reporter dispatch, Wheeling, Virginia, October 1861

The citizens and voters of 39 designated counties of Northwestern Virginia were scheduled to vote on whether the Restored Government of Virginia should become a new state of the Union, forever severing the original state into two. The *Wheeling Daily Intelligencer* printed an editorial expressing confidence that on Thursday, October 24th, people within the newly drawn state boundaries would decide to become a new state, tentatively named Kanawha, a word tied to both the Shawnee terms "water way" or "new water," and to the Catawba word meaning "friendly brother."

If the latter meaning was in the new state constitution framers' minds, their intentions for the new and old states to become "friendly brothers" would not soon be realized.

****

Chapter Twenty-Two

Nicholas County, Virginia, October 22, 1861

Daddy sent the money for the mules, which he said were better for pulling wagons over hilly country. We packed as light as we could. The only furniture we put in the wagon was the rocking chair, which Mama reasoned we would need to soothe the little ones from time to time along the journey. We used flour sacks for pillows and took enough plates and cups for what we figured would be a three- or four-day trip, depending on the weather and the bushwhackers.

Fog puffs filled spaces between trees along the hills, a few straggler leaves hanging from mostly bare branches. The road was rutted and the mules were balking. We rocked side to side in the back of the wagon. Will had the reins and Mama sat next to him. We were headed to Kanawha Falls, southeast of Charleston, and would stop there for the night.

Aunt Nancy and Aunt Sarah drove their wagon behind ours. Aunt Nancy was pregnant and had her three boys, George, Clark, and Dixon. My cousins Chrissa and William were older and could help drive when needed.

Little Peg cried and hugged Barney's furry neck when we dropped him off at Aunt Caroline and Uncle Frank's house. I had to leave my books at home, but Aunt Caroline gave me a new one before we left, *Great Expectations* by Dickens. I was fine until she hugged me goodbye; that's when the tears fell.

"You will be better off in Ohio, Lydia," she said softly into my ear as she smoothed my hair. "God be with you. We will be praying for you and want to hear all about your new home after you get there." She let go of the hug and reached into a satchel for a packet of paper, a pen, nibs, and bottle of ink. "Here now, you write when you can."

As we rumbled through Cross Lanes, we came upon a clutch of grey-capped pickets standing in the middle of the road. "Whoa!" Will shouted to the mules. I stuck my head through the canvas flap and recognized John Williams as one of them.

"Halt!" one barked. He was tall and pot-bellied, a thin grey beard sprouting along his jaws. John looked at me and walked up to the stopped wagon.

"Miss Lydia, where might y'all be going?" he asked. His hat brim looked like it had taken a bullet.

"We are on our way to Ohio," I answered. "We have a home there now."

He let out a low whistle. "Leaving Panther Mountain? Well, that's a shame," he said, shaking his head.

"Yes, well we might not have to leave if not for Jeff Davis' wretched war," Will said, his neck turning beet red.

"Son, you best not forget that this is *Lincoln's* war," Greybeard shot back. "We were living in peace until he threatened our way of life! How *old* are you, boy?"

Mama put her hand on Will's arm and squeezed. "Gentlemen, we have many miles to travel today, so if you would be so kind, we will be on our way."

"Not till we get a look at the inside of your wagon," Greybeard said, walking toward the wagon.

John held up a hand. "That's alright, Lieutenant. I can handle this." He walked around to the back. I stumbled over children's legs and packing crates to get there before he did.

"Now listen, John..." I began.

"How about you listen to me, Miss Lydia? I'm the one holdin' a gun, if you haven't already noticed." He had a peach fuzz outline of a moustache over his upper lip. I stared at his face, focused on his blue eye.

He lifted the musket and aimed it at me. I froze. I knew from my squirrel hunting days with Daddy that a little old Kentucky long rifle like the ones we used to hunt with did not pack the power of the higher caliber Confederate-issue Richmond musket pointed at me.

Just then, John gave me a wink and nod, lowered the gun, and turned back to his comrades. "All's clear, Lieutenant!" he called out.

I clutched my shawl and breathed out. *Thank you*, I mouthed.

96

It was almost dark when we reached Kanawha Falls. We pulled up to the Glen Ferris Inn, a place I had heard of but never seen. It was a stately brick mansion set near the Kanawha River with five Ionic columns, like the ones described in *The Marble Faun*, like Atlas' whitewashed arms holding up a pebble-studded triangle of roof. Mama climbed down from the driver's bench. Will stretched out his arms and yawned.

I called after Mama. "Do you mind if I go with you? I need to stretch my legs a bit"

Mama said yes. I hiked up my skirt, clambered over the bench and jumped off, landing with shooting pain in both ankles. I heard Caroline whining inside the wagon. "I need to stretch, too!"

"Just stay there for now, you'll get a turn shortly," I called back. I looked through the iron gate along the side porch and saw a line of shiny Morgan horses tied to hitching posts.

The lobby smelled of beef, beer, and cigar smoke. We walked up to the polished mahogany front desk and Mama asked about lodging for the night.

"Ma'am, I am mighty sorry, but we are full up," the innkeeper said. He was balding, with bristly red sideburns. A Union soldier leaned against a nearby wall on one elbow, chatting with a young woman who was working behind the desk.

"Full up?" Mama asked, raising one eyebrow. "Sir, how can that be so at this time of year?"

"Officers, ma'am. Union big wigs. They've taken up every room we have."

"Oh dear." Mama's voice sounded like it was hanging by its last thread. She had a panicked look.

If we couldn't get even one room at the Glen Ferris, we would have to sleep in the wagon. If we pulled over to the side of the turnpike, we'd surely get stuck in the mud. With all the mosquitoes, flourishing as they were in the wet weather, we'd be eaten alive. We'd have to huddle together so as not to freeze to death. And then there were the bears. And Rebels roaming about, who might not let us pass as John's unit did, who might force Will to sign the oath.

"Mama," I said as she turned from the desk. "Mama, we can't stay in the wagon tonight."

"We have no choice, Liddy," she said, frowning.

"I have to try this one more time," I said, and rang the front desk bell. The proprietor, who had stepped into a back room poked his head out.

"Look here, sir," I said, ""We've just come all the way from Panther Mountain and have got seven young'uns to feed and put to sleep. My aunts and cousins are on their way here too. We can't possibly stay in our wagons all night.

The soldier turned his head and stood up straight. "Did you say Panther Mountain, ma'am?" he asked, eyebrows arching over his big brown eyes.

"Yes sir, I did," I answered. "We are from those parts and are on our way to Ohio."

"Well ma'am—ladies," he tipped his hat at both of us, "I am mighty grateful to the people of Panther Mountain. Without their help, a lot of us might be Rebel prisoners... or worse."

Mama and I looked at each other and our mouths dropped a little.

"I should introduce myself," he said, smoothing his straight dark hair with one hand, hat in the other. "I am Private Dan Judson, Ohio Volunteer Infantry. Some of your neighbors hid us in their home and fed us after we escaped."

"Well I'll be," Mama said. "They were not just our neighbors, they were our *family*!"

The three of us chuckled while the innkeeper stared at us, unsmiling. He cleared his throat. "Ahem, well nevertheless, we cannot keep you for the night, so...."

"Oh, sir," Dan said, "you don't have a spot to spare?"

"Full up, as I told the ladies just now."

Dan turned to us. "My company is camped nearby, at the Falls. While we cannot offer you the comforts of this fine inn, I am certain we could give you and your families some space in our tents. That is, if you don't mind roughing it a bit," he said, lowering his chin and searching our eyes for reactions.

"That is mighty kind of you, Private," Mama said, "but we wouldn't want to intrude..."

"Not at all, madam!" he exclaimed. "The least we can do is return the hospitality your family so graciously showed us when we were in dire straits!"

It turned out that Private Judson was among the stragglers who ended up at Grandma and Grandpa Grose's that night back in August. When Aunt Sarah and Aunt Nancy caught up with us at the inn, he offered them hearty handshakes and they laughed about how quickly they'd scraped together biscuits and jellies for him and his comrades in the middle of the night.

The soldiers camped near the inn were polite and kind. They watered our mules and cleared out two of their largest tents for us. I put the little ones to sleep straight away and then joined the group around their campfire. The night air was crisp and chilly. Mama, Will and I, my aunts and older cousins huddled on logs around the campfire and ate Army-issue salt pork and hard tack, washing it down with campfire-brewed coffee.

Most of these men were from Edgar's regiment, I realized. Could he be here?

"Beg pardon, Private Judson." I leaned toward him. "Do you know a Private Condit? Edgar Condit?"

"I certainly do, Miss Renick," he answered, smiling. "Oh, fine fella, fine fella. I'm sorry to say I don't know what has become of him. Many of our men came down with typhoid and were hospitalized in Charleston. I'm sorry I can't tell you more about his whereabouts. You know Condit, ma'am?"

"Yes, he and two other Ohio volunteers, Fred and George, hid on our property. We kept them for about two weeks."

I looked into the fire, as if its crackling embers could provide me with an answer.

****

"I have not had either opportunity or inclination to write in my Journal for several days. Today is a most bitter cold day and have suffered more from cold than I have since we left Cleveland. Yesterday we had the honor of entertaining the women who fed us on our retreat from Cross Lanes. They are going to Ohio. I fear they did not receive as much good from what they got of us as we did from their warm bread and apples. I hope I may meet them again at some future time."

--Private Daniel Judson, Company C, 7th OVI, Charleston, Virginia, Oct. 23, 1861

Chapter Twenty-Three

Along the James River and Kanawha Turnpike, October 23, 1861

As we loaded up our belongings the next morning, Private Judson spoke with Mama and my aunts. "Ladies, please be very, very careful traveling, particularly as you approach Charleston. We have reports of rebel forces hiding up in the hills along the river."

They thanked him, and we all exchanged warm goodbyes and God blesses with the group of Ohio soldiers who saw us off with fresh coffee and apples.

It was our plan to drive at least to the outskirts of Charleston before nightfall. This was the first time I had ever traveled outside of Nicholas County, and as I sat next to Will on the driver's bench, I was amazed by how many little hamlets lined the turnpike. Houses of log, wood and brick dotted the hillsides along the Kanawha River. A world I hadn't known about, just miles from my home.

The closer we got to Charleston, though, the scenery changed. Roadside weeds were flattened and matted with mud. Tree branches and stones were scattered across front lawns. We passed a logging crew with horse teams pulling a fallen tree, lassoed with chains, off of a tavern roof.

"What in the world do you suppose happened here?" I asked Will. "Looks… like…. it flooded," he said, straining to turn the mules away from the workers and horses.

We rolled through a town called Kanawha Salines later that day. Mud lines on houses and stores told the tale of the September flood. Many storefronts were boarded up, but we found a boarding house that was open for business. The owners, Mr. and Mrs. Bailey, had rooms available.

"You poor things, traveling without your menfolk," Mrs. Bailey said, clucking her tongue. She stood in the front doorway as we pulled our bags from the wagon. She was broad shouldered and heavily endowed. Her gingham dress with its dainty lace collar seemed a bit delicate for such a sturdy body.

She backed away from the threshold as we made our way in, and in doing so, revealed Mr. Bailey, a slight, thin man wearing a suit coat, vest, and tie as if he were going to Sunday meeting. They were an absolute contrast to each other, she being the bulkier one, he more like a fence post.

"The rooms are upstairs, down the hallway to your right," Mr. Bailey instructed, waving a hand upward. "Supper is served at five o'clock, so you'll have some time to wash up."

Flowered wallpaper lined the wall of the staircase. We clambered up, little ones grabbing our hands and skirts, and I opened the first door I saw.

I made out two brass beds, a chair and a wash stand in the dim light. The curtains were closed. I knocked a knee against a chest at the foot of one bed as I walked over to pull them open.

"Only two beds!" Caroline cried out. "I claim one!"

"Now, Caroline," Mama said, "We must all share and some will have to find spots on the floor. It's a sight better than sleeping on the cold ground in an Army tent as we did last night!"

The corners of my younger sister's mouth drooped. Frankie and Sis climbed up on the chest and jumped onto the bed like little frogs.

"Come now, you two, off," I said. I picked Sis up and Frankie slid down the bedpost. The wash basin was full. "Everybody come here and roll up your sleeves."

Mama went down the hall to see the aunts' and cousins' accommodations. Will flopped down on the cloth rug, stretched and yawned. "I ain't never drove any pack animal as long as I have those mules."

"Haven't ever," I corrected as I soaped up little hands. "If you're going to make a good impression in Ohio, you'd best stop talking like an unschooled ridge runner."

His head jerked back, strands of dark hair tumbling over his forehead. "Hmph!" he answered, "Who do you think you are, talkin' to me like a schoolteacher?"

"I'm just saying, we are going to have to make all new friends, you know!" The thought of strangers making judgments about us made my chest ache a little.

****

"Liddy," Mama said to me later, "I heard you from down the hall scolding your brother Take it easy on him. He is just as sad as you are to leave friends and family behind, whether you realize it or not." She looked at me with that iron gaze that could always shut me right up.

There was a knock at the door. "We are going on down, Peggy," Aunt Nancy called. We were all hungry, but she was probably even more so, seeing as how she was eating for two.

Fried chicken aroma drifted up as we walked down the stairs. My stomach growled. Candlelight gave a rosy glow to the Bailey's dining room. Mr. Bailey sat at the head of a long cherry wood table and we pulled out our chairs. There was a small table, like one for playing cards, for the youngest ones.

Mrs. Bailey carried in bowl after bowl of vegetables, tureens of gravy and platters of chicken drumsticks and breasts, and set them on the table.

"Fred, would you bless the food for us?"

We bowed our heads and Mr. Bailey held forth in prayer, his voice rising and falling like a preacher's. "Heavenly Father, we thank you for this food...."

And on he went, and on and on. I clenched my fists under the table, *Hurry up!* I thought. *Oh please, hurry up!*

Then, finally. "Amen!" "Amen!" we all answered. Serving spoons clattered in dishes.

Mrs. Bailey broke the silence as we chewed. "Tell me about where y'all come from and where you're going."

Aunt Sarah chose her words carefully, not knowing if the Baileys supported the Yankees or the Rebels. "Our families have decided it's best to move to Ohio while the fighting is going on. Safer for our children."

104

"So you're figuring on coming back to Virginia in the end?" Mr. Bailey asked, his cheeks packed like a chipmunk's.

"Yes," Mama said. "We pray this fighting will be over soon and we can get back to our farms."

Mrs. Bailey nodded. Her blue eyes were watery as we told her about our church being ransacked, our horses stolen, how we ran out of food. "It is indeed terrible, this fightin'. Neighbors against one another. We don't know from one day to the next if we'll be run by the Yankees or the Rebs. They go back and forth. Right now, it's the Yanks." I still couldn't reckon whose side they were on from what they were saying.

There was a knock at the back door. "You'll excuse me, please," Mrs. Bailey said. From the dining room, I heard the sound of footsteps shuffling in. More boarders? I wondered.

No one came into the dining room. We finished our supper and passed our plates to the right. Mama scraped sop, crumbs and kernels onto a single plate and stacked the others. "Lydia, Will, could you please take these to the kitchen?"

My brother and I picked up the dishes and lugged them into the steamy kitchen. Coffee was brewing on the stove. Mrs. Bailey cut slices of pound cake and placed them neatly onto a glass dish.

The clink of silverware on plates in the pantry caught my attention. I looked across the room to see four dark-skinned men, dressed in filthy work clothes, digging into their meals.

I looked up at Mrs. Bailey and asked, "Are they your slaves?

She caught my puzzled gaze and nodded, jutting out her chin. "Oh no, not ours," she said softly. "They're hired out as salt packers by their owners."

There were a handful of folks in Nicholas who had slaves or what they called servants working for them, but not many. I looked back into the pantry and saw hard, muscled forearms resting on the table top.

"They can't work right now because the flood washed away so much of the salt works. We give them a bite to eat. They have so little."

I pressed my lips together and nodded. Will stood next to me, staring at the men who didn't notice that they were being watched. I poked him in the side with my elbow. He snapped his head around and scrunched up his nose.

One of the men came out of the cramped pantry, empty plate in hand. He stopped suddenly and stared hard at Will. His eyes were on guard, bloodshot, with deep creases underneath. Will took a step back, giving the man space to pass by him and across to the stove.

"These folks are our guests, Mr. Armstrong, just traveling through on their way to Ohio. Will you have more?" Mrs. Bailey asked, walking over to take the plate from his hands.

"Won't turn it down, Miz," he answered, bowing his head. I heard chairs scrape the floor and the other three men came into the kitchen, holding their plates.

"Of course, gentlemen, there is plenty," she said as she scooped beans onto their dishes. What kindness she showed them. Not only were the Baileys feeding the poor souls, they spoke to them with respect.

"Thank you, ma'am," a man in a dirty tan shirt said. "We will gladly pay you once the salt works are up again."

I ate my dessert and then took the younger ones up to bed. Once they were cleaned and dried and tucked here and there around the room with pillows and blankets, I went to sit by the window. In the distance I saw a bonfire, shadows of people warming their hands at it. I wondered if they were also slaves, salt workers, who had been flooded out of work, out in the cold. I stared at the flickering flames, feeling drowsy. When Mama came into the room, I woke with a start. I had fallen asleep, head on my arm, on the windowsill.

Chapter Twenty-Four

Point Pleasant, VA, October 25, 1861

A chilly wind blew across the river. Bells clanged and steamboats hooted, churning the brown water into foam as they passed the slower coal barges. I looked over the boardwalk rail to the landing below, where Will and George were tying the mules to the sides of the flat boat. The rivermen pushed and pulled our wagons onto the boat.

I shaded my eyes and looked across the river to Ohio. We would see Daddy at last and be together as a family again. I wondered what living in a town would be like, what the new house looked like. Would I have a real bedroom and not just a loft, separated by the thinnest fabric from my sisters? What would our neighbors be like? I hoped they were friendly. At least in Ohio, we would be away from the guns and cannons, away from the war for a time.

A newspaper flapping in the breeze on a boat dock bench described an ambush on the Kanawha.

Unsuccessful Rebel Attack on a Steamer

The Government steamer Mary Cook was fired into last night at Cannelton, on the Kanawha River, by about three hundred rebel cavalry. About one hundred shots were fired into her, wounding one man belonging to the boat. The fire was returned by the boat, and one rebel horse crippled.

The rebels followed the boat several miles, but she succeeded in escaping.

--Cincinnati Daily Press, October 25, 1861

A shiver ran through me. Had we not left on our journey on the day we did, we surely would have been caught in the crossfire as we passed through Cannelton, a dingy coal mining town. We were protected by guardian angels; Rebels up in the hills may have had us in their sights all along our route.

We were nearly a hundred miles downriver from the scene of the attack, having arrived at Point Pleasant, where we could see Ohio across the water. Boatmen told us we were just a little bit upriver from Gallipolis. Mama and my aunts stood nearby on the dock, pulling out pages of letters that Daddy and my uncles had sent on where to meet when we arrived in Ohio.

"Covey wrote that he'll meet us in the town square, just up the riverbank from the dock," Aunt Nancy said, her dress stretched across her bulging belly.

"A.J. said he would be with the others," Aunt Sarah added, blonde curls sprouting from beneath her bonnet.

Mama held up her hand, "Well wait a minute, now, James writes 'I will greet you on the riverbank with open arms…' I wonder if he means…

Aunt Nancy put a hand on Mama's arm, "Peggy, we will just have to trust that our husbands will be there, one way or the other." Mama nodded. "Well, I know my brothers, and I know that they sometimes don't plan very well." She cracked a little smile and my aunts nodded in agreement.

****

Part Two: Exile

--Excerpts from *Gallipolis, being an account of the French five hundred and of the town they established on La Belle Riviere*

As the tide of migration grew, an immense traffic in men and goods developed all along the Ohio. Boats could hardly be built fast enough. Even a comparatively small place like Gallipolis had its ship ways. Trade boomed amazingly, and Gallia County farmers had no trouble in selling their fruit, vegetables, and grain. The steamboats brought artists and entertainers to the town.

The Civil War temporarily interrupted this genial tempo. Gallipolis was made a supply depot for the Union Army. Immense warehouses for storing equipment went up on Public Square, and the marketplace became an ammunition dump. The Union School building was turned into a military hospital, and when it proved inadequate, additional hospitals were erected upon the grounds in the northwest corner of the town. Several military companies of local men were organized for border service.

****

The list of sick and wounded soldiers at the hospital in Gallipolis numbers over 400, all from [Brigadier Generals] Rosecrans and Cox's division. Several hundred have been taken to the [Cincinnati] Marine hospital, there being no room for them here. How many more are yet to come God only knows. Every boat is loaded with them. The prevalent disease seems to be camp fever, brought on by exposure and excessive fatigue in climbing those wild mountains which seem only intended for the wild beast, not for civilized men. The heat during the day, and extreme cold of the nights, added to the malaria peculiar to that region, renders the service there arduous, and destructive to life and health.

-- *Gallipolis Journal,* **October 17, 1861**

****

Chapter Twenty-Five

Gallipolis, OH, October 1861

I turned 18 in our new home, a two-story clapboard house with four gables jutting out of the roof. Daddy had found us a nice place and was excited to show us around. It was set off from the road and the grounds included pens for sheep and horses, a large garden and chicken coop. Red roosters strutted about and turkey heads bobbed, wattles wobbling. Butternut and black walnut trees grew here and there. There was a feeling of safety in our new home. For now, at least, we were in peaceful territory.

I wasn't sure I could get used to the flat riverside land. I missed the deep cut valleys of Virginia and ached for the snug comfort of being surrounded by high peaks, for the high perch of our home on Panther Mountain.

Mary Ann and Jonathan were living in a small frame building on the property that Daddy helped them fix up. It had been used as a schoolhouse before the war. It was nice to have them so close to us.

We rented from a woman whose husband had enlisted with the Union and gone to fight down south. She and her children had to move in with her parents. They took their personal belongings but left much of their furniture, much to our advantage, as we had left all but a rocking chair behind in Virginia. Before the first hard frost, we harvested the last of the corn and wheat that they had planted.

The house had a good-sized dining room, just off the entrance hall. A sturdy walnut table and chairs gave us plenty of room for visitors. Soon after we arrived in Ohio, Mama and I went to town to buy a tablecloth and take a sack of corn to the miller. It was quite a thrill to be able to walk to stores and do our shopping, much more convenient than our accustomed way of driving the wagon to and from Summersville.

Public Square was bustling with activity. Hammers rang out, pounding nails into skeletons of warehouses. Horse hoofs clopped along the brick streets. We strolled along the town's wooden walks, past the druggist's, the dry goods stores, the watchmaker, and the jeweler. Items that were all under one roof at Hardman's in Summersville had entire shops of their own here— shops just for boots and shoes, for magazines and newspapers, groceries, and hardware.

I spotted a photography studio, which reminded me that I promised Edgar I would have a photo taken of myself in the not-yet-sewn silk dress. "Mama, when we are fully settled, might we work on that dress for me?" I asked as we walked, and she agreed.

On our way home from the markets, we stopped at the post office, a small house on a dirt side street. I mailed letters to Aunt Caroline and Logan.

"Dear Aunt Caroline and Uncle Frank,

Daddy found us such a lovely house here, and we are working to set it up nice and proper. There are beds in the rooms upstairs that suit us all just fine. You would be surprised to see how lively this town is. We live close enough to walk to the market. There is much foot traffic on the streets and many boats coming and going on the river."

Please give the boys kisses and hugs from me. I miss you all dearly.

Love,
Lydia"

"Dear Logan,

I find myself wondering daily and nightly where you are and how you are holding up. I hope you are over your recent sickness and can perform your duties, awful as they are. At least some fresh mountain air and a walk around camp might lift your spirits, if nothing else. I am praying always that God will keep you safe from harm.

Our new home is quite nice although very different from our little farmhouse in Virginia. We have more space here, but I find myself homesick for family and friends and the beautiful mountains. I hope our stay here is short and that when the fighting ends, we will see each other again under bright, sunny skies.

Your faithful friend,
Liddy"

Chapter Twenty-Six

Eyewitness report, Summersville, Va., November 1861

Summersville, Virginia was mostly deserted when the 36th Regiment of the Ohio Volunteer Infantry arrived to set up winter quarters. Most of the town's 40 houses were standing empty. By late October, only four families remained.

Board fences that had once squared off tidy homes were picked apart and used to build soldiers' bunks; rail fences were dissembled and used for firewood. One company of soldiers took up residence in the Summersville Hotel, another in the saddle and harness shop where Logan Stephenson had once worked. The rest of the commissioned and non-commissioned officers occupied abandoned houses.

The jail and clerk's office, both made of stone, survived early assaults. Colonel George Crook set up a contingency plan for the occupying troops. In the event of a Confederate attack, all buildings containing U.S. Government property would be set on fire.

The town's brick Catholic church was converted to a regimental hospital, which General William Rosecrans, a devout Catholic, ordered guarded around the clock. A handful of men died of typhoid in their first days at Summersville. Each casket was marched to the graveyard of the Methodist Episcopal Church, South, where it was lowered into the ground. The Chaplain read a few words from Army regulations for funerals, after which soldiers fired three rounds of blank cartridges over the grave and then marched back down the street.

****

Renick home, Gallipolis, OH, November 1, 1861

I was just hanging up my cloak in the entryway after a brisk fall walk when Mama came down the hall.

"Leave it on," she said in a loud voice, pulling on a sweater. "We've got a baby to deliver!"

The baby's head was crowning by the time Mama and I got there. Jonathan had one elbow on the bed, clutching Mary Ann's hand and allowing her to squeeze the life out of his.

"Push, girl! Push!" Mama said loud and firm. She washed her hands and set about her delivery work. She did not have formal medical training but had studied with a midwife and delivered quite a few babies back in Nicholas. "Lydia, get a cool cloth for her face."

After an hour more of labor, the little nugget slid out and Mama's capable hands caught it. "Towel, please," she said to me. Wiping the infant off, she announced, "Mary Ann and Jon, you've got yourselves a fine baby boy!"

They named him James Harry Pierson, James for Daddy.

"We've got an Ohioan in the family!" Daddy declared after he walked in. He was the first, but wouldn't be the last, Panther Mountain baby born in Ohio.

114

Chapter Twenty-Seven

Renick home, Gallipolis, OH, November 1861

My family hosted the Thanksgiving feast. The weather was shifting quickly from fall to winter. Snowflakes drifted past the windows as Mary Ann and I set the table.

Cousins, aunts, and uncles arrived, and what a spread they brought with them. The sideboard was piled with potatoes, squash, green beans, biscuits, and pies. Daddy carved the turkey on the table, gently pushing away my little sisters' fingers as they picked at the slices. Mama's face was relaxed in a way I hadn't seen in quite a while. She held her first grandson Jimmy as she walked around, greeting everyone. She loved having the family together and though she still worried about our kin in Virginia, she was happy in that moment.

Grace said and plates passed, the conversation turned from the weather and the food to what was happening in town. My cousin Chrissa said she had gone to the Army hospital that was set up in a school, to deliver some food and socks she had knitted. "A nurse took the basket but would not let me enter the place," she said between bites, "I suppose I shouldn't have expected a royal welcome, but she strictly forbade me to set foot in the hospital. Said it was too dangerous."

"Well, darling, I'm sure it is," Aunt Nancy said, dabbing at the corners of her mouth with a napkin. "The place is filled with disease. They cannot allow townspeople to be exposed to the sickness."

"Even so," Chrissa said, "I felt such an urge to help at the hospital. I don't see how I can, though, without endangering myself and, really, all of you," she said looking at Nancy's pregnant belly.

"I would like to help there as well," I said, surprising myself. I hadn't really given it any thought until that moment. Although helping Mama with the young'uns was my real job at that time, I also felt a restlessness, a need to do more, especially for soldiers. Like Edgar and Logan.

"Oh, Liddy Jane, I'm afraid that won't do," Mama said shaking her head. "I know you are always looking to help others, but in this case, we must let the doctors and nurses do the healing work."

"Yes, actually, there was an item in the newspaper, right around the time you all arrived," Uncle Covington said. "The editor urged the ladies of Gallipolis who offered their help at the hospital not to do so, for fear of typhoid spreading throughout the town."

I sighed and slumped a little. *But what if Edgar was in that hospital, right now?* I thought. *How could I see him?*

They might stop me at the door, but I could still deliver a letter.

****

Gallipolis, OH, early December 1861

A stout matron with a ring of keys pinned to the waist of her black dress stepped out the front entrance. She must have seen me coming and guessed that I was one of the town ladies come to help the sick. "Please stop right there!" she barked. "Don't come any closer. No visitors allowed."

"Surely you might be able to take this to a patient I have written, to, in the event he is here," I said, and handed her the envelope."

A thick rust-colored curl escaped from her skinned-back bun and bounced on her forehead as she shook her head. "I am not able to tell you any names of patients," she said, her voice rough as gravel.

"I can't promise you anythin', missy, but that I will walk back through that door and put this here letter in the mail basket. After that, it's out of my hands."

I thanked her and prayed that my dear Edgar would be there to receive my letter.

> *"Dear Edgar,*
>
> *We, Renicks and Groses, have arrived in Ohio and are settled in Gallipolis. Along the journey in Virginia, we stopped and were welcomed by a number of your Company C fellows. They shared their food and tents with us. My heart nearly burst when Private Judson relayed to me that*

116

you had fallen ill. I worry that you are yet down with the fever and am wondering if you are recuperating at the U.S. Army hospital here in town? I have read reports that the sick and injured Union soldiers in western Virginia are being brought here and wondered if you might be among them? If you get this letter, please do write to me, so that I may know how you are.

Your faithful friend,
Lydia"

****

A few days later, I was watching Little Peg and Frankie practicing their letters on slates in the parlor. Caroline was playing teacher and had enlisted them to be her pretend students. My mother and father walked into the room. "Look, Mama, I spelled 'cat,'" Little Peg said, her voice squeaking with excitement.

"Very good, darlin'," Mama replied, smiling at her. "I reckon we'll need to find schooling for these two soon, James."

"Indeed," he agreed, "but what with the school being used as an army hospital, we may need to find other arrangements. Wait until after Christmas, shall we?"

"Yes, I suppose you're right," Mama nodded. "Did you go into town?"

"I did, and I stopped off at the post office on my way home," he answered. "Liddy, there is a letter for you on the kitchen table."

I excused myself and hurried to the kitchen. There, on the table, was an envelope with my name on it. The return address was "U.S. Army Hospital, Gallipolis, Ohio."

"Dear Lydia,

I have asked my comrade Martin to pen a few lines to you. In my current state of poor health, I am unable to sit upright and do much, let alone writing. The camp fever caught up with me on our march to Charleston. If not for the care of friends like Martin, I might not have survived. It has hit me hard.

What a joy to receive your letter! I am gratified to learn that you and your family are safe here in Ohio. Being a native son, I am partial, but I believe you could hardly be in a better place right now. I am sorry you had to leave your home and am guessing you may feel somewhat homesick from time to time.

For now, I must ask that we communicate only through letters. This place is full of sickness and I would be heartbroken if you were to fall ill, even though the sight of you would be sweet, very much so. Your good health and that of your family are of utmost importance. The doctors here have turned away many visitors and volunteers. It is most prudent that you stay away.

I will stop and rest for now. Please do write again when you have the time.

Fondly,
Edgar"

I clutched the letter to my heart. I could not believe Edgar was only a few streets away!

Chapter Twenty-Eight

Gallipolis, OH, early February 1862

The cold winter days passed slowly. Thick gray fog pressed down along the river, the sun peeking through only in quick, shiny spurts. I was stuck in the house with the children most days, cooking meals, mending, and knitting. In the evenings, I stood like a mannequin while Mama fitted pieces of green silk over my arms or pinned up the hem.

My older cousins had gotten jobs. Chrissa worked as a cook at a busy tavern. Cousin William found carpentry work in town. Will was helping build government warehouses. For me, nothing was changing or moving forward. Their jobs made me want one of my own.

One night, as Mama was at the sewing machine, I asked her, "Is my work here important? My work here at home?"

"Why, Liddy, why ever would you ask such a thing?" she said, feet pedaling, eyes steady on the bobbing needle. "Of course, your work is important. You are helping our family in so many ways."

"But with the war going on, I feel as though I could be doing more to help."

"You, who just knitted a basketful of warm socks for the poor soldiers? Who takes our extra eggs to the cooks at the hospital? You, my darling, are helping in the war effort more than you realize."

I sighed. *No*, I thought, *those are just little things.*

"And do not forget, you are helping to cheer poor Edgar up as he lies in his hospital bed with little to do as he recovers from the fever."

I had written to Edgar several times, and he had dictated to Martin two letters in return. His stamina was slowly returning, he said, but he was not sure when he might return to his unit.

Aunt Caroline had written to me. I was grateful for news from home. There had been a battle in Summersville back in January, between Ohio soldiers and rebel forces, which we read about in the Gallipolis newspaper. She wrote that many of that regiment, the 36th, were very sick, with camp fever, measles, and other diseases. Quite a number had died and were buried in the cemetery at the ME Church, South.

Every letter from home arrived with the promise of news about Logan, but none of the envelopes that came that winter mentioned him. Logan was sacrificing his dignity, his very life for this war. There had to be something I could do to contribute.

****

To the Women of Ohio, Indiana and Kentucky:

There is a service you owe your country, which she now calls upon you to perform. It is to make full provision for the relief and comfort of our sick and wounded soldiers. From every city and town and neighborhood these brave men have gone to defend our National honor, and we feel assured that you—their wives, mothers, sisters, daughters—will need no other appeal to awaken all your interest and activity than the simple statement that many of them are now lying sick and wounded in the military hospitals, enduring sufferings and privations which it is in your power to relieve.

--Cincinnati Branch of the U.S. Sanitary Commission, February 1, 1862

Chapter Twenty-Nine

Late February 1862, Gallipolis, OH

After communion one Sunday, the pastor called upon a woman in the congregation to make an announcement. Dressed in a maroon cape dress and crinkly bonnet, she calmly walked up onto the altar.

"Thank you, Reverend Ryan," she said, loudly and clearly, leaning forward over the pulpit. "For those of you who don't know me, I am Annabelle Tucker. I speak to you today as a representative of the Southern Ohio Ladies Aid Society. We are asking for volunteers to use their time and talents to support our brave soldiers. Many of you have said farewell to husbands, sons, brothers and friends as they marched off to fight, and you know from their letters that their needs are great. Would you, ladies, be willing to join our quilting or knitting circles, to make mittens, socks, blankets, and the like? You may find the time and location for our next Society meeting posted near the church entrance, or, if you wish, please direct your questions to me after the conclusion of this service. Thank you and may God bless us and our loved ones who are so courageously fighting for the Union and the just cause of ending slavery."

The following Wednesday night, Caroline and I took our baskets and walked down to Mrs. Tucker's house to join the Ladies' Aid Society Knitting Circle. The house was not far from ours, but much grander. A decorative black iron gate guarded the walk up to the wrap-around porch. Lights shone from nearly every window of the house. Mrs. Tucker greeted us and we went inside.

A welcome gust of warm air felt good on my chilled cheeks. My sister and I handed Mrs. Tucker our wraps and took seats on a parlor bench near the fire, next to a cluster of ladies and girls, needles clacking, lithe fingers looping rough strands around the tips. I took out my yarn and joined in with their rhythm.

A girl who looked to be about my age leaned over to watch my work. "Socks or mittens?" she asked. Her rose-tinted face, a creamy full moon, was friendly.

"Socks," I answered. "And what are you working on?"

"Also socks." She smiled and stuck out her hand. "My name is Josephine. Everyone calls me Josie."

I shook her hand. "I'm Lydia, and this is my sister Caroline. We have a friend who is a patient at the Army hospital and needs something to warm his feet."

"Oh, my mother works at the hospital. In the kitchen."

We continued to knit and chat. Josie told me about growing up in Gallipolis and how she was named after her French grandmother

"I hope to finish as many socks as possible before Saturday," Josie said, flames flickering in her brown eyes as she looked at the hearth. "Even though townsfolk are not allowed to enter the hospital, my mother would be glad to meet us there and take the socks to the soldiers. She can make sure yours get to your friend."

My heart flipped at the thought of Edgar. "That would be lovely, thank you."

"I will meet you in front of the hospital…and we can deliver our donations together."

At the appointed time that Saturday morning, I walked up Fourth Street. The sky was clear, the air crisp. I waved at Josie, who was standing out front.

We took the stone pathway around the side of the building and back to where the hospital kitchen was located. Josie's mother opened the door and invited us in. Pots hung from iron hooks over the stove, bottoms sweating from the rising steam of broth pots. We set our baskets of socks on a table, which was nothing more than a wooden door set across two sawhorses.

Mrs. Laurent wiped her hands on her apron and extended one to me. "Hello, Lydia, a pleasure to meet you." Her hair was dark and thick, piled on top of her head in a knot.

"Mother, Lydia would like to have two pairs of socks go to a certain soldier she knows," Josie explained. His name is…." She looked at me. "I forgot to ask you his name."

"Edgar. Edgar Condit, ma'am," I said to Mrs. Laurent. "He is with the Ohio Volunteer Infantry. Or was."

"But of course," she answered. "I will see to it that Mr. Condit receives your gifts. I am sure he will be most appreciative."

"I hope so," I said, looking down. My eyes suddenly watered and I wasn't sure if it was from the chopped onions piled on a nearby wooden board or the frustration of knowing I was so near to where Edgar was but couldn't be with him to comfort and cheer him.

Josie and I walked back out to the street. She assured me that she would ask her mother for a report on Edgar's condition and we parted ways.

The next morning at church, Josie caught up with me in the line of people waiting to shake hands with the pastor. "Can we talk over there?" she asked, pointing to the last pew in the back of the sanctuary. I nodded.

"I asked Mother about Edgar," she began slowly. "She spoke with the nurse on his floor. He has checked out of the hospital. Unfortunately, he didn't get the socks you made for him."

"Oh," I said quietly. "Oh. Well, I suppose that means…he was well enough to leave. But where did he go?"

****

Captain C.M. Moulton has received instructions from headquarters to erect a Government Hospital at Gallipolis, as soon as practicable. This will afford employment to our mechanics and be the means of disbursing a large sum of money, where it is most needed. Being easy of access from all points, the terminus of navigation on the Kanawha, together with freedom from any danger of high water, no place in the Ohio valley is so well calculated for a hospital for the Mountain Department as Gallipolis.

--Gallipolis Journal, May 8, 1862

****

Chapter Thirty

Gallipolis, OH, May 1862

"My dearest Lydia,

I hope you are well and adjusting to your new home. I am writing to let you know that I have been discharged from the Army hospital and am now convalescing in Oberlin. Friends have taken me in and are showing me great hospitality and kindness. I fear I have many miles to go toward my recovery. Typhoid is a ferocious disease and even after receiving the best of care at the hospital, I am not yet cleared to rejoin my comrades in the Seventh.

What a sad irony that we were in the same place but were not able to see each other. I keep all your letters and have read them many times. How good it is to hear that you have found someone to photograph you wearing the dress. Please do send the photo as soon as possible, so that I may put it on my bureau and be reminded of you.

Please write when you have the opportunity.

Yours,
Edgar"

"My dearest Lydia." I read it over and over. "Yours, Edgar."

Mine. *Mine?*

I folded the letter and stuffed it between the pages of a book. Stepping lightly down the creaky staircase, I heard Will and Daddy loudly discussing something in the boys' bedroom.

I went into the kitchen and sat down with Mama at the table. She was peeling apples. I snatched one from the bowl and took a bite. "Now you, you leave those alone," she said, pretending to slap my hand. "You'll ruin your appetite for supper."

"Mama, I would like to apply for a job at the new army hospital. What do you think of that idea?"

"Jobs? My goodness. Haven't you got enough to do around here?"

"You know I have wanted for so long to do something to help in the war effort, Mama."

"Yes, you have said as much. But you mustn't expose yourself to the sickness there, dear. We could all come down with the fever."

"I would be very careful, I promise. I read in the newspaper that there are jobs that are not on the sick wards, like in the laundry and the stables.

She looked up from her paring knife and into my eyes. "There is a very important reason why we must all stay as healthy as possible in this family."

I dropped my apple on the table. "You mean...."

"Yes, dear, I am expecting."

We call attention to the advertisements of Capt. C.W. Moulton. Six good wagon makers and six good blacksmiths can find employment by calling immediately. Also a number of teamsters and laborers wanted to go to Gauley. Thirty dollars per month and rations will be paid teamsters and laborers. Call at the Assistant Quartermaster's office, Gallipolis.

--*Gallipolis Journal*, May 8, 1862

Chapter Thirty-One

Renick home, Gallipolis, OH, May 1862

"No, son, it's just too dangerous," Daddy said, shaking his head, as he walked into the kitchen, Will trailing behind him.

"Look, Daddy, please just read what the newspaper says," Will pleaded, handing him a copy of the *Gallipolis Journal.*

Daddy grabbed the paper from him, sighed, and sat down at the table, pushing his glasses higher up on his nose. "Yes, I see, they need workers at Gauley Bridge. But a Renick man returning home now would be in great danger. Have you forgotten the reason we had to leave?"

"No, of course not. But if I worked at Headquarters, I would be safe. Don't you see?"

"What on earth are you two discussing?" Mama asked."

"Your boy seems to think he's not doing enough to help the Union. Since we won't allow him to fight"—Daddy looked hard at Will—"he wants to go back and help build at headquarters."

"What? Son, what has gotten into you?" Mama asked.

"Mama, please listen to me. You know I have not felt at home here. I want to go back to Virginia. Please. I will be surrounded by the Yankee army."

"But what if you go off half-cocked like you sometimes do and decide to sneak away to visit the mountain?" I broke in.

"I won't. I *promise,*" Will shot back at me, his eyes darting back and forth between Mama and Daddy.

"We will not be deciding this right here and now," Daddy declared. "Now get back to your chores, son."

Will blew out a loud breath and left the kitchen. One thing I knew for sure about my brother. When he wanted to do something, he was like a dog with a bone. He would not give up.

130

Chapter Thirty-Two

Gallipolis, Ohio, early June 1862

The mad chirps of bobolinks outside the bedroom window woke me. Someone had blown out the candle next to my bed. The book I was reading the night before slid off my chest and onto the floor as I shifted to my side and raised up on an elbow. This was the day.

It was the day we said goodbye to Will. He had convinced our parents that returning to Virginia to serve with the U.S. Army laborers was the right thing to do—for now. But Daddy made clear to him that he was not, under any circumstances, to leave Camp Gauley on his own. Mama wrote a letter to Aunt Caroline about Will's return and asked her to share it with the rest of the family.

The sun was high in the sky, waves lightly lapping the shore as Daddy and I walked my brother down to the riverfront. A U.S. Army steamer was waiting, gangplank stretching from dock to main deck. Will took a small knapsack, with just enough clothes, an extra pair of shoes and a Bible.

He tugged on his cap, turned, and looked at us, eyes welling up. "This is not for long," he said, wiping his nose with his sleeve. "God willing, the fighting will stop soon and you all will be back home soon."

Daddy nodded and wrapped his arms around Will's shoulders. I touched Daddy's arm and we prayed for safe travel and God's blessings.

I didn't expect to be so sad to see my brother go. After all, he would be serving our country, working to help preserve the Union. I felt a little sting of jealousy, too. The army hospital was supposed to open in May, but there was a delay and they couldn't say when it would begin taking in patients. I felt restless.

Will walked across the plank and turned to wave at us from the ship's deck. I waved back with my handkerchief.

On the way home, we stopped at the photographer's studio to pay for my picture. I had posed in the studio wearing the new green dress made from the pattern Edgar sent. I didn't much like looking at myself in a photo, but I had to admit, the dress suited me pretty well. It had a high collar, cinched waist, and flared skirt. Smart, I thought. Mama had braided my hair and pinned the pigtails into glossy buns. For a mountain girl who would rather racehorses in her work clothes than get all gussied up, I had come a long way.

****

Secessionists (both male and female) should be more discreet in their remarks and sympathies toward rebel prisoners in the Hospital at this place, else duty will compel me to forbid all visiting or communication, by such persons, with said prisoners.

--Letter to the Editor, *Gallipolis Journal*, from James R. Bell, Surgeon, U.S. Army General Hospital, Camp Carrington, Gallipolis, OH, July 3, 1862

Chapter Thirty-Three

U.S. Army General Hospital, Gallipolis, OH, early July, 1862

I forked fresh hay into Prince's stall while he grazed out in the pen. He was my favorite, by far, a beautiful black Morgan, shiny and strong. I was fortunate to get a job working in the stable.

After the main hospital ward buildings and stables were opened, I was called to the quartermaster's office. It was a hot, dry June day and I was nervous about my interview with Captain Moulton.

He sat behind a bulky oak desk and stroked his beard, studying me. "Hm. I have always hired stable boys, never a girl..."

"I see..." I began, thinking it curious that he would say such a thing. He knew I was a girl when he called me in for the interview. "I can assure you, Captain, that I have a great deal of experience taking care of my own horses and also the neighbors' back home."

"And where is 'back home'?" he asked me.

"Virginia, sir," I answered, weighing in my mind whether I should explain the story of how and why we ended up in Ohio.

He broke in before I could say another word. "Well, these are trying times, and most of the boys around here are needed to fight or help on the farm. I suppose I can make an exception."

He asked me to sign a piece of paper and said I could begin work the next day. Mama and Daddy had given me their blessing since I would not be working near the sick soldiers.

A spider dangled from a cobweb strand hanging from the stall ceiling, almost as if he was watching me pitchfork clumps of manure into the wheelbarrow. Through the bars of the stall door I saw Charlie coming up the walk, arms full of saddle and tack. His dark eyes matched his dark skin, and both shone in the hot sun.

"Wait till ya hear this one!" Charlie called out. I looked down and chuckled, shaking my head. Charlie, 18, was the son of one of the nurses. He always had good gossip on what went on in the hospital.

"What have you got now, Charlie?" I called back.

"I'll tell ya after I put these away! It's a whopper!"

He put the saddle down and hung up the bridle and bit. "Seems Doc Bell is feeling the heat!"

"Do tell."

"A boatload of Reb prisoners are up in the ward where Momma works. Rowdy bunch. Complainin' about the food, about how they whupped the Yankees at Greenbrier, how they can't wait to get back to the front to whup some more."

"Yeah?" My jaw tightened. "What's that got to do with Doc Bell?"

"One of 'em was hootin' and hollerin', upset the other patients, and Doc got hot under the collar, told 'em to quiet down or he'd send for some of the Yankee guards down on town square."

"Don't blame him! Good enough for 'em!"

"But here's the thing. One of 'em said he was writing a letter to the newspaper that says the food that folks from town are bringing to the hospital isn't getting to the patients. Like somebody's stealing it!"

"Do you think that's true?" I asked.

"Well, I can't prove it but I've heard tales. That kind of news'll make Doc look real bad."

"I suspect those ornery Rebs are just lying. I don't think Doc would let such a thing happen."

"I reckon you're right," Charlie agreed. "You've seen more Rebs than I ever have. How many did you have to go through to get here to Ohio?"

"A few at first, close to home. But we were helped along the way by a company of the very soldiers, fellers from Ohio, who we helped when they escaped to our mountain."

****

Letter from Capt. Giles Shurtleff, 7th OVI, to Charles G. Curtis, Pvt. Daniel S. Judson's brother-in-law and guardian, Flint, Mich.

Austinsburg, OH

"Dear Sir:
Your note of inquiry about Daniel S. Judson was not received until a few days ago. Mr. Judson was wounded in the ankle, his limb inflamed was amputated, mortified and caused his death. He died in a hospital near Port Republic.

Judson was a noble young man. I never had to correct him or prompt him in the slightest. He was brave, moral, devoted and obedient. I sympathies [sic] with his affected friends and assure them that there are few men whom I admire more than I did D.S. Judson.

May God heal your affected hearts.

Yours sincerely,
G.W. Shurtleff"

Chapter Thirty-Four

Eyewitness report, Summersville, Virginia, July 1862

On a sweaty July morning, teenager Nancy Hart stood at her cell door in the Summersville Jail, hands dangling over cool iron bars. She began flirting with the guard, flattering him about what a great marksman he must be. He walked over to her cell and struck up a conversation with the attractive brunette.

Nancy convinced the guard that she could never even hold a gun straight, let along shoot one. He laughed at the thought of her pale, tiny hand wobbling under the weight of his heavy revolver and even held the gun butt out to her. Seconds later, the guard lay dead on the concrete floor, blood gushing from a gunshot to his forehead. Nancy reached for his ring of keys and unlocked the cell door. She climbed out a window, shimmied down a tree and ran for the nearby woods.

In a few hours, Nancy Hart, Confederate spy, returned to Summersville, leading a pack of more than a hundred and fifty Rebel soldiers and bushwhackers on a slick roan horse.

****

AN ATTACK UPON SUMMERSVILLE, VA.
Lynchburg, Wednesday, July 30, 1862

A special dispatch to the Republican, dated Narrows of New River, July 28, says: "The gallant Maj. Bailey, commanding four companies of cavalry--in all about 150 men, sent to the rear of the enemy by Col. McCausland--stormed Summersville, the county seat of Nicholas, Friday morning at daylight, and killed and captured the entire garrison, including the Lieutenant-Colonel commanding, named Starr, three other commissioned officers, and sixty-two non-commissioned and privates--killing a large number."
--Correspondence of the Richmond (VA) Examiner, reprinted in *The New York Times*, Aug. 7, 1862
****

Gallipolis, Ohio, early August 1862

"Extra! Extra! Read all about it! Attack on Summersville, Virginia! Rebels take Union Colonel prisoner!"

I handed the newsboy a coin and took a paper. "That's where my family is!" I said to Josie, who stopped alongside me on the sidewalk. She moved in to look at what I was reading. The paper rattled in my hands.

I read aloud: "A few prisoners were paroled. Not being able to bring away the large quantities of Commissary, Quartermaster, and ordnance stores found at the place, Major Bailey committed them to the flames. Major B. brought to this place a large number of Enfield rifles and mules. The prisoners arrived this morning at the Salt Sulphur Springs."

I looked up at her. "What if my grandparents or aunts or uncles or cousins were in town when it happened?" My voice was high and thin.

Josie put a hand on my shoulder. "Oh dear, I am so sorry to hear about it. Maybe we should head back home. You'll want to show your parents the news. We can try the new ice cream parlor another time."

"Yes, I think you're right," I said, nodding.

We turned and walked back toward my street. "You must miss your family terribly," Josie said.

"Oh yes, I...". My eyes filled up. I couldn't say anymore. I plucked my handkerchief from my purse.

"Well, here we are," she said as we caught sight of my house. Josie gave me a hug and her kindness caused me to let out a sob on her shoulder. "I should go," I said, sniffing, "I don't want to stain your lovely dress with my silly tears."

"Not at all," Josie replied. Her smile was lovely, her lips like rose petals. "I can't imagine being so far away from my home. You have every right to shed a tear or two."

I smiled. "Thank you. You are a good friend."

I ran up the walk and burst through the front door. "Daddy! Mama!" I called out.

"In here, dear," my mother answered, "in the parlor."

"Have you heard? Have you heard the news about Summersville and..."

Daddy was sitting at the desk. He turned with a jerk. "What news? Summersville?"

"Here." I handed him the newspaper. Mama struggled a little to get up, off-balance because of her swollen belly, pulling herself forward by gripping the couch arm.

"Mercy," Daddy said quietly as he read.

"What does it say, James?" Mama asked.

He read: "The notorious renegade and spy, Dr. William Rucker, is among the prisoners. The telegraph office was destroyed, and the Government operator captured. This affair is regarded as the most brilliant exploit of the war in this section. Its successful execution spread the wildest consternation and dismay throughout the Yankee army in the neighborhood."

Just then, the younguns came in from school. Little Peg skipped over to the desk to see what Mama and Daddy were looking at. "What's that?" she asked.

"Just the daily news, darlin'," Daddy said, folding up the newspaper. Little Peg was nine years old and was a pretty good reader. He didn't want her to see the war news. Peg, Frankie, who was seven, and Caroline, who was then 12 years old had begun attending the Union School after the hospital there was no longer needed. Caroline laid her books on the lamp table. "What's going on?" she asked.

"Daddy is just finishing up reading today's paper," Mama answered, "and now we need to leave the room, so he can go back to keeping the books. It's harvest time, you know!"

Frankie sighed. "Yeah, we know. We have to pick it all."

His bedraggled look made me giggle. Daddy said, "Come on now, son, it's not so bad," taking my brother's chin in his hand. "If you work fast, we can go fishing down t' the river after supper."

"Alright, everyone, change into your work clothes and help me pick some beans," Mama called out over her shoulder as she walked out of the parlor.

****

A few days later, a letter arrived from Grandma.

> *"Dear Peggy and James and children,*
>
> *I am writing just a few lines to let you know that none of us was in Summersville on the day of the raid. We are fine, just a bit shaken. The fire was so big we could see the smoke from here. The telegraph office is gone and we don't know when it will be back up. Please do not worry about us. Peggy, take good care of yourself and get lots of rest. We will be eager to hear when the baby comes.*
>
> *God bless you all,*
>
> *Mama (Grandma)"*

Chapter Thirty-Five

Gallipolis, OH, mid-September 1862

I picked up the mail at the post office on my way home from the stable. My heart did a little jump when I saw Will's handwriting.

At home, Mama read the letter to us at the dining room table.

> *"Dear Mama and Daddy and Everybody,*
>
> *There is a lot of news to write about. First, let me say that I am well and most happy to be back home. Kernel Lightburn and his troops came through here days ago after an attack from Loring."*

Mama looked up. "I thought that boy was schooled better than that," she said, shaking her head. "He spelled Colonel wrong!" She continued reading out loud:

> *"There were several Yankees shot in the fight and brought here for treatment. We just finished a hospital building and they were treated there, even though not all supplies have arrived from the quartermaster's. The Rebs burned down the U.S. bridge here and tried to burn the stores along the dock, but those fires were put out before all was in ruins. We got word that Lightburn and his men went on down the Kanawha to Charleston and rolled as many salt barrels as they could into the river to cut off the supply to the Confederates.*
>
> *The fellows here on the work crew have been nice enough. Seeing as how most all of them are from Ohio, I am helping them find their way around the area. We are now building a shed for the ambulances.*
>
> *What a surprise it was to see Logan turn up here at headquarters yesterday...."*

Mama stopped reading and looked up, mouth open wide. "Logan! He's there with Will!" she cried out, putting a hand to her cheek.

"Hooray!" Caroline shouted, waving her fists over her head, and the rest of the young'uns joined in. Daddy cracked a big wide grin. "Attaboy," he said.

"What else does he write, Mama?" I urged, "What about Logan?"

"Okay, I'm getting to that," Mama said as she picked the letter up off the table.

> *"Logan was in rough shape. He walked all the way from Camp Piatt and had walked there all the way from Charleston the day before that. He got shot and had a minie ball lodged in his shoulder. They took him to a hospital in Charleston but the doctor there was not at all helpful, said his was just a sick hospital and sent him to another place where they treated wounds. A surgeon at Piatt got the slug out of him, but he sent him on to Gauley. So now here he is, resting and feeling better. He says to say hello to you all and that he will write soon as he is able…"*

After that, Mama continued to read, but thundering heartbeats filled my ears so I couldn't listen. Logan was shot, he could have died. But he didn't. Oh, sweet Jesus, thank you for keeping him alive!

But was he still a Confederate?

****

Chapter Thirty-Six

"Do you not know, Mr. Langston, that this is a white man's government; that white men are able to defend and protect it, and that to enlist a negro soldier would be to drive every white man out of the service? When we want you colored men we will notify you."

--Ohio Governor David Tod

"Governor, when you need us, send for us."

--U.S. Representative, Attorney and Abolitionist John Mercer Langston

****

U.S. Army Hospital stable, Gallipolis, OH, mid-September 1862

I sneezed as I brushed the dust from Prince's coat. I stopped and clawed through my pocket for my handkerchief. Wrong pocket. I pulled out Edgar's letter.

"Dearest Lydia,

I find myself back in Virginia, in a part of the state where the locals are not nearly as hospitable as those on Panther Mountain. The boys and I have just made it through a most terrible, bloody battle near Sharpsburg, Maryland. I am sorry to report that many of my comrades in the 7th did not make it, and many more were wounded. We were up against Lee's troops, and though our final charge, in a thick wood, sent the Confederates into retreat, it was a horrible cost to pay for what ended up an unclear victory. My dear chum Martin was not with us, as he was recovering from a hand wound suffered at Cedar Mountain. Lucky fellow to have missed the carnage at Antietam Creek.

As the officers reconnoiter our position here, I find myself exhausted, yet with just enough energy to write a few lines to you. I trust your family is happily awaiting the new baby's birth and I do hope your mother is well. I have your photo with me, tucked safely away. It is a balm for my soul to look at your lovely face, especially in the aftermath of such destruction. I do ask for your continued prayers and am praying for you as well. I hope caring for the horses is a happy duty for you, knowing how you love them so.

I must close for now. Please write when time permits and give my warmest regards to your family.

Yours,

Edgar"

Here I am, I thought, *18 years old. Other girls are getting married or looking to. Should I be looking too? Do I consider Edgar a beau? On the one hand, Edgar is with his regiment in eastern Virginia. On the other hand, Logan, has turned up at Gauley and has signed the oath of allegiance to the Union. Both are in danger, their futures unsure.*

And what about my future? Will I have a home and family one day? How many children might I have? I hope to have at least one boy and one girl. I'll read to them and teach them how to garden and ride. They will go to proper schools and be well educated. But where? I have no idea. Back home, I hope.

"Uh, daydreaming, Lydia?" I startled at the sound of Charlie's voice. He was standing on the stall gate.

"What? Oh, I guess I was a million miles away. Are you done for the day?"

"Mm-hm. Going down to the square to sign up!"

"Sign up? For what?"

"The United States Army, of course!"

"But...I didn't...I thought..." I began.

"I know, you didn't think a black feller could be a soldier. That all changed back in July. The government passed a law that allows us to enlist with the Union. I expect I'll go up to Massachusetts."

"Massachusetts? Why so far away?"

"Right now, that's where the only U.S. Colored Troops regiments are. Free men like me and slaves who have been freed are allowed to join."

"Oh, dear," I said, sticking out my lower lip. "I shall miss you terribly if you go. And what about your mama?"

"She is proud of me for wanting to serve," he answered, looking down at the stall floor. "But she cried a little when I told her."

I nodded. I knew that sadness.

"Well, see ya around," he said, jumping off the gate.

On my way home, I stopped at the post office to pick up the mail. There was a letter for me. From Maysie. I sat down on a bench under a shade tree and read:

> "*My dear friend Lydia,*
>
> *How are you getting along in Ohio? Did you know Logan was back home?"*

Yes, I thought, *I knew before you did.*

> "*Oh, I was so delighted when I found out. At first we were not supposed to know and could not tell anyone because he was hiding out at the farm. He signed the Union oath! How wonderful that he is able to fight for our side now! He walked me home from church the other day and told me all about the dreadful time he had being forced to serve with the Rebs. What a handsome figure he cuts in his brand new Yankee blues! I thought I should be the one to let you know how he's doing, since he's probably too busy right about now to write to you..."*

My face burned. Good ole Maysie, never one to miss an opportunity to spend time with Logan and let me know about it. *"My dear friend Lydia."* My foot!

****

Dr. O. E. Davis of Lancaster has superseded Dr. Jas. R. Bell as Surgeon in charge of the Gallipolis General Hospital. This was brought about chiefly by Dr. Bell himself, who retains his position in the business department, Dr. Davis taking charge of the surgical department.

--Gallipolis Journal, October 30, 1862

Chapter Thirty-Seven

Renick home, Gallipolis, OH, December 7, 1862

I was getting the children ready for church when Daddy called out: "Liddy! It's time! Fetch some water!"

I stopped braiding Lizzie's hair and rushed downstairs, grabbing a pitcher from the kitchen as I ran outside. I broke ice off the pump with a hammer. Fingers stiff and freezing, I was able to push a trickle out, little by little.

By the time I put the kettle on and fetched clean towels, I could hear my mother. "EEEEEEE!" "Breathe, Mama! Breathe!" Caroline coached.

Once I was in the room, I could see that all was not well. My sister looked up at me from the foot of the bed, panicking. "I think the baby's feet first!" she cried.

Mama had taught me, when I went with her on a few births back in Nicholas, how to knead a woman's belly to turn a baby around. "Mama, hold on. I am going to do what you showed me to do when such a situation happens." Sweating and red-faced, Mama nodded, eyes shut tight.

I motioned to my sister to get on the other side of the bed, lifted Mama's knees and placed a pillow underneath them. I blew on my hands to warm them and gingerly touched the top of Mama's belly. I found the baby's head.

"This is a little like kneading bread but has to be done much slower," I said to Caroline "Once I start guiding the head sideways, I will need you to help move the legs."

We gently worked on my mother's tight stomach, encouraging her to breathe so her muscles would relax. I heard my father's voice behind me. "How is she?"

"We are doing our best to move the baby," I said, not taking my eyes off my work. "He or she is going to be fine if we do this just like Mama would."

Daddy massaged Mama's feet as we worked on the tiny body inside the womb. Slowly and surely, we turned the baby right way around.

"Baby's ready, Mama," I whispered, bending down to her ear, stroking her hair. She exhaled and began to push again.

It took a couple of hours, but she finally pushed her last and out came our new brother. I wiped him off, put his tiny head to my ear to make sure his breathing sounded clear, wrapped him up tight in a cotton sheet, and put him in Mama's arms.

"Well, Peggy," Daddy said, smoothing her forehead with his thumb. "What shall we name this young man?"

She breathed in and out slowly. "Why not name him for two of the finest men I know? James Edgar."

I looked at my fresh, rosy baby brother and grinned.

****

--Letter from the President of the United States of America

December 23, 1862

"Gentlemen of the Cabinet: A bill for an act entitled 'An Act for the admission of the State of West-Virginia into the Union, and for other purposes,' has passed the House of Representatives, and the Senate, and has been duly presented to me for my action.
I respectfully ask of each [of] you, an opinion in writing, on the following questions, to wit:

1st. Is the said Act constitutional?

2d. Is the said Act expedient?"

Your Obt. Servt.
ABRAHAM LINCOLN

****

The new State question is now reduced to very narrow limits. With the people of West Virginia themselves rests its decision. The other party to the contract, the United States Government, has already signed the bond and it only remains for us to say amen. Shall we do it?

--Editors, *Wheeling Daily Intelligencer*, December 31, 1862

****

America:
A Proclamation.

Whereas, on the twenty-second day of September, in the year of our Lord one thousand eight hundred and sixty-two, a proclamation was issued by the President of the United States, containing, among other things, the following, to wit:

"That on the first day of January, in the year of our Lord one thousand eight hundred and sixty-three, all persons held as slaves within any State or designated part of a State, the people whereof shall then be in rebellion against the United States, shall be then, thenceforward, and forever free;

--Emancipation Proclamation, issued January 1, 1863

****

Chapter Thirty-Eight

Gallipolis, OH, mid-February 1863

What a year 1863 was turning out to be, and it had barely begun. Our part of Virginia was carved out and broke away from the rest of the state, and the proposed new state had the approval of the United States government. President Lincoln, God bless him, took the first step to free all people from slavery in his Emancipation Proclamation. And Charlie was on his way up north to train for service as a Yankee soldier.

There was change for me as well. The hospital needed more help in the kitchen, as the numbers of incoming patients increased weekly. Because the kitchen was separate from the sick and wounded, I took a job as a cook's helper with my parents' blessing, working with Mrs. Laurent and Mrs. White, who was hired to direct the special diet kitchen at the hospital. At first, I missed caring for the horses, but I could visit and help around the stables anytime I wanted, so that made it easier.

At home, my baby brother was healthy and had plenty of older siblings to help look after him. Sis, being only three, didn't quite know what to think of Jimmy. Her place as baby of the family had been taken and she was a bit out of sorts about that. She looked at him as if he were a stranger who just dropped out of the sky and into our house. "Who that?" she would ask with a pout.

Despite being in her last months of pregnancy, Mama had managed at harvest time to can and put up a shed full of fruits and vegetables, meats and soups, and she gave me generous quantities to take to the hospital kitchen. The need for healthy food for patients was quite great; it was so important that the governor of Ohio wrote a letter to our newspaper asking citizens to contribute whatever nutritious foods they could.

Will continued to write to us about what went on back home. Uncle Billy and Aunt Becky kept an eye on our farm and told Will that Logan had officially signed up for military duty with a Union cavalry regiment. That suited him well, considering his knack for riding.

Edgar had had a rough time of it, having been wounded in the left leg at the Battle of Dumfries just after Christmas. He was taken to a field hospital in Alexandria, where conditions were dreadful.

> "*The official name of this place is Camp Convalescence, but we call it Camp Misery. We are housed in tents with no floors, just dirt, in the freezing cold, with no wood for fires.*"

He was promoted to Sergeant during his recovery, but his wounded leg did not heal properly, and he was discharged due to disability.

> "*I will not stop looking for ways to serve the Union cause but for now, I will head back west and tend to my health.*"

I did not see much of Josie around that time, except sometimes at work. She had become a nurse's aide and was working in the wounded ward. She had a new beau, Alfred, who was home on furlough from his regiment and was courting her quite avidly. So she had less time for me.

****

The Ladies of the Soldiers' Aid Society, request that the Ladies throughout the county, while canning their usual supply of fruit, do not forget the sick soldiers, and prepare a few extra cans for our brave boys who may be languishing in hospitals. This is praiseworthy and we hope the hint here given will be acted upon.

--Gallipolis Journal, **August 1862**

****

Chapter Thirty-Nine

Kitchen, U.S. Army General Hospital, Gallipolis, OH, mid-February 1863

I was peeling potatoes when I heard Rufus say something odd.

"Wonder how much money Wilson makes off those jars?" he asked Hank, the other cook.

Hank shushed him, and I saw out of the corner of my eye that he was tilting his head toward me.

Then I remembered. There were accusations printed in the newspaper about donated food from the community not getting to the patients.

I went about my work but kept my ears open around Rufus. He was a Kentucky soldier waiting out his time at the hospital as he recovered from a shoulder wound. His left arm was in a sling most of the time, so he did all his cooking right-handed.

After work one day, soon after I heard Hank say that, I was in the hospital business office picking up my paycheck. I saw Charlie's mother putting on her bonnet at the end of her nursing shift. She spotted me and smiled. "Hello, Lydia," she said. Her voice was soothing, like hot tea on a cold day.

"Hello, Mrs. Delaney, how are you today?"

"Just fine, dear, now that I'm about to go home and rest," she answered with a chuckle. She pulled on brown leather gloves. "I hope you are well."

"Yes ma'am, I am liking my new job in the kitchen."

"The kitchen you say?" she said, her eyes widening as if she had just realized something."
"Yes, it's good work. Keeps me busy. What do you hear from Charlie?"

"That boy is taking to soldierin' like a duck to water. He writes that drills go on forever and the days are long, but he seems quite satisfied to be wearing the Yankee uniform."

"I know you must be very proud of him."

"Oh yes, mighty proud," she replied. "Say, Lydia, may I ask you something? In private?"

"Sure, Mrs. Delaney. We could go over there."

"Let's do that," she agreed, and we walked through the door and into a dingy hallway.

In the dim light of a dirty, cracked window, she stood close to me and asked quietly if I knew anything about any shenanigans in the kitchen.

"Shenanigans? What sort?"

Chapter Forty

"Take nothing on its looks; take everything on evidence. There's no better rule."

--from *Great Expectations* by Charles Dickens

Kitchen, U.S. Army General Hospital, Gallipolis, OH, mid-February 1863

The next day, I decided to do a little detective work in the kitchen. I looked over the pickle jars lined up along the pantry wall. Rufus walked in and picked a jar off the shelf.. "Whatcha doin', missy?" he asked.

"Just checking on the jars I brought in from home," I answered, not looking at him. "Funny thing, though. I'm not finding my mother's pickles. The patients must really be gobbling them down."

"No, no, them's your mama's pickles," Rufus corrected me. "The ones you brought in t'other day."

"Well, that can't be," I replied, looking at him straight in the eye. "Because none of these pickle jars have spice bags in them. My mama always leaves the little linen spice bags in hers when she cans them."

His eyes got wide and then squinted tight. "Then maybe you are right. Maybe your mama's pickles already got 'et up." He slowly backed out of the pantry, banging his bad elbow on the door frame. A pickle jar slipped from his hand and dashed into pieces on the kitchen floor. "Dagnabbit!" he cried out.

I didn't say any more to Rufus about it. But since he was likely to mention it to Hank and the two would try to square their lies, I went straight to the business office after my work was done that afternoon.

"Doctor Bell?" I stood at the head surgeon's door.

"Yes? What is it?"

"Dr. Bell, I want to report some missing supplies?"

"Missing supplies?" he blurted, twitching his handlebar moustache.

"Well sir, I have heard rumors...."

"Just the facts, please, Miss...Miss..."

"Renick, sir. Lydia Renick. I'm a cook's assistant in the kitchen."

"Please proceed, Miss Renick."

"Sir, my mother has provided many canned goods to the hospital, which I bring in every work day. She is quite dedicated to the cause and has shared a great deal of our harvest with the kitchen."

"Very laudable," he nodded. "Get on with your story then."

"I was doing an inventory of the canned goods in the pantry and noticed that none of the pickle jars I brought in just two days ago are there. It's not that there are no pickles on the shelf, but that I know they're not hers."

"And how on earth can you tell that?" he asked.

"My mother always includes small bags of spices in her pickle jars, sir, but I can find no jars containing spice bags. So, either all ten of the jars I recently brought in have been consumed by patients in an unusually short period of time, or...."

"Or what?"

"Or maybe someone has done something else with them."

He exhaled loudly, took off his glasses, and rubbed the bridge of his nose. "I see. Well that is a very serious allegation, young lady. And I'm not surprised to hear it."

I was confused by his reply. I thought I was about to be scolded for accusing someone of wrongdoing, but instead he seemed to accept the story as I told it.

"Miss Renick, I am glad you have brought this to my attention. Your mother's sacrifices from your own larder are much appreciated. The highest form of patriotism. That they have gone missing is an affront to her generosity. I promise you I will follow up on this matter and do a thorough review of pantry supplies. Thank you for coming in."

He put his glasses back on and returned to his work. "Thank you, Dr. Bell," I said, as I sidled out the door.

In a few days, Rufus, Hank and Wilson were called in to Dr. Bell's office, and the next thing we knew the three were ushered out of the hospital, never to be seen within its walls again. By June, Dr. Bell was once again the surgeon in charge.

****

This day ushers into being the new State of West Virginia and adds the thirty-fifth star to the constellation of the American Union. Today is the beginning of a new order of things with us here. The old government goes out and the new one comes in.

--*Wheeling Daily Intelligencer*, **Saturday morning, June 20, 1863**

Chapter Forty-One

Gauley Bridge, Virginia, June 10, 1863

"Dear Liddy,

Please forgive me for not writing to you sooner. I know Will told you about my being shot and escaping from the hospital down in Charleston. I am just now feeling up to snuff and have signed up with a West Virginia cavalry regiment. You of all people know just how glad I am to be on the Union side now.

How is life in Ohio? I trust you are occupied with your hospital work. I am proud of you, Liddy. You always have been smart and strong and even though it must be hard to be away from home, you have found a grand way to serve the cause.

Everyone here is excited about West Virginia joining the Union as a state that will eventually be free not slave. There is a big celebration planned in Summersville for June 20th, and there will be a parade with bands and a big picnic on the green. I wish you could be here for that, Liddy. I truly do. Do you think now that West Virginia is broken away from Virginia that your family could come home? That would be wonderful if you could.

I am sure you are happy to have another baby in the family. I hope little Jimmy is growing healthy and strong. Give my kindest regards to your Ma and Pa and the children. I will write again soon as I can.

Fondly,
Logan"

Gallipolis, OH, June 18, 1863

"Daddy?" I asked, tugging on my handkerchief in my lap.

My father looked up from his logbook. "Yes, darlin'?"

"Now that Nicholas is part of the new state, does that mean we can go back home?"

Daddy got up from his desk and sat down next to me on the sofa. "You're about to wear that handkerchief out," he said with a smile.

"I wish I could give you an answer. It is good news that our part of Virginia has severed ties with the East, no doubt about it. But the war is not over. We must pray that it will end soon, of course. But until the battle is won and we are at peace, I can't guarantee when we will return." His put his hand on mine, his weathered skin rough and warm.

"I understand, Daddy. Thank you for giving me an honest answer. Even if it isn't the one I was hoping for." I gave him a weak little smile and tucked strands of hair behind my ear. *What I wouldn't give to go back home and see Logan,* I thought.

****

We did our best to toast the new state on June 20th with our Ohio family and friends. The girls and I strung red, white, and blue banners between the trees in the back yard and stuck patriotic pinwheels in the yard. We baked apple and blueberry pies and served coffee and lemonade. Uncle A.J. brought his ice cream freezer and the little ones took turns cranking the handle and sprinkling salt around the metal cylinder inside. We topped the creamy delight with sliced strawberries. Neighbors walking by waved. "Hail Columbia!" they shouted. "Hail West Virginia!"

> *Hail Columbia! Happy land!*
>
> *Hail, ye heroes--heaven-born band,*
>
> *Who fought and bled in Freedom's cause,*
>
> *Who fought and bled in Freedom's cause,*
>
> *And when the storm of war was gone*
>
> *Enjoy'd the peace your valor won.*
>
> *Let independence be our boast,*
>
> **--"Hail Columbia," by Joseph Hopkinson**

War report, Gettysburg, Pennsylvania

In one short week, the tide of war turned in favor of the Union. On June 30th, 1863, A large body of Federal cavalry reached Gettysburg and took possession, capturing a number of Rebels. By July 3rd, a major battle had been fought in Cashtown, Pennsylvania, a town between Gettysburg and Chambersburg. Though the Yankees suffered heavy losses in officers and men, General Robert E. Lee's army suffered worse casualties and was put on the defensive.

On July 3rd, Union Major General George Meade reported the he and his men held Gettysburg and that the Confederate troops had left large numbers of killed and wounded behind on the field of death. General Lee asked for a temporary cease fire to bury his dead and gather up the wounded. General Meade rejected the cease fire. He replied that the only option was unconditional Confederate surrender.

****

The President announces to the country that the news from the Army of the Potomac to ten o'clock p.m. of the third, is such as to cover the army with the highest honor; promise a great success to the cause of the Union and claim the condolence of all for the many gallant fallen. For this he respectfully desires on this day, that He whose will, not ours, should be everywhere remembered and reverenced with the profoundest gratitude.

--Proclamation from President Abraham Lincoln, July 4, 1863, Washington, D.C.

****

"It was felt that the same day that witnessed the birth of the nation might also prove either the day of its salvation or of its destruction."

-- Rector, Gettysburg Christ Church, July 4, 1863

****

Chapter Forty-Two

U.S. Army General Hospital, Gallipolis, OH, July 6, 1863

Everything felt heavier that day. After lugging bushels of apples in from the dock, I could barely lift my arms to commence peeling them. It was a hot, humid day but the pressure on my chest was less from the thick kitchen air and more because of Gettysburg.

The reports trickled in slowly, over telegraph wires and into newsprint. We didn't have any real idea how many Ohio or West Virginia soldiers were there, or how many were hurt or killed. Everyone at the hospital braced for incoming sick and wounded. Even though we were hundreds of miles away from the battlefield, we knew that the bloody fight could dislodge healthier hospital patients to make room for the many critically wounded in Pennsylvania.

There had been much crying and praying at church the day before. Josie was worried sick that Alfred's unit might have been at Gettysburg. Reverend Ryan tried his best to soothe the congregation, pulling out Proverbs and reminding everyone how King Solomon reigned in peacetime after his father David's war-torn kingdom, and that we should expect and pray for that same peace that comes only from God.

"Lydia, are you alright?" Mrs. Laurent leaned down to face me and I realized I had stopped peeling and was staring at the burners on the stove.

"Oh...yes, ma'am, sorry, I just...." Words would not come out.

She patted me lightly on the shoulder. "We must work double-quick in the event troops come pouring in," she said. I nodded and got back to the apples.

****

I will never forget the moment when I found out. I was just home from work and had gone to the bedroom to fetch a book. Mama came to the door.

"Caroline and Peg, would you please go down to the cellar and bring up potatoes and onions for supper?" she asked my sisters.

164

I knew she asked them to leave the room so that she could talk to me alone.

"Liddy," she said softly, sitting down on my bed. I looked into her eyes. They were filled with tears.

"What's wrong, Mama?" A chill ran through me on that muggy afternoon.

"Come sit," she said, patting the mattress next to her.

"Oh no, oh no...." I started.

"I have some news. Some bad news," she said, tears spilling down her cheeks. "Darlin', no other way to put it...Logan has gone to be with our Lord."

Something inside me crumbled. It seemed as though time stopped "No, no, no!" I cried out. "It can't be! God wouldn't let it happen!" . My fists tightened around my pillow.

Mama put her arms around me and I sobbed, deeply, moaning in a voice I didn't know was mine. I'm not sure how long she held me tight, her tears and mine dripping down our faces and necks.

She wiped her face and sniffed. "Aunt Caroline sent the news. I got the letter today. He died at Gettysburg. She knew your heart would be broken."

All of me was broken.

****

Remember me when I am gone away,

Gone far away into the silent land;

When you can no more hold me by the hand,

Nor I half turn to go yet turning stay.

Remember me when no more day by day

You tell me of our future that you planned:

Only remember me; you understand

It will be late to counsel then or pray.

Yet if you should forget me for a while

And afterwards remember, do not grieve:

For if the darkness and corruption leave

A vestige of the thoughts that once I had,

Better by far you should forget and smile

Than that you should remember and be sad.

--"Remember," by Christina Rosetti

Chapter Forty-Three

Gallipolis, OH, Spring 1864

Life limped along after Logan was gone. I have to say—and I'm not proud of this, but it's how I felt—that my hatred for Confederates grew even stronger. It wasn't enough that they had forced him into their gray uniform and marched him through who knows what, fighting against the very people he sided with. To have him escape and then wind up being killed by one of them, well, that was a little too much for me to accept.

There were secesh in our hospital, of course, and I was helping to make the very food they ate. When one died that fall, I was not even sorry to see the workers carry the blanketed body out on a stretcher. They had started all this trouble and now Logan was dead.

Sometimes, we would race Blackie and Miss Lou in my dreams. Sometimes we watched the sun go down and the lightning bugs rise. Sometimes we held hands and talked. But when I woke up, I could only hold on to the happy feeling for so long.

Edgar wrote that he, restored to good health, had signed up with an Illinois regiment. He was moving farther and farther away from where I was. I admired him, though. He was an ambitious man, had risen up through the ranks. A real leader. I liked that. When I prayed for him at night, I was not sure God would keep him safe. He took Logan; would He take Edgar from me, too?

Josie and Alfred got engaged after he completed a year of service with his Gallia County company. I was happy for her, to be sure, but her upcoming marriage served only to remind me that I might always be just a bridesmaid.

A new doctor was in charge at the hospital, and Mrs. Delaney was quite pleased to find out that he had been a surgeon with the 54th Massachusetts, one of the two Colored Troops regiments formed in Boston. Dr. Stone assured her that the troops, including Charlie, had shown their bravery many times over and made their officers very proud.

Will was still at Gauley Bridge, building whatever the U.S. army needed. We had to make peace with the fact that he sometimes went along on scouts and visited Grandma and Grandpa on occasion. The thought of him traveling through Fayette and Nicholas made Mama and Daddy very uneasy. But Will could be very bullheaded when he had set his mind on something.

The first state elections were scheduled for fall, and some of the men who stayed in what was then West Virginia were out campaigning. Aunt Caroline wrote to me that she was unsure about one or two of them, who were known to have worked for the Confederate army.

I asked Daddy one day what he thought about that. He was in the shed, tying feathers to fishhooks. I sat on the anvil next to his workbench.

"Do you think it's right for men who sided with the Secesh to run for election back home?"

"What do you think?" he asked, looking at me out of the corner of his eye.

"Well, it right burns me up," I answered. "Who do they think they are? Our part of Virginia broke away and now it's a Union state, and seein' as how they started the whole thing, I don't think it's fair for them to run things."

Daddy looked up, glasses low on his nose. "Do you remember that day in town when Ben Dorsey was almost choked to death by a Union man?"

"Sure I do. What's that got to do with Rebels running for office?"

"You asked me afterward why I helped him. Do you remember what I told you?"

"Something about him being our neighbor and God wanting us to be kind. But still, that doesn't change the fact that he's fighting against our side."

"Well, no he isn't at the moment. Ben got shot at Droop Mountain and was captured. He's sittin' in a Union prison. So he has paid a price."

"At least he's still alive."

"Yes, and God may have a purpose for him yet. We don't know. But what we do know is that the holy scriptures tell us that we must love even our enemies. I know it's very hard to do, but those are Jesus' exact words. Sometimes our enemies are also our neighbors."

"But do we have to give them back all their privileges? After what they've done?"

"Liddy, this is war, and war is downright awful. There is killing being done by both sides. Of course we believe in the Union cause, that hasn't changed. But being for the Yankees doesn't mean we stop being for God."

I tilted my head back, feeling a little sore at Daddy for not taking my side of the issue. He was so wise, it sometimes made my head hurt.

****

Near Richmond, VA, Sunday, April 9, 1865

Moved in good season. Marched hard. Woods on fire, filling the air full with smoke, making it disagreeable indeed. Rebs are being picked up all along. Saw & heard a man talk concerned who had lost an arm at Seven Pines, said Lee passed with about 10,000 men on that road, terribly scattered, many were deserting to their homes & said that no Virginians would fight out of their state. The woman living there had lost her husband in battle, he was buried in the dooryard, Found one Reb with his family by the roadside, a deserter, who said he was surprised to see how kindly "you all are"...

--diary of Wiliam T. Patterson, Quarter Master Sergeant, 116th OVI

VICTORY!!!

GLORY HALLELUJAH!!

LEE SURRENDERED

His Entire Army Captured!

Grant Dictates Terms

The End Draws Nigh!

--Cleveland Morning Leader, Monday morning, April 10, 1865

Chapter Forty-Four

U.S. Army General Hospital, Gallipolis, Ohio, April 10, 1865

There was a lot of hollering coming from the East Dining Room. I ran out of the kitchen to see what the ruckus was about.

"Hooray! Hooray!" Soldiers and surgeons, lunch left on their plates, were on their feet beside the tables, punching their fists into the air. A newsboy stood on a chair, waving a telegram over his head.

"What on earth?" Mrs. White followed me into the dining area.

"War is over! Praise the Lord!" came more shouts.

Men were shaking hands all around the room, some bandaged, on crutches and in casts.

"Mrs. Davis!" Dr. Stone called out. "Might we break out a few bottles of wine for a toast?"

The kitchen manager's forehead wrinkled as she thought for a moment. "I see no harm in it, if just for a toast!" she called back. "Lydia, please ask the steward to bring us a case of Catawba."

I clutched my skirt and ran to the steward's office. Maybe we were finally going home! I felt like flying. Soon enough, though I didn't know it at the time, I would fall back down to earth with a painful thud.

****

ABRAHAM LINCOLN

President of the United States, assassinated in the city of Washington, April 14, 1865.

A martyr to the cause of Virtue, Liberty and Independence, he died at 7:20 A.M., of the 15th of April, full of honors, mourned not only by the nation, but by the civilized world. His memory will live forever in the hearts of his countrymen. His enemies will find in his death, their severest loss.

"One of the few, the immortal few, that was not born to die."

--*Gallipolis Journal*

Chapter Forty-Five

Methodist Episcopal Church, Gallipolis, OH, Easter Sunday 1865

Easter lilies lined an altar table draped in black. In row after row, many heads were bowed, faces glossy with tears. Reverend Ryan did not preach the Easter sermon he had prepared.

"Brothers and sisters, it is right and fitting that we should mourn this Easter morning. Our country has lost a great man, a leader whose work was not quite finished. Some have called Abraham Lincoln his country's second savior, liberator of the oppressed."

"Lamentations 5 speaks of the deepest grief humans can imagine:

'The joy of our heart is ceased; our dance is turned into mourning. The crown is fallen from our head: woe unto us, that we have sinned! For this our heart is faint; for these things our eyes are dim.'"

"There is great sorrow in the land today. But there is also a promise of great rejoicing. The words of Jesus Christ assure us:

'Verily, verily, I say unto you, That ye shall weep and lament, but the world shall rejoice: and ye shall be sorrowful, but your sorrow shall be turned into joy.'"

****

O CAPTAIN! My captain! Our fearful trip is done;

The ship has weathered every rack, the prize we sought is won;

The port is near, the bells I hear, the people are exulting,

While follow eyes the steady keel, the vessel grim and daring;

But O heart! heart! heart!

Leave you not the little spot,

Where on the deck my captain lies,

Fallen cold and dead.

--from "Oh Captain, My Captain," by Walt Whitman

Chapter Forty-Six

--letter from the Department of West Virginia Medical Director's Office, Cumberland, Md.

May 7th, 1865

To Surg. L.R. Stone USV
In charge US Gen. Hosp.
Gallipolis, Ohio

"Doctor,

It having been brought to my knowledge that men have been returned to their Regiments from General Hospitals who, under recent orders from the War Department should have been mustered out of Service, I beg leave respectfully to call your attention to said Order, and to request that you will use all diligence and circumspection in carrying them out to the letter.

No man fit for duty except Veteran Volunteers, Veterans of the 1st Corps and Regulars are to be so treated, but will as requiring no further medical attention be discharged from the service, in muster out as prescribed.

Very Respectfully,

Your Obedient Servant

A.N. Dougherty
Surg. And Col. U.S. Vol.
Medical Director"

****

U.S. Army General Hospital, Gallipolis, OH, June 1865

I saw Mrs. Delaney in the steward's office just after handing in my resignation letter to the secretary.

"Oh my, we certainly will miss you, Lydia," she said as she took my hand. "I guess we'll all be gone from here very soon."

"Yes, it appears the hospital is preparing to close," I said. "Times are changing, for the better. Have you heard anything from Charlie?"

"His regiment is still holding Charleston, South Carolina, but he believes they will be discharged in the fall." Her eyes looked tired but there was still light in them.

"Please tell him that my family...I...we are returning to Virginia. West Virginia, I should say. We have a new state now. May I have your address so that I can write after we're back home?"

"Of course, Lydia," she said and asked the secretary for a pen and scrap of paper.

"Here, dear. Please do let us know how you are doing. I imagine your town will have changed from when you left."

"Yes, much of what was in town burned to the ground. I suspect they will rebuild some of it. Thank the Lord, my family members survived and I cannot wait to see them again."

On the way home, I walked down the riverbank and sat on the grass. Hugging my knees, I looked across the water to West Virginia. The river belonged to both states, same trees on either side, same boats gliding back and forth, same blue sky. As much as Ohio had seen me grow and change, it could never take home's place. Uncle A.J. and his family were headed west, to new frontiers. The rest of us were on our way back to Panther Mountain.

****

Part Three: Return

Who Shall Vote in the South?

If anything is clear it is that the framers of the Constitution meant that each State should prescribe who should vote....

But again, the question recurs, is not all this changed in a State where the voters have voluntarily renounced their allegiance to the General Government? Can such a State renounce all its duties, and yet insist upon its rights?

--speech by John Sherman, U.S. Senator, State of Ohio, 1865

****

An Order Concerning Rebel Soldiers in West Virginia

Head-Qr's, Dep't West Virginia
Cumberland, Md, June 15, 1865

General Orders, No. 68

Hereafter paroled prisoners and others from the rebel ranks found wearing or carrying fire arms or concealed weapons of any kind, will be arrested and reported to these headquarters, and the arms and other weapons taken from their possession and turned over to the nearest Ordnance Officer. No person will be permitted to wear the rebel uniform, or any insignia designating rank or position in the late rebel army.

--by command of Brevet Major General Emory

Chapter Forty-Seven

'You ought to be ashamed of yourself,' said Alice, 'a great girl like you,' (she might well say this), 'to go on crying in this way! Stop this moment, I tell you!' But she went on all the same, shedding gallons of tears, until there was a large pool all round her, about four inches deep and reaching half down the hall.

--Alice's Adventures in Wonderland **by Lewis Carroll**

Panther Mountain, Nicholas County, West Virginia, September 1865

There is nothing quite like the smell of dry, fallen leaves baking in the sun. It's a musty scent, earthy and good. There is nothing like standing at the edge of our property and looking out over the red-orange dotted hills and hearing the rush of the Gauley down below. Nothing is as crisp and clear as a fall day on Panther Mountain.

It was fitting that I returned to the spot, the tree, where I had read letters from Logan and Edgar in years past, during the war. Now the first letter of peacetime had arrived. Edgar had just mustered out of his Illinois unit and was considering returning to his family's Iowa farm.

> *"...and now, for the first time in four years, I am a regular citizen again. What to do with myself? That is the question. My friends have invited me back to Oberlin for a reunion. Though I did not complete my degree as most of them did, they seem inclined to include me nonetheless. Kind of them.*
>
> *I am delighted for you that you are finally back home. What a long, difficult separation you had from your family and friends. And now you return to live in a different state than the one you left! How many people can claim that accomplishment? Few, to be sure. Please do send my best, warmest regards to your mother and father and the rest of the family. I remain ever grateful for you and your brave sacrifices on behalf of myself, my comrades and the Union.*

Please write when you have time.
Yours,
Edgar"

****

The grief flooded over me the first time I saw Becky after we returned to Nicholas. We were both overcome and held each other, crying, mourning for Logan. Bushwhackers had stolen Miss Lou during the war, so I cried for her, too. So much loss. So much death.

It should have been a happier time, returning to our little home and loved ones on the mountain, but the weeds in the wheat field and empty barn stalls bit into me. Nothing was as before. There was no north star to guide me. Friends had married and moved on or away. Rebel stragglers hung on fenceposts like tired scarecrows, homeless, property seized by the Union, unable to find work. Most of those early days felt like long muddy trudges that took every bit of strength to complete.

Mama worried about me. "You look so tired, darlin'," she fretted, watching me move through the kitchen. "What can we do to lift your spirits? I thought coming home would be good for you, good for all of us." I would nod and shrug, but words would not come.

I had lost my place again. In Ohio, I had a purpose, a job that helped the war effort. Back home, I was back to helping around the house and farm, but with no future prospects. I was not about to marry just to get out of my parent's home as some did. When I decided to marry, it would be because I found a man whom I could respect and admire and love. Not until then.

It grated on me that folks in town looked at me strange. I saw Maysie at Hardman's one day. She had married a boy from Fayette County and was in town shopping.

"Lydia Ja-ane, how are you?" she exclaimed, putting her hands on mine and squeezing a little. Her pinky cheeks were rounder than I remembered. "How wonderful to see you again!" The charm oozed out of her like molasses.

"Hello, Mays. Doing just grand, thank you," I lied. "And how about you? I hear you caught yourself a feller?"

She giggled. "Oh, yes, James! Met him at a barn dance and he stole my heart! And now we are expecting! Oh, Liddy, marriage is just the peachiest!"

I nodded, forcing a smile. I cleared my dry throat, "Ah, splendid. And when are you due?"

"Spring, Doc says. But you know, they never know for sure. I hope it's a little girl I can spoil and dress up like a dolly!"

"Wonderful," I said, tilting my head, hoping it would appear that I was truly, truly happy for her.

"And how about you, dear? Still swatting those boys away like flies?" Her eyes were wide open, in the way a person's eyes are when they are just flattering you.

"Oh, ha! Hardly that," I answered.

She leaned in and grasped my forearm. "Now you listen, don't be bothered about the boys around town. They are just leery of a girl who has traveled, gotten an Ohio education. You know how they are. They'll come around," she said with a wink.

An Ohio education? I thought. What do they think, that I've been away at boarding school?

"Um, oh, yes, I surely do know how they talk," I said, hiding the fact that I did not know at all how they talked.

Sure enough, as I walked back to the wagon to meet up with Will, I heard whispers from the front porch of the Alderson Hotel. They thought I couldn't see or hear them from behind the potted ferns on the porch rail. Snapping their suspenders, hocking chewing tobacco into bronze spittoons, they were talking. 'Ssps, ssps, Ohio…ssps, ssps uppity…' They reminded me of Rufus and Hank back at the hospital kitchen. Rubes.

This was the lot I had to choose from?

Chapter Forty-Eight

Backus home, Panther Mountain, early November 1865

"Let me bring you some tea, dear." Aunt Caroline's voice was silky, soothing.

I sat stock straight on the davenport, right hand gripping the doily laid across the plump arm. A fire crackled beneath a mantel heaving with crocks and vases. I counted book spines on the shelf to occupy my mind while she was in the kitchen.

She brought out her finest china on a tray. Steamy wisps rose from the teapot spout. "Tell me about Edgar's letter," my aunt said, sitting down in the wingback chair next to me.

"He wrote about a woman named Elizabeth. Eliza for short. They are engaged."

Aunt Caroline eyebrows squeezed up together like praying hands. "Engaged. Has he known her very long?"

"They were classmates in college," I answered, taking a sip of tea. "They met again at a reunion at Oberlin. She is from Ohio. Her father is a judge."

My aunt picked up her cup and saucer and held them on her lap. "Oh, my darling. I know how you feel about him. I am so sorry."

"Thank you," I said. My throat was tight but I was determined not to cry. Too many tears had been shed of late and enough was enough. "I suppose it was foolish of me to believe we might be together after all these years of war, separation." *How could he just forget me after all we'd been through together?*

"You had every good reason to think that he might be the one," she said, leaning forward to pat my arm. "After all, he was quite taken with you from what I remember."

"Well, he is taken with someone else now," I said, looking at the rug.

"Did you know, Liddy, that I was much older than you when your Uncle Frank and I were married?" she asked, blowing on her tea.

"No. How much older?"

"I was 29 years old on my wedding day, and not only that, I was—and am—seven years older than Frank. I was a confirmed spinster at that age. But look how well that has turned out," she said, smiling.

I was so surprised to hear her say that, and my face must have shown it, because she started to laugh.

"It's true! No one believed I would ever leave home. You must take that as encouragement. You have many years to go before you best my record!"

I smiled and exhaled. "If my beautiful aunt can wait for her best mate, I suppose so can I."

"He will come along, Liddy. I promise."

****

Chapter Forty-Nine

MARRIED

Condit—Bell—At Seville, Medina Co., Ohio, Feb'y 8th, 1866 by the Rev. James Gray, Mr. E.M. Condit, of Anamosa, Iowa, and Miss Eliza Bell, daughter of the Hon. James A. Bell.

--marriage announcement, *Lorain County (OH) News*, February 14, 1866

Renick home, Panther Mountain, Nicholas County, West Virginia, early April 1866

Mama held the newspaper clipping next to the lantern on the table to read it better. "I reckon his bride is a lovely gal," she mused, holding her spectacles up to her eyes without putting them on.

"Mm..." I said, "Nice of him to send the announcement from the paper." I shoved a pan of cornbread into the oven and slammed the door shut.

"Now, Liddy, I know your nose is a little out of joint about Edgar getting married," Mama said in that matter-of-fact tone of hers. "It's only natural you should feel that way."

"I *am* happy for him, Mama," I replied. "The news just comes at a bad time, that's all."

"Bad time?"

Just then, there was a knock at the door. "I'll get it," Daddy said. I was glad the knock ended a conversation that would likely lead to me saying I was an old maid and Mama assuring me that I was not.

Daddy opened the door. "May I help you?" he asked.

I could hear a man's voice as I listened from the kitchen. *Running for sheriff. General store, rally soon at Cross Lanes.*

I was so curious about the visitor I couldn't help myself. I got up from the table and walked into the front room. There stood a tall, handsome man in a

Union coat. His eyes were the clearest shade of light blue I had ever seen. His eyes left Daddy's face and lit on mine.

"Hello, ma'am," he said and nodded respectfully.

"Mr. John Malcolm, this is my daughter Lydia. Lydia, Mr. Malcolm owns land down in Cross Lanes. He is here campaigning for sheriff and is going door-to-door on the mountain to explain what makes him a good candidate.

"Hello, Mister…Candidate…Malcolm," I said with an awkward nod. My mind raced. What was I wearing? Was my hair a mess? I swiped a few loose strands from my face.

He smiled and I could have sworn those eyes were twinkling at me, as if a flame were flickering inside them. "I was just explaining my credentials to your father."

I knew little to nothing about politics but decided this handsome man might have gotten my vote, had I had one.

"I was just telling him that my family were among this county's first pioneers, and that I served for two years as a private and second lieutenant in the Nicholas Scouts, under both Captains Brown and Ramsey. I hope that will provide sufficient evidence of my dedication to the Union cause and my intention to keep the people of Nicholas County safe.

"Well, it sure sounds like you have done your Yankee duty, Mr. Malcolm," Daddy said.

"Oh yes, sir. And please, call me John."

"Alright, John. Well pleased to meet you and I will be sure to attend the rally."

"Much obliged, sir," John Malcolm said. Turning to me, he added with a rakish smile, "And of course your wife and lovely daughter are invited as well."

"Thank you! I mean, thank you for the invitation." Why was I acting so silly?

After Mr. John Malcolm was out the door, Mama called out from the kitchen. "Who was it, darlin'?"

"Oh, just a politician," Daddy called back. I wiped sweat from my cheeks with a corner of my apron.

Chapter Fifty

Renick farm, Panther Mountain, June 30, 1866

"Hurry up, Liddy!" Mama called from the front yard.

I was wearing my Sunday dress and good shoes. I could not get my hair right. No matter how hard I tried with the hair iron, the humid summer air wilted my blonde curls and all fell straight and stringy once more.

We were on our way to a picnic. Not just any picnic. This was a political occasion, a public rally for Candidate John G. Malcolm. It was being held at the Malcolm family's farm.

I took one last look in the mirror, pinched my cheeks pink, and let out a big sigh.

We headed downhill in the wagon. Mama sported her best bonnet and Daddy had spit-shined his shoes. I didn't mind going along. I would probably see some friends and cousins, uncles, and aunts, and maybe there would be good food. I also made myself a promise that I would, if given the opportunity, mention how uninvolved I felt in the political process because as a woman, I had no vote.

The Malcolm farm sprawled across gentle green fields. A neat, two-story house and barn and general store dotted the landscape. There were tables and a wooden platform in the apple orchard. Folks were milling around, drinking lemonade and fanning themselves.

Daddy tied the horses to the gate and helped Mama and me out of the wagon. I spotted a white-haired gentleman walking toward us.

"Good day! Welcome!" he called out. He shook Daddy's hand. "Good to see you, James."

"Well thank you, John. Good to be seen!" he answered cheerfully. "This is Mr. John Malcolm, father of the candidate," Daddy explained to us. "May I introduce you to my lovely wife Peggy and my daughter Lydia?

"Welcome, ladies and thank you so much for coming. I hope you will enjoy the afternoon here. Please, make your way to the refreshments," he invited, extending his hand in the direction of the orchard.

As we made our way through the cool shade of the apple trees, I saw John G. walking toward us. "Ah, the Renicks are here. Greetings!" He shook Daddy's hand. "Ladies, you're looking pretty today."

He was a sharp dresser, that was for sure. His brown hair was combed back and he sported a neatly trimmed goatee. He wore a dark blue suit, a round-collared shirt and red tie. I felt a tingle run through me when he took my hand.

"Why thank you kindly," Mama said. "Oh, James, there's Caroline and Frank over there. Would you please excuse us?" She took Daddy's arm and they left me and John standing there.

"Could I get you some lemonade?" he asked.

"Certainly, that would be nice."

He walked over to a long table topped with pitchers and glasses and poured me a drink. "What a fine dress you're wearing," he said, handing me the glass. "Do you do your shopping in Charleston?"

Shopping in Charleston was something well-to-do ladies of Nicholas did, not farm girls like me. "Uh, I have not been there in quite a while, actually," I said, hoping to sound appropriately vague about my big city experience.

"Well, I highly recommend a visit. The town has really begun to bustle since the war ended. Although there is still much rebuilding to do, the city is shaping up nicely. There is even speculation that the state capitol might move from Wheeling to Charleston."

"Do tell?"

"Indeed. And how convenient it would be, if I am fortunate enough to be elected sheriff, to conduct business closer to home. Traveling to Wheeling is quite a difficult undertaking without decent roads and railroads in such disrepair. Oh, but listen to me going on and on. This must be very boring for you."

"I agree, it is so important that we rebuild our community and have strong advocates representing us in the state capitol. I'd have more to add to this conversation if I were actually able to vote." John's hand jerked and some lemonade dripped on his waistcoat. "Where do you stand on giving women the right to vote?"

"Women? Oh, well, heh, heh, that's a very good question. I believe that might be a politically unpopular idea right now and we have such bigger fish to fry, what with putting the country back together again. But—*but*—and I say this with all respect, I firmly believe there are many women who have the intellect to vote."

"Well, it's nice to hear you say that," I said. "I hope you win, John Malcolm. Maybe you could use your considerable influence and standing in the community to put forth such ideas in the future."

He clearly did not know what to make of me and that pleased me, although I was absolutely drawn to him at the same time. He projected a kind of energy, a broad-shouldered, confident posture. But even confident men didn't always take kindly to outspoken women. I figured I had put him off by sharing my ideas on women's suffrage.

"Perhaps I should join my parents."

"Of course, by all means." He nodded and smiled. "Please do enjoy yourself. I will have to take my leave and address the crowd soon. Silly political stuff, you know. But I would very much like to continue our conversation. May I see you again?"

"Why, yes. Yes, that would be nice."

"Splendid," he said, softly, tilting his head ever so slightly as if he were admiring me on a museum shelf. "I shall follow up with a proper invitation very soon."

I excused myself and headed toward my family. *Maybe I hadn't put him off after all.* "You seemed to enjoy talking with our next sheriff," Aunt Caroline said as she pressed her cool hand to my cheek. Then my family chuckled

I let out a nervous little laugh.

****

Chapter Fifty-One

"Dear Josie,

I hope this letter finds you and your family well. You may have gotten a head start on me in the marriage race, but who knows? I might catch up with you.

I have found myself a charming suitor. His name is John and he is a real high-flyer. He is running for county sheriff here and I, of course, am supporting his candidacy, having attended many of his campaign speeches. He may well win and so might I.

Love,
Lydia"

By election time, John George Malcolm had become a regular Panther Mountain visitor. Our courtship was moving quickly. After a September supper with my family and a walk around back to look at the brassy leaves, he put an arm around my waist and leaned in to kiss me. I giggled.

"What's so funny?" he asked, looking bemused.

"Your beard is ticklish," I said, scratching my chin.

"Is it now? Well, my gal, you had best get used to it!" he said, dipping me down backward with dramatic flourish, and pulling me back up, close to his chest, for more kisses.

"You're a cheeky devil," I purred.

I had come to admire him long before Election Day. He was ambitious and energetic. He was a natural leader and knew how to negotiate and reach compromise with business partners and political rivals alike. He bought a patch of land from his father and began building a house on the Cross Lanes property. "I want it to be ours," he told me that cool autumn night. I sucked in a sharp breath. "Well, you'll have to ask Daddy first."

We went back inside and he asked my father for my hand in marriage. Later, under the lantern light on the front porch, he cupped my hand in his larger one and placed a gold band in my palm. It caught the light and shone like a star.

And on November 8th, 1866, I was officially engaged to a lawman. He had won the race. I didn't realize then what a high-speed gallop through thick forest our love would be.

Chapter Fifty-Two

Bethel Church, Nicholas County, WV, December 11, 1866

"Hold still, Liddy, I'm not done buttoning," Mama said. "I know you're nervous but settle down, please."

Aunt Caroline had loaned me her glamorous satin wedding gown. The buttons that ran down the back of the dress were tiny and plentiful.

Walking down the church aisle, clutching Daddy's arm, was like being in a dream. John looked so handsome standing there, smiling at me. Pastor Jordan, who had come to our circuit after the war ended, began to speak. I could barely remember my vows.

"Do you, Lydia, take this man, John, to be your lawful wedded husband?" I paused and realized everyone was waiting for me to speak. "I do!" I blurted out. I heard Grandma giggling at my slow response.

After the ceremony, the Malcolms hosted our wedding reception in their stately home. It really hit me then that I was marrying into some money, into a family richer than my own. I wondered how marriage would change me and how money might play a part. I said a little prayer that God would keep me the same person I had always been.

****

The kind of men we want for the Legislature, as well as for the other offices to be filled, are: First—Unconditional Union men, who have shown their faith by their works; who have been consistent in the adherence to that party and are still manifesting their devotion to that cause.

--*The West Virginia Journal*, July 11, 1867

Chapter Fifty-Three

Kessler's Cross Lanes, Nicholas County, WV, July 1867

In those first weeks and months of our marriage and my pregnancy, John and I were living with his parents. It was only a temporary arrangement until our house on a nearby property was finished, but it brought with it complications: lack of privacy, my mother-in-law's sometimes unwanted advice on child rearing, my father-in-law's habit of holding forth after supper, often to excess, on any number of political or social topics.

Soon after the new house was ready for us to move into, I went into labor. Our firstborn came into the world on a blistering hot July day. Mama, pregnant again herself, brought Mary Ann and Caroline along to assist with his birth. My sisters brought buckets of cool water from the spring and dipped cloths in it, wiping my forehead and arms as I sweated and pushed.

We named him Melvin Phoenix Malcolm. John was at that time enchanted by stories he had read about the Arizona territory silver mines and wanted to give our firstborn an exotic middle name that reflected the pursuit of precious elements.

The world slowed down in those first days of Melvin's life. I was completely infatuated with my first child, watching him as he nursed, as he slept. My heart was bursting with love for him. I was amazed by everything he did— his little smiles (Mama said they were likely gas, but I didn't care), his tiny fingers opening and closing, tiny toes flexing.

In those early days of motherhood, I was short on sleep and feeling isolated. My mother-in-law suggested I hire a nanny, but I bristled at the idea. Although I was new at mothering, I had helped raise my own brother and sisters, so I knew a thing or two about babies. Now and then, my aunts and cousins would drop in to visit, bringing me baby quilts and bits of motherly wisdom. *Don't let him sleep on his stomach*, one would caution. *He'll probably sleep better on his stomach*, another chipped in. *He'll let you know when he's hungry. Don't wait too long between feedings.*

I wished John had had more time to spend with our newborn boy, but soon after Melvin was born, he was on his way to Wheeling in his official capacity as sheriff. He went asked the legislature to suspend county tax collection for the last year of the war. So many Nicholas Countians had fled, abandoning their homes that it was difficult to assess what had been for years empty properties, farms that did not yield the usual crops. Also, those who sided with the Confederates returned home hoping to find some peace and quiet, only to find that their homes had been confiscated by Union-backed authorities and they had nowhere to go. How were they to be taxed, let alone to be held accountable for property that was no longer legally theirs?

It was lonely when John was away, whether he was traveling or attending to county matters, law and order and all that. I was housebound much of the time, as young mothers are, trying to keep the baby and myself cool. I kept the curtains closed to keep out the sun. Sometimes on especially hot days, I carried Melvin to the spring house, where I would sit in a chair next to the shelves of canned goods and hold him, and he would fall asleep to the sounds of the gurgling water running beneath the floor.

One night, after I had put the baby in his crib, I went downstairs to do some unpacking. I carried a lantern through the hallways and found myself in John's study. I set the lantern down on his burly oak desk and sat in his thick leather chair, running my finger through the dust settled on the blotter.

I set about opening a box with a letter opener from the desk. I lifted out an accordion file and papers spilled out into the box. As I leaned over to gather them, I saw what looked like a receipt.

The heading read: **The Confederate States**

    To: John G. Malcolm

    Date: Oct. 26, 1861

    For wagon as Teamster for Army of Kanawha from 11 Sept. 1861 to date, 1 Month and 15 Days at $16.00 per month. Total: $24.00

    Received at Lewisburg, Va., the 16th day of January, 1862, of Major A.W.G. Davis, Quartermaster, C.S. Army the sum of Twenty-four Dollars and No Cents, in full of the above account.

            Signed,
            John G. Malcolm

It was John's handwriting. My heart beat fast and hard. The man I married was a self-professed, staunch Union man, loyal to the United States through thick and thin. And yet here was proof on paper that he aided the enemy.

How could he be an officeholder in a county where formerly disloyal citizens were barred from being elected or even voting? How could he have kept this a secret?

Why hadn't he told me?

****

Jo devoted herself to Beth day and night, not a hard task, for Beth was very patient, and bore her pain uncomplainingly as long as she could control herself. But there came a time when during the fever fits she began to talk in a hoarse, broken voice, to play on the coverlet as if on her beloved little piano, and try to sing with a throat so swollen that there was no music left, a time when she did not know the familiar faces around her, but addressed them by wrong names, and called imploringly for her mother.

--from *Little Women*, by Louisa May Alcott

Chapter Fifty-Four

Renick home, Panther Mountain, October 1867

"Sister is sick," Mama said, rings of worry around her eyes, when I arrived that fall day.

"What is it?"

"Don't know yet, but I'm going over to help with the young'uns. Could you make up a pot of chicken soup and bring it over later?"

"Of course." I put on an apron and pulled out the soup pot.

Mama called only one of her sisters "Sister." Caroline.

I learned from Mrs. White in the army hospital kitchen how to make good chicken broth, broth that was both nourishing and easy on soldiers' stomachs. I had memorized the recipe: Boil separated chicken joints in a gallon of water, skim the fat, add six crushed crackers and a cup of fresh milk, salt and pepper.

One of the few times I was on the sick ward was just before the hospital closed. There were very few patients left and most of the hospital workers had been let go. Mrs. Davis asked me to deliver soup to some patients who were sick with the flux. I held my breath as I entered the room, having been warned that the smell inside would be foul. The men were so pale, their skin parched, and they cried out for water.

After the broth cooled on the window sill, I wrapped the kettle and set it into a picnic basket. I carried it to Backus's house, hoping to find Aunt Caroline sitting up in bed, ready to eat. That is not how I found her.

"Liddy? Is that you?" she rasped. The room was dark, the curtains drawn.

"Yes, it's me, Auntie Caroline," I said, taking her hand. She was smaller, the skin of her face dry and taut, dark circles beneath her eyes, cheeks sunken.

She took a long breath in and spoke with difficulty. "I must look a fright." The words squeaked out of her dry throat.

"Shh, now, please don't try to talk too much." I smiled at her. "You are always beautiful. I brought you some soup, the kind we made for the soldiers at the hospital."

She nodded her head. Her dark hair splayed across the pillow like barren tree branches.

Mama came to the door. "Caroline," she said softly, "Frank is going for Doc Rader. He will have what you need to get back on your feet again."

Aunt Caroline's thin lips turned ever so slightly upward. "You all are..." she whispered, "taking good care of me. Better than any doctor could."

"I am going to get you a bowl of broth now," I said, squeezing her hand. "Don't run off now, y'hear?"

She squeezed her eyes shut. "Mm," she managed.

I lifted spoonsful of soup to her lips. She strained and stretched her neck up like a baby bird until she couldn't manage anymore, falling back on the bunched-up pillows. I wiped her mouth with a flannel and set the bowl down. I had just seen her, healthy, a week before. How quickly she had shrunk. I had to get back to Mama and Daddy's house to fetch Melvin, but hesitated to leave, as if my staying there could make her well.

I returned to my parents' house. Mama sat at the kitchen table, face buried in her hands. "Doc mixed up some powders for Sister. Said they usually clear up the flux. But...." She looked up at me and shook her head slowly. "Lucy is sick now, too."

****

Dysentery, or as it is usually termed in the country, Bloody Flux, is a serious and often dangerous disease, if not properly treated--often prevailing in certain districts as an epidemic; that is to say, extending generally over the country, frequently attacking several members of the same family. It is a disease that is not likely to disappear of itself, and very often proves fatal; yet, if properly treated--which may easily be done--it is one of the easiest diseases cured in the world!

--Gunn's New Domestic Physician, or Home Book of Health

****

All doctors have to put on a bold front...I am not ashamed to confess that I do not know it all. Probably never will. I do try to use the best things and methods that rational science has to offer. All medicine has much yet to learn.

--diary of Dr. Amos Betterman, Northeast Ohio country doctor, 1868

Chapter Fifty-Five

Malcolm home, Kessler's Cross Lanes, October 14, 1867

I paced back and forth across the parlor, rocking Melvin in a baby sling, hoping he would fall asleep for at least a couple of hours so that I could get some rest. The day before, I had taken a shift caring for seven-month-old Rufus, along with his older brothers Adam, Billy and Bloomfield, while Doc and Mama tended to Aunt Caroline and Lucy. Doc's black leather bag was filled with elixirs, compounds, and powders. Mama ground up blackroot and golden seal, which Doc mixed with grains of morphine and gum arabic and then shaped into pills. Mama brewed flaxseed tea and kept bowls of warm water in the sick room, dipping and squeezing out flannel cloths to lay across the patients' midsections.

Despite Doc's best efforts, Aunt Caroline was getting worse. She was doubled up under the blankets, unable to lay flat. Her skin had a gray cast. Bedpans were lined up along the floor beside her bed, taken out carefully in hands covered with heavy leather gloves, emptied in the johnny house, rinsed thoroughly at the pump outside, returned, and taken out again.

Uncle Frank hacked away at logs on the stump out back, cutting away at his tension with every fierce swing of the axe. He read the Bible to his wife and daughter every morning and night, and prayed to God to heal them. He hired a woman to help take care of his young sons, hoping he could soon send her home and have his family back to normal.

I heard John come in through the back door.

"I stopped by the Backus' to see if I could help with anything," he said, taking his hat off.

"How are they doing?"

He shook his head. "Not well, I'm afraid. They've called for Reverend Jordan."

"Oh no..." I stopped in the middle of the room. "I must go..."

John held up his palm. "No, darling. No. I think it's best if you don't. She's...not...really there."

"Not really there?"

"It looks like the end, I'm afraid."

I crumbled to the couch, cradling Mel's fluffy little head against my cheek.

****

Caroline Grose Backus funeral, Bethel Church, October 17, 1867

"Almighty God, we mourn the loss of our sister Caroline, but we rejoice in the knowledge that she is with you now in her heavenly home. Please comfort her husband and children, her mother and father, sisters and brothers, nieces and nephews. All who knew her will miss her kindness and faithfulness. We are comforted remembering that she knew Jesus as her Savior, and that she can now see Him face to face. In the words of the Apostle Paul in First Corinthians,

> *But now is Christ risen from the dead, and become the first fruits of them that slept.*
>
> *For since by man came death, by man came also the resurrection of the dead.*
>
> *For as in Adam all die, even so in Christ shall all be made alive.*
>
> *O death, where is thy sting? O grave, where is thy victory?*
>
> *The sting of death is sin; and the strength of sin is the law.*
>
> *But thanks be to God, which giveth us the victory through our Lord Jesus Christ."*

--Rev. Louis H. Jordan, Methodist Episcopal pastor

****

Kessler's Cross Lanes, W.Va.
December 1, 1867

"Dear Edgar,

I write to tell you about events of great sadness in our family. My beloved Aunt Caroline, my mother's sister whom you met during your time with us, has passed. I am at a loss for words to describe the anguish her death has caused for her husband and children, and of course, for me and my family. She fell ill in October. We were certain that her disease could easily be cured, with the right medicines and nourishment. Her daughter Lucy contracted the same illness shortly afterward. The doctor tried his best, and we all united to help, feed and comfort them and the rest of the family. But God had other intentions. Caroline went to be with Him on October 15, and Lucy followed, joining them in Heaven just ten days later. My Uncle Frank is left with four boys, one but an infant and the oldest having just turned twelve. Naturally, our hearts are broken. Please do keep us in your prayers, if you would be so kind.

I hope you and Eliza are well and that your farm yielded a plentiful harvest. We think of you often. Mama and Daddy send their best wishes, as does John.

I will write more later.

Fondly,
Lydia."

****

In 1865, during West Virginia's first election after the Civil War, voters selected a number of former Confederates for state and local offices. Though a "Voter's Test Oath," designed to eliminate those who served in the Confederate Army or who supported the Confederacy had been enacted in February 1865, election officials misunderstood or simply ignored the legislation.

Those who had been elected were required to take an oath that they had not served in the Rebel army nor had given aid or support to the Confederate cause. The legislature meeting in January 1866 would not seat some delegates and senators who would not or could not take the oath.

--excerpt from "Anthony L. Rader and the Test Oath: A Nicholas County Tale" by Kenneth R. Bailey

For two or three years, political matters in Nicholas County have been under the control of a few men from the North who have gone into that county claiming to be the only "loyal" people there, and of some influential ex-rebels who became Radicals when the Confederacy proved a failure. Of these two classes, one Captain [Thomas G.] Putnam from New York, and John G. Malcolm, formerly in the rebel service but now "loyal" sheriff of the county, may be taken as fair representatives...Malcolm and his deputies announced that no man who did not support the extreme Radical [Republican] ticket should remain upon the registration lists...

--*Wheeling Daily Register*, October 18, 1869

Chapter Fifty-Six

Malcolm home, Kessler's Cross Lanes, October 1869

John and I were having breakfast in the dining room when I finally asked.

"John, what is the meaning of this reference to you in the paper as 'formerly in the rebel service?'" Of course, I remembered finding the Confederate States of America receipt, years earlier, after it fell out of the folder, but I had never questioned him, being afraid to hear the answer. Now, the subject could no longer be avoided.

John looked up from his plate. "Oh, now, you know how those Democratic papers are. Just rags full of nonsense. They're sore about the election." He took a bite of egg and wiped his mouth with his napkin.

"Of course," I continued. "You couldn't have served in Ramsey's guard if you were in league with the Confederates, could you?"

"No, if that were true, they would sooner have captured me and sent me to Camp Chase than sign me up. You know that, Lydia," he said, one eyebrow lifted above his cold blue stare.

"So you're saying the newspaper is lying?"

"Please, darling, just ignore that news article. The Democrats can't stop fighting the war. They will say anything to get their voting rights back. To my mind, they don't deserve the privilege."

****

Notes from a Nicholas County observer

John Malcolm had good reason to discredit the newspapers. Letter-writers to the pro-Union *Wheeling Daily Intelligencer* complained that voter registration was being suppressed in Nicholas County. Supporters of Dr. Anthony Rader, Liberal, running for a seat in the West Virginia House of Delegates, alleged that their candidate actually was more popular and had more potential voters in the county than Radical Republican Thomas Putnam, an attorney and New Yorker who had recently transplanted himself in West Virginia.

The Democratic-leaning (and therefore pro-Confederate) *Wheeling Daily Register* published a statement of affairs in Nicholas, "which showed that a gang of scalawags and carpet-baggers, with this fellow Putnam at their head, were riding rough-shod over the people, managing [voter] registration to suit themselves, making a farce of election and taking fraudulent, if not forcible, possession of the offices of the county."

Putnam won the election. Soon after he began serving as a Nicholas County delegate at the State Capitol in Wheeling, land deeds revealed that he had friends in powerful places. He and Sheriff J.G. Malcolm were doing business together, Malcolm having sold Putnam 9,300 acres of land.

****

IV. Reunion

The years went by, but never without a letter or two passing between Miss Renick (long since Mrs. John G. Malcolm) and myself.

--Excerpt from *An Episode of the Battle of Cross Lanes*, by Edgar M. Condit

Chapter Fifty-Seven

Kessler's Cross Lanes, late August 1878

"Melvin! Please! Stop!"

My eldest had spilled an entire shaker of salt out on the dining room table in a long, straight line and was running his finger through it.

"But Mama, I'm building roads!" he answered, looking up at me, freckled cheeks flushed with excitement.

"Oh no you don't, not on my oak table," I said, waving a feather duster at him. "Now skedaddle!" He jumped down from the chair and ran out of the room. I sank down in the chair and stared at the spilled salt road, sweating and exhausted.

Mothering four active children and an infant meant I was tired most of the time, and in the summer heat, more than just a little aggravated when one of them made a mess or threw a tantrum. I was anxious to make sure the house looked perfect because soon, Edgar and Eliza would be arriving.

Edgar sent letters to me and Mama asking if he and his wife might come for a visit to mark the 17th anniversary of the Battle of Cross Lanes and the beginning of his friendship with the Renick family. We wrote back to say yes, by all means, do come, and Mama invited everyone on Panther Mountain, family, and friends, to an August 26th picnic in Edgar's honor.

I would have a chance to introduce Edgar in person to his namesake, my five-month-old daughter, Lydia Condit Malcolm.

Cory helped me wash, dry and iron my good linens and bedding for the occasion. She was tiny and quick, with a thick Irish brogue. I had hired her as our live-in servant after Blanche was born, and I don't know what I would have done without her to help with housework and taking care of the children. The Condits, traveling from their home in Iowa, would be staying for two weeks. Mama would host them the first week and they would stay at our house the second. I was anxious for everything to be perfect. It would be the first time I had seen Edgar since he, George and Fred left Panther Mountain, under cover of darkness, seventeen years before.

On the day of their arrival, John drove the carriage to the train station at Gauley Bridge to fetch the Condits. After dropping them off at Mama and Daddy's, he came home to get me.

"We were barely up the Sunday Road before your father met us on horseback!" he announced as he came into the parlor.

"That's grand," I said. "This is the first time Daddy has ever met Edgar. It doesn't surprise me he wanted to give him a warm welcome."

"Well, my gal, get yourself freshened up and we'll join them."

I was excited to see Edgar again and nervous to meet his wife. When we walked into the front room of my parents' house, the dashing soldier I fell for during the war was standing right in front of me, looking nearly the same as he had, except for a sun-tanned face and a few streaks of grey in his thick dark hair.

"Lydia," he said, arms open wide, and embraced me. "It is a delight to see you again. Your husband and father gave us a grander reception than General Grant himself could have hoped for!"

I laughed. "Well-deserved," I said. I turned to see an elegant, well-coiffed and dressed lady. "Hello, you must be Eliza. I'm Lydia. Welcome to Panther Mountain." Her auburn hair was caught up in a neat bun, her nails polished.

"Thank you, Lydia. Edgar has told me so much about you." She had the smooth fair skin of a woman who carried parasols with her everywhere she went.

Our guests sat and I brought out a tray of coffee and cookies. "What a long journey you have had," Daddy remarked. "You must be plum tuckered out!"

Edgar chuckled. "It was one of the longer train trips we have taken, to be sure, James. But the comforts of Pullman cars have greatly improved over the past few years. Now the cars have gaslights, fine dining, sleeping berths, and many other luxuries. You and Peggy really must take a train and come visit us in the Midwest!"

Mama sighed, "Oh, wouldn't that be wonderful, James?" She reached over and patted his arm.

Daddy nodded. "Would be quite an amazing adventure," he agreed. "But maybe a little dear for our budget."

"Well, Daddy, start saving those pennies now," I chimed in. "Our carriage trips to Charleston and back would be nothing compared to a trip on a fine locomotive! And think of how much of the country you would see."

"Oh my, yes," Eliza offered. "We were dazzled by the scenery, going from our flat lands through the river valleys and on to these majestic mountains. I've never seen the like."

We sipped coffee and chatted well into the evening before taking our leave. I found myself studying Edgar's face, looking for changes or features remembered. Still the same strong jaw, the warm brown eyes. He was handsome as ever.

John and I said our goodbyes and headed home in the carriage. "You enjoy his company?" he asked.

"Whatever do you mean by that?" I could feel a heat rising up from the small of my back.

"I couldn't help notice how you look at him," he continued, clearing his throat. "I'm sure you have some fond memories of the past."

"I don't know what you're talking about, John. I hope you're not insinuating that there is more than a friendly reunion going on here. We are *all* happy to see our friend, someone who did so much for our country, whom we were privileged to help in his time of need." I pulled a handkerchief from my purse and dabbed sweat from my upper lip.

It was dark, but I could see John's chin jutting out, lips scrunched. His voice was flat. "Of course. It has been a long time since you last met." We rolled along in silence after that, wagon wheels hitting every rut in the road, rattling me to the bone.

****

Chapter Fifty-Eight

Between the two families—the mother and daughter—we spent about two weeks, feasting on ripe peaches, fresh cider, fresh eggs, young chickens, etc. We spent the seventeenth anniversary of the Cross Lanes battle with the mother, and we slept in the identical "loft" of the old log cabin I had occupied when a soldier. On the anniversary day of the battle the family and invited guests held a picnic at the cave. During the afternoon we carefully removed the debris within this stone chamber to see what we could find.

--from *An Episode of the Battle of Cross Lanes*, by Edgar M. Condit

"Well, look what we have here!" Edgar cried out. He swept leaves off the cave floor with pine branches. "See what I've found!"

He stood up in the very cave where he and his comrades hid nearly 20 years before, and held up a U.S. Army bullet casing between his forefinger and thumb. "I recall that in absence of paint, we mixed the powder from a bullet like this one—maybe this is the one—with water to paint our initials on the ceiling." I looked up to see the evidence: "E.M.C." was painted on a rock overhang. And he had carved his initials near the opening of the cave as well: "E.M.C. '61."

Everyone from the picnic who had clambered into the cave broke into loud applause, claps echoing through the rock chamber. Friends and family turned the scene into a scavenger hunt, picking up peach pits and corn cobs from the cave floor, perfectly preserved since they were disposed of by the soldiers 17 years earlier.

We returned to the picnic, tables laden with every type of meat and vegetable and fruit. Sis walked up to Edgar and Eliza, carrying her chubby toddler on her hip.

"Who have we here?" Eliza cooed, her voice soft and warm.

"This is my newest baby," Sis answered, looking at his sweet face and smiling. She stuck out her hand to shake Eliza's. "Thanks to your husband, my name is Nora."

Everyone laughed and Edgar blushed a little. "Why yes, I've told you about Nora, darling. She was about two years old when I met her and she needed a name. I was honored to be asked to christen her 'Leonora.' "

"Mr. Condit, we still haven't come up with a good name for our boy here. Would you be so kind as to do the honors once again?"

Edgar looked at his wife and back at the baby. "Why....oh, my, I am so touched that you would ask me once again to do that honor! May I?" he asked, reaching for the boy and taking him into his arms.

"Well now, ahem...." Edgar paused, eyes glistening in the afternoon sun. He put his left index finger up to his lips. "I am thinking of names of my comrades and acquaintances...Martin? No, doesn't fit. Joseph? How about Eugene?"

"Yes," several voices cried out in the crowd gathered around. "Perfect! He looks like a Eugene!"

That is how my nephew Eugene Carlton Drennen got his name on that day in 1878.

Out of the corner of my eye I saw John pluck our baby daughter from her stroller. He carried her over to us. "To make sure that the friendship between the Condits and the Drennens and the Malcolms and the Renicks carries on to the next generation, may I present to you Lydia Condit Malcolm," I said, taking her from John. Edgar folded his hands as if praying and held them up to his lips. He smiled but did not say a word.

Before night fell, John took the children back home. I stayed behind at my parents' house. My sisters and I were putting away food and cleaning in the kitchen. Edgar climbed down from the loft and began gathering up dishes, scraping off bits of food. Eliza joined us in the kitchen shortly after. "*Well*, if I could only get him to help me with my kitchen chores the way he's doing here!"

After all was put away, the family began to drift into the front room. Eliza excused herself, saying she was still quite tired from traveling and would be going to bed.

I put the last dish in the drying rack. Edgar stood next to me at the sink and said, "I haven't seen fireflies like the ones on Panther Mountain since leaving here that night years ago."

"Why don't we sit on the back porch and watch them again? For old time's sake?"

We sat on a hardwood bench my Grandpa Grose had made. "I can hear the river," he said, inhaling the fresh evening air.

"Mm-hm," I said. "It's comforting. Always there."

"After everyone left the cave today, I went back with a hammer and chisel. Took me the better part of an hour, maybe more, but I added '78 to the 1861 carving."

"That's splendid! Well done."

"Lydia, I apologize for being tongue-tied earlier when you brought your baby over. I was overcome…with emotion. You see, Eliza and I …that we cannot have children of our own. So to know that there is a child, a beloved child, daughter of a dear friend, who carries on my family name, well…I am deeply touched."

Caught up in the moment, I took his hand and squeezed it. We sat there for a while, holding hands, and watching the lightning bugs rise up across the horizon.

Chapter Fifty-Nine

Malcolm home, Kessler's Cross Lanes, West Virginia, 1885

Years passed after the Condits' West Virginia visit but we continued to write letters back and forth and exchanged cards at Christmas. John was not eligible to run for a third term as sheriff. An end to his official duties meant I no longer needed to show up on his arm at every church bazaar and dinner while he glad-handed with potential voters. The visits to Wheeling on county business subsided; I had grown weary of them anyway.

My focus returned to the children and keeping our home. I sometimes helped out at the store, sorting mail and taking orders from customers. John was appointed Kessler's Cross Lanes postmaster and he continued to look for other ways to hold office, whether by political appointments or through his leadership in the Summersville Masons chapter.

I began collecting photos and pasting them into scrapbooks; it was a good way for me to preserve our family history. I spent hours positioning pictures on pages. There were numerous photos of John that told the story of his public service and business successes. One showed him in his sheriff's uniform. There was a carte de visite portrait of him, gold Masonic compass pinned to his lapel, his hair and whiskers white.

A newer album was filled with Maud's baby photos, taken at the Richwood Studio. A snapshot of Melvin, Chando, and Maxwell, dressed in Sunday best and posing next to daffodils on Easter before church. A portrait of Blanche and Lydia, posed next to me on either side of the wingback chair, taken by a traveling photographer.

I leafed through the pages from Edgar and Eliza's visit years before. John had photos taken of himself and Edgar as they toured the county courthouse, which was then John's domain and a place where he could show off his accomplishments. Eliza and I posed in front of the Hale House Hotel in Charleston, where we stayed overnight on a shopping trip. A street photographer captured us wearing jacketed silk dresses we bought at Frankenberger's and sporting broad-brimmed hats with feather plumes from Donnelly's Millinery.

There were photos of Josie and Charlie and their families. During my last visit to Gallipolis, Charlie and his wife Elise welcomed me to their home for tea. He had become quite a successful merchant and she was a music teacher. Their son and daughter were students at the colored school. Charlie amused us with stories about some of the characters who had been Army hospital patients, and I told them how Charlie's mother had helped me bring the kitchen thieves to justice.

I stayed with Josie and Alfred that trip. They took me to the Gallia County fair. Their three sons, who attended Gallia Academy, won a blue ribbon for their calf in the livestock competition, and Josie's needlework earned her a red ribbon. In addition to the agricultural exhibits, we attended a horse race, which of course put me in mind of Logan and how he would have enjoyed competing in such an event.

I bought a postcard at the fair that showed the hot air balloon ride. Looking at it brought back the sounds and smells of sawdust, cotton candy, popcorn popping, cows mooing, race fans cheering in the grandstand, cups of cool lemonade, colorful quilts on display. Mama loved county fairs. Perhaps I could bring her to the Gallia fair someday.

Blanche bounced into the parlor, breaking into my daydreams.

"Mama, could you put this ribbon in my hair?"

"Of course, darling." She handed me her mother-of-pearl handled brush. I gathered up a swatch from each side and wound an elastic band around to fashion a high ponytail.

My oldest daughter was quite my opposite. Where I had been a tomboy who had to be reminded to brush my hair or change into my good clothes, Blanche was very girlish, always careful about her appearance. She loved dresses, the frillier the better. "Pretty is as pretty does," I would say to her, but I never doubted that she was as sweet as she was beautiful.

"Will Daddy be here for supper tonight?" she asked.

"I hope so. He said he would try."

By the time the dinner bell rang, John was, once again, not there to eat with us. We had gotten used to his absences. To my way of thinking, he simply took for granted that I would be there to keep house, fix the meals, make sure the children did their homework. He believed he didn't need to show up for every supper as long as I was taking care of things. Now and again, he would compliment me on what a good mother I was, which sounded in my ears like an abdication of his responsibility as a father.

Blanche brought one of her dolls to the table and placed her in her father's chair. "Arabella can sit in Daddy's place until he gets home," she announced.

The next afternoon, I was adding more photos to albums when there was a knock at the parlor door.

"'Scuse me, Mrs. Malcolm?"

"Hello, Cory. What is it?"

She tucked a lock of red hair behind her ear. "A letter has arrived for you. It's postmarked from Chicago."

I tilted my head. Chicago? She handed me the envelope.

It was Edgar's handwriting.

> *"Dear Lydia,*
>
> *I take a few moments to write you a line or two about our new plans. I have traveled to Chicago on business and am also looking for a suitable home for Eliza and myself. I have found a buyer for the farm and my company has asked us to relocate here. They are expanding their fire insurance business and asked me to open an office. It will be quite a huge change for us, moving from farm to city, and no small city at that.*
>
> *I will write again after we are settled and send you the new address. I hope this finds you, John, and the children well and happy. Melvin must be 16 now, and Chando 14. My how time flies! Please give my warmest regards to your mother and father.*
>
> *Yours,*
> *Edgar"*

****

A not admitting of the wound

Until it grew so wide

That all my Life had entered it

And there were troughs beside—

A closing of the simple lid that opened to the sun

Until the tender Carpenter

Perpetual nail it down—

**--"A not admitting of the wound,"
by Emily Dickinson**

Chapter Sixty

Kessler's Cross Lanes, March 1893

Cory had gone to her bungalow; I saw light streaming from her window as I sloshed through the mud toward the house. I stoked the fire and hung my drenched cloak near the mantle to dry. The house was still, the way it always was when John was not home and the children were either studying or in bed upstairs.

John made himself known when he was there, pacing about, smoking his pipe, muttering to himself. I remembered he had a meeting at the Lodge that night, so I went straight upstairs, put on my night gown, and washed my face.

My hair was still wet on the pillow when I startled awake. John stood in the bedroom doorway, candle flickering in his hand. "Lydia, darling! Please wake up!"

"What? What is it?" I strained my eyes into focus.

"There is a woman in town, in labor, who needs your assistance. She needs a midwife."

"Why me?" I hadn't delivered a baby in many years. "There are other midwives around, or someone could call Doc."

"My dearest, please. The woman needs your help. I need your help. Because...because...the baby is mine."

I pushed myself up on one elbow and shook my head hard, to make sure I wasn't dreaming. "What did you say?"

"Please forgive me. God help me. The baby is mine."

I don't remember how, but the next thing I knew, I was galloping toward Summersville, gripping a lantern, through a raging thunderstorm. Rainclouds blotted out the moon. There was almost no light at all along the road, save for occasional slashes of lightning and weak lantern glow through windows.

An old lady in a ragged shawl waved me into a tiny, broken-down house. I heard the low moans of labor coming from a back room and headed toward it with my birthing kit. A young woman, strands of dark hair plastered to her forehead, heaved and sweated beneath a sheet.

222

I put a hand on her head. It made me sick to touch this girl who had bedded my husband. How could he *do* this to me? And not only do this to me, but ask me to *help* this adulterer?

My sense of duty overpowered my rage. I asked the old crone to bring me a bowl of hot water and towels and began my work, coaching breaths and taking the woman's pulse. "Bear down! Breathe!"

"Annie! Oh, Annie! Tell me you're alright." The woman's voice cracked.

Huff. Huff. "Yes, Grandma. I….am…." She then let out a howl.

"Oh dear! Miz Malcolm, how is she doing?"

She knew my name. "She's dilated enough, the head should crown soon if all goes well."

Another hour passed before the tiny head was visible. The girl bore down with all her might and the tiny, ruddy infant slid out onto the sheets. I wiped her off, wrapped her and placed her on the mother's stomach, fished through my bag for scissors and cut the cord.

"You are going to need a few stitches," I told her. I packed wet towels between the girl's legs and took the baby from her.

Tears streamed down my face as I cradled the newborn. Her eyes were open wide. They were typical dull blue newborn eyes. She was calm. I put the baby down in a crate I found in the kitchen which I fitted with a blanket to make it softer.

The mother's breathing was shallow and her heart raced. "My head, Lord Jesus, my head," she murmured.

I put a palm on her forehead, then placed a thermometer under her tongue and paced the room as I waited for the mercury to rise and stop—104 degrees. *Dear Lord, I have got to get this fever down. She is burning up. She needs to get well, to take care of that baby.*

I rubbed her reddened abdomen with turpentine and mineral oil, covering it with hot soaked cloth. I turned to the old woman. "Ma'am, please go for the doctor. I'll stay here with them."

The young mother either passed out or fell asleep and I checked on the baby, who was sleeping in the crate. I sat down next to it and must have dozed off, because the next thing I remember is John standing over me, dripping wet, eyes bulging.

"How… is… the baby?" he asked, out of breath.

"She's fine," I hissed. "Aren't you going to ask about your mistress?"

"Lydia. I know, I am guilty. I am so sorry…."

"Little late for that now, don't you think?" I snapped.

I'd never seen him frightened before. I took no pity on him and wished my angry glare could knock him down to his knees.

After some time, the old lady opened the door and Dr. Summers appeared. He checked the girl's vital signs and got to work stitching her up.

"You were right to treat her for childbed fever best you could," he said to me after we finished. "Can you keep an eye on her for the rest of the night? I'll come back in the morning to see how she's doing."

"What about the baby? She needs to nurse."

"Try your best to have the mother feed her. Prop her up and help her hold the baby."

My head swirled. *I have to stay here. I have to help her feed this illegitimate baby.*

A ray of morning sun shone through a grimy window. John and I had fallen asleep sitting up in rickety chairs, the old woman on the floor clutching a blanket. The baby cried and I picked her up, patting her back. The mother was breathing hard and very pale.

Doc Summers came back mid-morning and checked on baby and mother. "Her pulse is too weak," he said of the mother. She's not going to pull through, I'm afraid." The granny wailed.

****

"Find someplace else to sleep," I hissed, shoving a pillow and blanket into John's arms once we were back at home. I was not too weary to be furious with him.

"I...I hope you can somehow forgive me, Lydia." His sad, bloodshot eyes bore a hole through me. He turned and walked out of the room. I called out to Cory and asked her to pull the crib out of the attic.

How would I explain this baby? No one who had seen me in the past nine months would believe I had been pregnant. My children were old enough to know better. It would have to be a story of adoption, of taking the child in because her mother had died. I thought I would die of embarrassment if word got out that she was actually the product of John's illicit passion.

The mother's last name was Alden. The grandmother's name was Mae. We named the baby after her.

****

I am sure word got around, though I don't know how. Neither John nor I told anyone about the true circumstances of Mae's birth. But I saw the stares, out of the corner of my eye, when I was out pushing Mae in the stroller.

Maysie, by then a grandmother many times over, caught up with me on the sidewalk in Summersville one spring day. "Lydia! I hear you have some wonderful news!"

I stifled a groan. "Hello, Mays, how are you today?"

"Very well, thank you! I just bought more yarn for the baby blanket I'm knitting for my new grandbaby. Another boy, can you believe it?"

"Mm, well congratulations," I said.

She grinned, wiping a gray curl off her forehead. "So tell me, how did you come to find out about the baby? I hear her mother was very poor and might not have been able to care for her even if she had, you know, lived."

I cleared my throat. "I helped with the birth. A friend of the family alerted me, because of my midwifing."

"Oh dear, you must have felt just *awful* that you couldn't save the poor girls' life!"

"Well, she had childbed fever. There was nothing Doc could do, she was just too sick."

"I hear there was no husband," she said leaning forward, one eyebrow raised. "Tsk, tsk. Shame."

"I'm not entirely sure about her circumstances really…" My voice trailed off. "I must run, dear. Nice to see you!"

I knew the longer I stood there, the more she would question me.

****

SECOND EDITION

CHICAGO WINS

She Secures the World's Fair on
The Eighth Ballot

--Chicago Tribune

****

Built in 1892-1893 the Yale is a seven-story Romanesque-style brick and limestone apartment building.

Before establishing his own practice and designing the Yale, John T. Long had worked for Adler & Sullivan and W. W. Boyington, architects who had designed distinguished Romanesque style buildings. With the seven-story Yale building, Long and his client Edgar M. Condit departed from the scale of the two-story wood frame houses that lined suburban Englewood's streets. The jump in scale reflected something of the boosterish optimism concerning Chicago's possibilities for physical and commercial expansion on the eve of the World's Columbian Exposition. Condit placed 54 apartments on a piece of land that would have accommodated at most two single-family houses if built according to the neighborhood's prevailing pattern. The Yale was clearly visible from Condit's own detached two-story wood frame house that stood one block away, on Harvard Avenue.

--United States Department of the Interior, National Park Service, National Register of Historic Places Registration Form

****

Chapter Sixty-One

Kessler's Cross Lanes, WV, August 1893

Edgar's letter, which someone—John, I suspected—had been hidden under a postal scale, invited Mama, Daddy and me to come to Chicago, to visit the World's Fair.

I ran upstairs as soon as I read it and began packing.

"What will we do while you're gone?" John asked. "Who will watch Mae?"

"You'll just have to figure that one out," I snapped.

John had the first switchboard in the area installed in the store, but Mama and Daddy didn't have a telephone so I couldn't call them in those days. I saddled up Jonathan and rode up the mountain road to tell them.

Mama was sitting out on the front porch when I reached the house.

"You'll never guess what, Mama!" I called out, tying my horse to the post. I held up the letter. "Edgar wants us to come to Chicago!"

"What in the world?" Mama replied, putting her knitting down in her lap. "My land. Who? Who's going to Chicago?"

"You and me and Daddy! He is sending us the money for train tickets. He and Eliza would like us to come and stay with them and go to the World's Fair!"

She blinked hard, as if to check whether she was awake or in a dream. "You don't say? Wait until I tell your father!"

Daddy was pleased to have been invited, but couldn't join us since we would be traveling to Chicago at harvest time. We planned to head out in early October.

In the meantime, I read everything I could about what to wear and see and do at the World's Columbian Exposition.

****

Hints to Lady Travelers—How to Journey Comfortably

"What shall I take for the night in the sleeping car?" is by no means a superfluous question to the woman who proposes a trip to Chicago.

First of all, do not be afraid of too much hand baggage. In addition to the traveling satchel, which contains the small wares of daytime travel, a shawl strap or large bag to hold the larger pieces for use at night will save no end of annoyance.

-- Wheeling Daily Intelligencer

****

Chesapeake & Ohio Gauley Bridge Depot, October 7, 1893

Daddy drove us to the station. John had sulked so much about the trip, I thought it best that he not come along to see us off.

The three of us waited together on the platform. A chill ran through me as the train whistle blew off in the distance. Mama grabbed my hand and squeezed. "Can you believe it? This will be my first time on a railroad train!"

I laughed. Though John and I had traveled by rail, my dear mother had never set foot in a train car. Daddy patted her shoulder. "Easy there, Peggy," he said with a chuckle.

At sunset, the shiny black locomotive chugged into view. The brakes squealed, the pitch so intense we had to cover our ears. Daddy kissed us both goodbye. The conductor placed a wooden step on the platform and I held onto my hat as I climbed up.

Edgar had spent lavishly on our train accommodations. Highly polished overhead cabinets shone, reflecting dozens of brass-encased lights. A burgundy carpet lined the way to our private, well-appointed Pullman berth. Thick velvety seats pulled out into plush beds. Mama's eyes looked like they might pop out as she gazed at the royal compartment.

By the time we got to Chillicothe, I was weary. Mama, on the other hand, sat chin in hand, gazing through the window, transfixed by the sights along the Ohio portion of the C & O Railway. "Will you look at that?" she would say every now and then.

230

"Mama, how can you see anything? It's pitch black out there."

"Oh, but I can see into the windows of the houses. Those aren't lanterns they're using. These Ohio folks have indoor gas lights. You can tell. Very bright."

"Mm-hm," I replied, laying my head down on the pillow. My mind drifted as I pictured our West Virginia home, where candles flickered and oil lamps burned, but gas lighting and electricity were still a dream away.

"I don't think I'll sleep a wink until Chicago!" Mama announced.

Morning came and Mama was slumped in her seat, softly snoring. I had to smile. She was like an exhausted excited child. I draped my blanket across her. We were stopped at a station in Illinois. It wouldn't be long before we'd see Edgar and Eliza in Chicago.

Chapter Sixty-Two

Chicago, IL, October 8, 1893

A jaunty straw hat perched on Eliza's head, her blouse neatly tucked into a flowing skirt as she and Edgar stood on the platform waiting for us. He was grayer than last time I saw him, which made him even more distinguished looking. I touched my own graying hair and realized how much time had passed since we first met, at 17 and 21.

There were hugs all around. "I have come all the way to Chicago to see a man that can be grateful for thirty-three years!" Mama exclaimed. The Condits guided us through the bustling train station and onto the street where Edgar hailed a carriage.

Chicago sidewalks teemed with people, market stalls bursting with fresh produce. News boys wove through the crowds, hawking papers. Horses clopped alongside streetcars that streamed along electrified rails. We rounded a corner and magnificent Lake Michigan came into view, its shimmering waters slicing the horizon.

We arrived at their house, a stately wood frame home with a gabled roof. As Edgar helped us out of the carriage, he added, "Wait until you see our new apartment building! It stands but a few blocks from here, on Yale. You'll soon find out that our streets here are named for the big Eastern universities."

In fact, their street sign read "Harvard Avenue."

After Eliza showed us to our rooms, I took some time to freshen up, then joined everyone downstairs in the parlor. "Tomorrow may well be the biggest day of the entire World's Fair," Edgar told us. "It's Chicago Day, and most of the city's businesses are closing so that employees can attend. Have you ever been in a crowd of thousands of people before, Peggy?"

"Never. Not even close! I have been around thirty, forty, maybe fifty folks at a camp meeting."

Eliza brought in tea and pastries as Edgar explained how he came to purchase the land for the apartment building, The Yale, and how a famous Chicago architect designed it for him. It was seven stories tall and had an elevator that lifted tenants to more than 50 apartments, all designed to accommodate travelers from around the world who came to the Fair.

Edgar showed us an ad in the *Chicago Tribune*:

> To Rent—Elegantly furnished room in the "Yale," corner Yale Ave. and 66th St; all the latest and modern conveniences; café, etc.

"A café? I can't wait to dine there," I said.

"We'll have the chef cook our specialty for you, Lydia," said Eliza.

"Specialty?"

"Pork barbecue. Fresh from the stockyards right here in the city."

My mouth watered at the thought.

****

World's Fair Grand Columbian Carnival

The World United in Chicago

October 9th, 1893. Anniversary of the Fire.

Monster Concert – Grand Chorus – Most Gorgeous Display of Fireworks Ever Seen in America

Forming in its entirety the most significant and grandest spectacle of Modern Times

--Chicago Day Poster, World's Columbian Exhibition, October 9, 1893

****

The next morning, we gathered for breakfast in the dining room. Mama yawned again and again. "Please excuse me. I'm just sorry I couldn't sleep on the train. I'm plum tuckered out."

"Peggy, if you find you're too tired to go to the Fair today, I could escort Lydia while you stay home and rest a bit," Edgar said. "Eliza, you would be happy to stay here with Peggy, wouldn't you, dear?"

"Be *delighted* to, dear," Eliza answered with what looked like a forced smile.

"What say you, Lydia? Will you brave the sea of humanity with me as your guide?"

I nodded and winked. "I'm always ready for an adventure."

After breakfast, I grabbed my bag and hat and we were off. We squeezed into an elevated train car, practically cheek by jowl with fairgoers sprawled across leather seats and hanging onto straps as the car lurched forward. We arrived at the main entrance, the Midway Plaisance beckoning us with its turreted palaces, pagodas, and villages. In the center of the midway was a gigantic steel wheel with spokes, wooden cars hanging off it like jewels. The sight of it took my breath away.

"It's called the Ferris Wheel," Edgar explained, shading his eyes against the bright sky. "We must go up in it after dark and watch the fireworks!"

"How high up will we go?" My voice wavered.

"At least two hundred feet! That shouldn't be too much for you, my dear. Aside from the fellows of the Seventh Ohio, you're the bravest person I know," he said with a wide grin. He offered me his arm and we stepped forward, bit by bit, slowed by the crush of the crowd.

Before me stood whitewashed buildings whose columns and pillars lined a lake, out of which rose a majestic bronze statue of a woman, robed, a wreath around her head. She held an orb on which an eagle was perched in one hand, and a staff in the other with the word "Liberty" inscribed on it. Boats glided in the lagoon around her, American flags flapping in the breeze, and fountains spewing sparkling water.

There was a building for each state in the union and almost every country in the world. We climbed to the top of the Manufactures and Liberal Arts Building. The entire fair spread before us from our balcony perch.

Down on the fairway we saw bare-chested Samoan warriors and belly dancers seductively wiggling. We drank strong black coffee at a Turkish café as we watched Bedouins ride past on white-as-snow Arabian horses.

"You know, Lydia," Edgar said, taking a sip of coffee from a demitasse cup, "the fellows thought I was a blooming chump for letting you go all those years ago."

"Go *on*!" I said.

"I'm not making it up," he insisted. "Jud Cross...I don't believe you ever would have met him...he was wounded at Cross Lanes and then captured, was a POW before being recaptured by Rosecrans at Carnifex Ferry. We stayed in contact over the years and he visited us in Iowa.

"He gave a speech years after the war, a copy of which he sent to me. In the speech, he recounted my story about how a very pretty Union girl helped hide and feed us in the cave."

"Really?"

"Yes, really. He then went on to tell the audience about my return visit to the cave in '78 and that we visited 'the girl,' meaning you, who was by then the wife of a wealthy farmer. He confided to the group that he could not understand why I hadn't married you. He even told Eliza that story." Speckles of light, reflecting from a café chandelier, danced in his coffee-colored eyes.

I touched my cheek, hoping to somehow cool it down. "Well, I am so, um, flattered. Oh dear. I hope Eliza wasn't offended. I would feel terrible about it if she were."

He shook his head. "No, she was not insulted at all. At least I don't think so. If she was, she never said so."

"I suppose she could have taken it as a compliment, couldn't she? That you married her instead of me?" The image of me weeping on Aunt Caroline's shoulder after getting the news that Edgar and Eliza had married flashed in my mind.

He smiled slightly, looked down at the table. "My wife is a good woman and she has made a comfortable home for us. I suppose we'll never know what might have happened if you and I had made it to the altar together."

****

Starbursts sparkled in the night sky. We watched the fireworks from the Ferris Wheel, packed into a windowed, wooden car with dozens of other people. I was thrilled by the display, and that is the only excuse I have for what I did next. Way up high on the wheel, glorious flashes of light spilling through the stars. *I am just so happy to be here with him.*

And then, Edgar leaned in to kiss me. I kissed him back, and held that kiss for a good, long while.

****

Chapter Sixty-Three

He that covereth his sins shall not prosper: but whoso confesseth and forsaketh them shall have mercy.

-- Proverbs 28:13

Malcolm Farm, Kessler's Cross Lanes, March 1894

Jonathan's muzzle was warm against my cheek. I could see my breath as I sobbed in the cold barn. My horse's giant kind eyes were at once both comforting and upsetting, as I wrestled with the memory of my betrayal.

After Chicago Day, our stay with the Condits continued as if nothing had happened between Edgar and me. The four of us visited the fair nearly every day. We walked their neighborhood streets, marveling at the majesty of The Yale. Mama got her first elevator ride there, and the café barbecue was succulent. No acknowledgement of anything wrong passed between me and Edgar.

But it had. Months had gone by, yet I was still weighed down by my indiscretion. One could have argued that I was simply evening the score with John for cheating on me. But I couldn't shake the guilt. And that was why I saddled Jonathan up and rode to the parsonage in Summersville to talk to Reverend Beckley. I told Cory that I had some shopping to do in town, and that I would be having tea with Bethel's minister. In truth, he was not expecting me.

I ached to write a line to Edgar asking for his forgiveness, but I didn't dare commit the words to paper, for fear they would be seen by someone other than the intended reader.

Not that I thought John would really even care. Our lives had taken different paths, with him spending more and more time on managing the farm, store, and hotel, forming a railroad corporation, selling off parcels of land to lumber companies, and his continued flirtation with public office. I threw myself into my children's lives; traveling to Louisville to visit Melvin at medical school, planning Blanche's wedding, keeping the books for Maxwell's dairy. There were few times when my husband and I were even in the same house at the same time. I doubted that a single kiss at the World's Fair would have made him the least bit jealous.

But there was a sort of scraped out, hollow feeling that would not leave me be. I realized it would not go away without my confession.

Mrs. Beckley invited me into the parsonage and offered me a seat in the parlor. As I waited for the Reverend to come out of his office, I gazed at the many books on the shelf. *The Book of Common Prayer. A Form of Discipline for the Ministers, Preachers and Members of the Methodist Episcopal Church in America. The Official Recognition of Woman in the Church. Bruder Concordance to the New Testament.*

"Good afternoon, Mrs. Malcolm." The pastor's deep voice was a testament to his gift for public speaking. "What a pleasant surprise to have you drop by."

"Hello, Reverend Beckley." He grasped my outstretched hand. "I hope I'm not interfering with your work today."

"No, not a'tall," he answered. Fluffy silvery tufts peeked out behind his ears, the only hair on his balding crown. "Please have a seat. How may I be of service to you today?"

I pulled at my handkerchief and unspooled my story. I told him about my indiscretion and the deep sorrow I felt about it. He listened intently, nodding, pushing his glasses up his nose with a finger now and then.

"Reverend, I know that God is loving and forgiving. Could it be, though, that I have done something so horrible that He will not forgive me this time?"

"Lydia, do you believe that Jesus Christ is the son of God?"

"Of course."

"And do you believe that Christ died on the cross for all of us, to wash away all of our sins with his shed blood?"

I nodded. "Yes, I have always believed that."

238

"Alright. And are you familiar with the scripture from the book of Matthew in which Peter asks Jesus about the precise number of times he should forgive his brother for his sin, and Jesus tells him to forgive seventy times seven?"

"I memorized that in Sunday School when I was a little girl."

"If we humans are told to forgive seventy times seven, how many more times will God forgive us? I hope you see my point."

I looked down at the floor.

"Lydia, if you ask God to forgive you—for this or any of your sins—knowing in your heart that He sent His only Son, who died and was buried and rose again to life to be the sacrifice for us, then He will surely forgive you. The Bible tells us so."

I felt a little lighter after he said that, but another question still nagged at me. "Does God require me to go to my husband and confess and ask for his forgiveness?"

"James 5 does tell us to confess our faults one to another. But are you hoping that by confessing the act, you will absolve yourself from guilt? Or is your motivation to let him know you have gotten even with him, so to speak?"

"I suppose that is my motivation."

"Wouldn't the act of confession, then, be a second selfish act to the first one?"

I rocked back and forth a bit, nodding. "Thank you, Reverend Beckley. I am grateful to you for your wisdom. I still have much thinking to do."

Chapter Sixty-Four

John and I stayed together because of our religious beliefs. Divorce was out of the question. We both stayed busy and presented a united front in parenting and in front of the community.

At the dawn of the new century, I had much to be grateful for. Kelly, Maude, and Mae were still under our roof. I can honestly say that bringing Mae into our family was a good thing. She was sweet and kind and helpful. When she was old enough to decide, she took the Malcolm name. She was among the first class to graduate from the new Summersville High School; the cornerstone of the building had been laid by John and fellow Masons.

The store and hotel were both doing a good business, as was the farm. Lumber companies began buying up land in Nicholas County and we profited handsomely from sales of property and mineral rights. Financially, we wanted for nothing.

The new inventions of the early 1900s changed our lives for the better. Our wagons and carriages were replaced with automobiles. Edison's electricity lit up more and more cities. Theaters that hosted live entertainment added moving pictures to their schedules. Two brothers proved that man could fly through the air in a gasoline-powered glider.

There were tragic events as well, to be sure. President McKinley was assassinated. A terrible hurricane devastated Galveston, Texas, and in the years following, the great city of San Francisco was shaken by a deadly earthquake. In West Virginia, a coal mine explosion killed more than 350 men. Unrest in Europe rumbled into a roar, headlong into a world war.

Through it all, though, my faith grew and helped me keep my sorrows and fears in perspective. I confess my relationship with God was tested when Mama died in 1906. I was quite angry when He took her from us, and the following year, while my grief was still fresh, Daddy passed away.

As for Edgar and Eliza, we were never able to schedule another visit, either in West Virginia or Illinois. They sold their Chicago home, spent two years traveling around the world and retired to Daytona Beach, Florida.

Edgar wrote a book about their journeys and it was well-received by critics from New York to Los Angeles. The book's dedication was especially touching:

Out of a grateful memory the author desires to dedicate this volume to two friends who materially assisted Providence in saving his life during the Civil War, viz: To Mrs. James A. Renick, of Cross Lanes, W.Va., who secreted and fed him in a cave for two weeks and thus saved him from the horrors of a Confederate prison, and to his comrade and "bunkmate" M.M. Andrews, now of Bay City, Mich., who, at a later period, gave to him not less than a mother's care and love during a long siege of typhoid fever in an army hospital.

VI.

Blanche's Story

March 15, 1920

"Dear Mrs. Condit,

I am writing to inform you of my mother's passing. Knowing how firm a friendship you and your husband shared with her and our whole family, I wanted to be the first to tell you.

Mother had just been here for a visit and we had talked about you, wondering how you were doing in Florida and enjoying the memories of the most juicy, delicious oranges you sent us from your grove. After she returned home, Mother became ill. My husband, who is a physician, diagnosed influenza. She suffered for about a week before she died. We are all, of course, heartbroken.

You and your husband knew her as a friend, and I also wanted you to know what a great mother she was. She raised us all, oftentimes by herself when my father was away on business, to be good Christians and productive citizens. You may know that two of my brothers are prominent doctors. Melvin is the smallpox doctor for Kanawha County, a county commissioner and responsible for many miles of road improvement in West Virginia. Chando is a physician practicing in Huntington and a member of the Good Roads Committee. Maxwell Kelly, or Kelly as we call him, continues to farm as well as staying active in local politics and serving on the state board of agriculture. My sisters Lydia and Maude are happily raising their families, as am I, and our adopted sister Mae is married and living in Charleston.

Praise God, Kelly and two of my nephews did not have to fight in the World War. Sadly, my nephew George succumbed to the Spanish flu in 1918. He was only 25 years old.

We were very sad to hear of Mr. Condit's death two years ago. Although I was quite young, I do remember meeting him when the two of you came back to West Virginia and visited the cave where he and the other two soldiers hid during the war. We are very grateful not only for his service to the Union but for his and your steadfast friendship and generosity toward the Renicks and Malcolms.

I hope this letter finds you well. May God richly bless you.

Yours truly,
Blanche M. Coleman"

Epilogue

Panther Mountain: Lydia's Story is a work of historical fiction. Much of the story is factually true, but parts of it are the inventions of my imagination, based on historic accounts of the Renick family's life, conditions during those times in history and bits of information gleaned from genealogy websites.

Lydia Jane Renick Malcolm was my first cousin, three times removed. Her mother, Margaret Grose Renick, was my great-great-aunt and sister to not one but two of my great-great-grandmothers, Caroline Grose Backus and Mary Ann Grose Backus. I happened upon her story while writing my first book, *Panther Mountain: Caroline's Story*.

I am grateful to the soldiers of the Seventh Ohio Volunteer Infantry, because without their letters and journals about their time in western Virginia (later West Virginia), I would not have known just how much my ancestors supported them in particular and the Union in general. Most of my Civil War-era family members were Methodist Episcopalians who sided with the North when that denomination split in 1844 over the question of slavery. Due to their great faith and service to their church, they were in favor of freeing slaves and therefore supported the Union army and President Lincoln after Virginia broke away from the United States to join the Confederate States of America.

Edgar Condit was, in fact, helped by the Renick family during the Civil War, along with two other soldiers from the regiment. Condit wrote "An Episode of the Battle of Cross Lanes," which is Chapter 15 of a book about the Seventh OVI, *Itinerary of the Seventh Ohio Volunteer Infantry, 1861-1864*, edited and complied by Lawrence Wilson, First Sergeant, Company D, and published in 1907. Edgar's recollections of how he and his comrades escaped to Panther Mountain after the Battle of (Kessler's) Cross Lanes gave me great insight into not only his time being hidden and fed with the help of Margaret, Will and Lydia Renick, but also the lifelong friendship that formed between the Condits and the Renicks. If not for his documentation of that friendship, I would not have known about their continued correspondence, the reunions over the years, and Lydia and Peggy's visit to Chicago 32 years after they first met.

As for the Renicks' exodus to Ohio, I found evidence that three children were born there during the Civil War: James Harry Pierson, who was the son of Mary Ann Renick Pierson and Jonathan B. Pierson, born November 2, 1861 in Jackson County, OH; Joseph Tyler Grose, son of Nancy Walker Grose and Covington Grose, born in Gallia County, OH; and James Edgar Renick, son of Margaret "Peggy" and James Avis Renick, born December 7, 1862 in Gallia County, OH. With those facts, I theorize that the Renicks and Groses settled in Gallipolis for the duration of the Civil War. The fact that they left Panther Mountain/Nicholas County for Ohio is corroborated through *A History of Panther Mountain Community* by Andrew Jackson Legg, and through Edgar's recollections. The journey of the rest of the family to join James Renick there is also documented by Private Daniel S. Judson in his journal, which I found at the Oberlin Heritage Center, Oberlin, OH.

An interesting side note about Edgar Condit's Yale Building apartments: The building is still standing (in 2019) on Yale Street, in Chicago's Englewood neighborhood. When construction was first completed, it stood just blocks away from the hotel built and owned by Herman Webster Mudgett, also known as Dr. Henry Howard Holmes, the notorious serial killer. Unbeknownst to Lydia at the time she and her mother visited the Condits during the World's Fair, Holmes was luring innocent victims to hidden passages and rooms in his building and murdering them.

Were there sparks between Edgar and Lydia? His writings and a speech made by one of his comrades in the Seventh OVI, Lt. Judson Cross, indicate that she was very pretty and he was considered unwise not to have married her or at least begun a romance. After describing his safe return to U.S. Army Headquarters at Gauley Bridge, Edgar wrote:

> If my story should stop here a very interesting part of it would remain untold. By this time most of my readers would say, 'Of course this writer afterward married the girl.' That is the way the novelist would have it, but I did not. Had she been agreeable to any such proposition, I could not have done so without breaking faith with an earlier young lady acquaintance; however, the deeds and heroism of this young lady and her mother were not allowed to perish from memory.

Malcolm Family photo, date unknown

Lydia Jane Renick Malcolm, second row, third from left; to her right, her husband John George Malcolm.

Photo courtesy of Kathy Garritty

Sergeant Edgar M. Condit

portrait found in *Itinerary of the Seventh Ohio volunteer infantry, 1861-1864,* by Lawrence Wilson, found at Internet Archive:

https://archive.org/details/itineraryofseven00wils/page/n557

Acknowledgments

I am grateful to everyone who helped me bring Lydia's story to print. I believe the story is stronger thanks to Vicki Entreken's careful consideration of plot and characters and useful editorial feedback. Sheree Wentz, a talented designer from West Virginia, brought Lydia to life for the book cover and was a pleasure to work with.

If not for friendships forged via Facebook, I would not have nearly as much Renick family history to help reconstruct Lydia's life events. Many thanks to Marsha Humphreys and Kelly Renick for sharing their family stories and genealogical research.

Through ancestry.com, I connected with Mel and Carol Malcolm and their help has been invaluable. Mel is Lydia's great-grandson and his was the last family to live on the Malcolm farm. I'm grateful to him and his wife for sharing what they know about Lydia and John and family. They also put me in touch with Kathy Garritty, Mae Marie Alden Malcolm Redmon's granddaughter, who graciously agreed to let me publish the Malcolm family photo found in this book.

As I did in the acknowledgements for *Panther Mountain: Caroline's Story*, I want to again recognize and thank my cousin, Kitty Harter Parkins Palausky, for keeping our family history alive and for the countless hours of genealogy research she has done over the years.

It was through the Oberlin Heritage Center, Oberlin, OH, that I found Private Daniel Judson's diary, which confirmed that the 7th Ohio troops did indeed re-encounter Lydia and her family along their journey to Ohio, and also provided additional supporting facts. Thanks to OHC Executive Director Liz Schultz and Collections Manager Maren McKee for guiding me to the right resources on my Oberlin research trip.

I needed to tap others' expertise when writing about horses and guns, two topics I am not personally familiar with. Thanks to Laura Lee Baldwin for providing me with information on horse care, riding and even a tour of the Virginia barn where she works and rides. Also, thanks to LL's mom Beth for her hospitality on my annual trips to the Richmond area, and to Suzanne Lysak, my dear friend, research road trip sidekick and the person who led to my friendship with the Baldwins.

I could not write accurately about Civil War-era firearms without Robert Busse's help. He has served as a gun expert and resource for both of the Panther Mountain books. He also happens to be married to my best-pal-since-kindergarten, Sara, so he's quite a lucky guy as well. □

I am grateful for the genealogical resources available through ancestry.com. fold3.com, and familysearch.org. Thanks also to the helpful librarians at the West Virginia Archives, the Library of Virginia and the National Library of Medicine's Special Collections in Bethesda, MD.

Selected Bibliography

Blog posts

Cowsert, Zac. "A Very Spicy Little Sheet": *The Knapsack*, A Soldiers' Newspaper and the Politics of War," March 7, 2016. Part of series, "The Civil War in the Press," Civil Discourse blog, found online at: http://www.civildiscourse-historyblog.com/blog/2016/3/7/a-very-spicy-little-sheet-the-knapsack-a-soldiers-newspaper-and-the-politics-of-war

Gale, Neil, Ph.D. "Chicago Day, October 9, 1893, at the World's Columbian Exposition in Chicago, Illinois." October 22, 2017. Digital Research Library of Illinois History Journal, found online at: https://drloihjournal.blogspot.com/2017/10/chicago-day-october-9-1893-at-worlds.html

Norwood, Karyn. "A Fond Farewell and Oberlinians' First Battle of the Civil War," 2011. Oberlin Heritage Center Blog, found online at: http://www.oberlinheritagecenter.org/blog/2011/08/a-fond-farewell-and-oberlinians-first-battle-of-the-civil-war/

Books

Ainsworth, Brig. Gen. Fred C. and Kirkley, Joseph W. The War of the Rebellion: A Compilation of the Official Records of the Union and Confederate Armies. Washington, D.C.: Government Printing Office, 1902. Google e-book: https://books.google.com/books?id=-9g4AQAAMAAJ&pg=PA267&lpg=PA267&dq=%22D+O+Kelly%22+Nicholas+County+Virginia&source=bl&ots=bp5mRXT21E&sig=_-LBh4he3q9fwnSS24QwgXlGh7Y&hl=en&sa=X&ei=IQHVVJ23BMuqNuGDg_gP&ved=0CCMQ6AEwAQ#v=onepage&q&f=false

Alcott, Louisa May. *Little Women*. Cambridge, Massachusettts: University Press, John Wilson and Son, 1880. Google Books e-book. https://books.google.com/books/about/Little_Women_Or_Meg_Jo_Beth_and_Amy.html?id=oTdAAQAAMAAJ&printsec=frontcover&source=kp_read_button#v=onepage&q&f=false

Atkinson, George W., A.M. *History of Kanawha County*

Ayers, Edward L. *The Thin Light of Freedom: The Civil War and Emancipation in the Heart of America*. New York, London: W.W. Norton & Company, 2017.

Barnes, Joseph K., et al. *The Medical and Surgical History of the War of the Rebellion (1861-1865), Volumes 1 & 2.* Washington, D.C.: GPO, 1870-88. Digitized books, both volumes, found at

Beach, Wooster, M.D. *Beach's Family Physician and Home Guide.* Cincinnati, Ohio: Moore, Wilstach, Keys & Co. 1859.

Beecher, Catherine E. *Miss Beecher's Domestic Receipt Book.* New York: Harper & Brothers, 1846. Digitized book found at Internet Archive: https://archive.org/stream/missbeechersdome01beec#page/n3/mode/2up/search/pickles

Brown, William Griffee. *History of Nicholas County, West Virginia.* Nicholas County, WV: Higginson, 1954.

Callahan, James Morton. History of West Virginia Old and New in One Volume. Chicago and New York: The American Historical Society, Inc., 1923. Digitized book found at Internet Archive: https://archive.org/details/historyofwestvir01call/page/n7

Callahan, James Morton. *Semi-Centennial History of West Virginia.* Charleston, West Virginia: Semi-Centennial Commission of West Virginia, 1913.

Cameron, William E. *The World's Fair: Being a Pictorial History of the Columbian Exposition.* Grand Rapids, Michigan: P.D. Farrell & Co., 1893.

Carroll, Lewis. *Alice's Adventures in Wonderland.* London: Macmillan, 1865. Original text and page images found online at British Library's Online Gallery: Virtual Books: http://www.bl.uk/onlinegallery/ttp/alice/accessible/introduction.html

Childress, Richard T. *A Historical Lottery: Europe to Appalachia and Beyond—A Ramsey Family Through 1500 Years of Social and Cultural Change.* Pittsburgh, Pennsylvania: Dorrance Publishing Co., 2016.

Clarke, Alan R. *The West Virginia and Pittsburgh Railroad: The B&O's Road to the Hardwoods.* Charleston, West Virginia: Quarrier Press, 2008.

Condit, Edgar M. *Two Years in Three Continents: Experiences, Impressions and Observations of Two Americans Abroad.* Chicago, New York, Toronto, London, Edinburgh: Fleming H. Revell Company, 1904. Digitized book found at Internet Archive: https://archive.org/stream/twoyearsinthree00condgoog#page/n0/mode/2up

Cox, Jacob Dolson, A.M., LL.D. *Military Reminiscences of the Civil War, Volume I, April 1861-November 1863.* New York, New York: Charles Scribner's Sons, 1900. Digitized book found at Internet Archive: https://archive.org/details/militaryreminiscen01coxdrich/page/n9

Crook, George, Gen. *His Autobiography.* Norman, Oklahoma: University of Oklahoma Press, 1946. Digitized book found at HathiTrust Digital Library: https://babel.hathitrust.org/cgi/pt?id=uc1.b4374641;view=1up;seq=9

Dickens, Charles. *Great Expectations.* Leipzig: Bernhard Tauchnitz, 1861. Google books e-book: https://books.google.com/books?id=rmNCV4VX_FAC&printsec=frontcover&dq=great+expectations+charles+dickens&hl=en&sa=X&ved=0ahUKEwi-_NTykJ7hAhWrY98KHcZ0DIUQ6AEILzAB#v=onepage&q=great%20expectations%20charles%20dickens&f=false

Dornbush, C.E. *Regimental Publications & Personal Narratives of the Civil War: A Checklist.* New York: New York Public Library, 1961-1972. Digitized book found at HathiTrust Digital Library: https://catalog.hathitrust.org/Record/007027136

Duncan, Louis Caspar, Captain. The Medical Department of the United States Army in the Civil War. Washington, D.C.: Surgeon General's Office, publication date unknown. Digitized book found at Internet Archive: https://archive.org/details/cu31924030749588/page/n3

Emmick, David J. *The Amick Partisan Rangers.* New York, Lincoln, Shanghai: iUniverse, 2007.

Grace, William. *The Army Surgeon's Manual for the Use of Medical Officers, Cadets, Chaplains, and Hospital Stewards.* New York: Balliere Brothers, 1865. Digitized book found at Internet Archive: https://archive.org/stream/62510310R.nlm.nih.gov/62510310R#page/n3/mode/2up

Graham, Michael B. *On This Day in West Virginia Civil War History.* Charleston, South Carolina: The History Press, 2015.

Grant, Ulysses Simpson. *Personal Memoirs of U.S. Grant.* New York, New York: Penguin Books, 1885. Google e-book: https://books.google.com/books?vid=ISBN0140437010&id=gxTEk8ZvFLoC&printsec=titlepage#v=onepage&q&f=false

Greenleaf, Charles R., M.D. A Manual for the Medical Officers of the United States Army. Philadelphia, Pennsylvania: J.B. Lippincott & Co, 1864. Digitized book found at Internet Archive: https://archive.org/details/62510520R.nlm.nih.gov/page/n3

Gross, S.D., M.D. *A Manual of Military Surgery*. Philadelphia, Pennsylvania: J.B. Lippincott & Co, 1861. Digitized book found at Jefferson Digital Commons, Thomas Jefferson University: https://jdc.jefferson.edu/milsurgusa/

Gunn, John C. *Gunn's New Domestic Physician, or, Home Book of Health*. Cincinnati, Ohio: Moore, Wilstach, Keys & Co., 1857. Digitized book found at Internet Archive: https://archive.org/details/63570990R.nlm.nih.gov/page/n5

Hall, Granville Davisson. *The Rending of Virginia: A History*. Chicago, Illinois: Mayer & Miller, 1901. Digitized book found at Internet Archive: https://archive.org/stream/rendingofvirgini02hall#page/n7/mode/2up

Hall, J.H., Ruebush, W.H. and Ruebush, J.H. *Crowning Day No. 6. (hymnal),* Dayton, Virginia: The Ruebush-Kieffer Company, 1904.

Hall, Susan G. *Appalachian Ohio and the Civil War, 1862-1863*. Jefferson, North Carolina and London, England: McFarland & Company, Inc., 2000.

Hawthorne, Nathaniel. *The Marble Faun or, the Romance of Monte Beni*. Boston, Massachusetts: Ticknor and Fields, 1860.

Hayes, Rutherford Birchard. *Diary and Letters of Rutherford Birchard Hayes, Nineteenth President of the United States. Volume II—1861-1865*. Edited by Charles Richard Williams. Columbus: The Ohio State Archaeological and Historical Society, 1922. Digitized book found at Internet Archive: https://archive.org/stream/DiaryAndLettersOfRutherfordBirchardHayesNinet eenthPresidentOfThe_657/diary_letters_v2_Hayes#page/n3/mode/2up/sear ch/Summersville+Virginia

Holland, Mary A. Gardner. *Our Army Nurses: Interesting Sketches, Addresses and Photographs of Nearly One Hundred of the NobleWomen Who Served in Hospitals and on Battlefields During Our Civil War*. Boston, Massachusetts: S. Wilkins & Co., 1895.

Jeffrey, William H. *Richmond Prisons, 1861-1862: Compiled from the Original Records Kept by the Confederate Government*. St. Johnsbury, Vermont: The Republican Press, 1893. Digitized book found at Internet Archive: https://archive.org/stream/richmondprisons00jeffrich#page/n3/mode/2up/sea rch/Atkinson's

Lang, Theodore R. *Loyal West Virginia From 1861 to 1865*. Baltimore, Maryland: The Deutsch Publishing Company, 1895. Digitized book found at Internet Archive: https://archive.org/stream/loyalwestvirgin00langgoog#page/n4/mode/2up

Larson, Erik. *The Devil in the White City: A Saga of Magic and Murder at the Fair that Changed America.* New York: Vintage Books, 2003.

Lesser, Hunter. *The First Campaign: A Guide to Civil War in the Mountains of West Virginia, 1861.* Charleston, West Virginia: Quarrier Press, 2011.

Lowry, Terry. *September Blood: The Battle of Carnifex Ferry.* Charleston, West Virginia: Quarrier Press, 1985.

Lowry, Terry and Cohen, Stan. *Images of the Civil War in West Virginia.* Charleston, West Virginia: Quarrier Press, 2000.

Mollohan, Marie. *Another Day in Lincoln's Army: The Civil War Journals of Sgt. John T. Booth.* New York, Lincoln, Shanghai: iUniverse, Inc., 2007.

Mollohan, B. Marie. *By the Banks of the Holly: Notes and Letters from the Desk of Bernard Mollohan.* New York, Lincoln, Shanghai: iUniverse, Inc., 2005.

Myers, S. *Myers' History of West Virginia.* Wheeling, West Virginia: Wheeling News Lithograph Company, 1915. Digitized book found at HathiTrust Digital Library: https://catalog.hathitrust.org/Record/008651594

Otis, George A. and Huntington, D.L. *The Medical and Surgical History of the War of the Rebllion, Volume 2. (1861-1865)* Washington, D.C.: Government Printing Office, 1883.

Parker, Granville. *The Formation of the State of West Virginia and Other Incidents of the Late Civil War.* Wellsburg, West Virginia: Glass & Son, 1875. Digitized book found at Internet Archive: https://archive.org/stream/formationstatew00parkgoog#page/n12/mode/2up

Reeves, James E., M.D. *A Practical Treatise on Enteric Fever; Its Diagnosis and Treatment.* Philadelphia, Pennsylvania. J.B. Lippincott & Co., 1859

Rice, Otis K. and Brown, Stephen W. *West Virginia: A History.* Lexington, Kentucky: The University Press of Kentucky, 1985.

Rucker, Michael P. *Bridge Burner.* Charleston, West Virginia: Quarrier Press, 2014.

Shurtleff, Brig. Gen. Giles W. *The Colors of Dignity: The Memoirs of Civil War Brigadier General Giles W. Shurtleff*. Edited by Catherine Durant Voorhees. Bloomington, Indiana: AuthorHouse, 2013. Google e-book: https://books.google.com/books?id=LLAqDv93A_0C&pg=PA7&lpg=PA7&dq =The+Colors+of+Dignity+Giles+Shurtleff&source=bl&ots=PSpZmnJcto&sig =CmbuvolMBqoj5BxnrEn1Wd-ALyY&hl=en&sa=X&ved=2ahUKEwia26v6jYTeAhVE1IMKHanHANAQ6AEw A3oECAgQAQ#v=onepage&q=The%20Colors%20of%20Dignity%20Giles% 20Shurtleff&f=false

Souder, Emily Bliss Thatcher. *Leaves from the Battlefield of Gettysburg: A Series of Letters from a Field Hospital and National Poems*. Philadelphia: Caxton Press, C. Sherman, Son & Co., 1864. Google Books e-book: http://bit.ly/2DYFfiT

Steiner, Paul E., Ph.D., M.D. *Disease in the Civil War: Natural Biological Warfare in 1861-1865*. Springfield, Illinois: Charles C. Thomas, 1968.

Stille, Charles J. *History of the United States Sanitary Commission*. Philadelphia, Pennsylvania: J.B. Lippincott & Co, 1866. Digitized book found at Internet Archive: https://archive.org/stream/historyofuniteds00stiluoft#page/n3/mode/2up/sear ch/Gallipolis

Taylor, Susie King. *Reminiscences of My Life in Camp with the 33rd United States Colored Troops Late 18th S.C. Volunteers*. Boston, Massachusetts: published by the author, 1902.

Washington, Versalle F. *Eagles on Their Buttons: A Black Infantry Regiment in the Civil War*. Columbia, Missouri and London, England: University of Missouri Press, 1999.

Whitehill, Alexander Reid. *History of Education in West Virginia*. Washington, D.C. Government Print Office, 1902. Digitized book found at HathiTrust Digital Library: https://catalog.hathitrust.org/Record/001065166

Wilder, Theodore. *The History of Company C., Seven Regiment, O.V.I., Volume 1*. Oberlin, Ohio: J.B.T. Marsh, Printer, 1866. Google e-book: https://books.google.com/books?id=HpZBAAAAYAAJ&printsec=frontcover& dq=Sargent+William+Parmenter+Parish+Prison&hl=en&sa=X&ved=0ahUKE wjA-dqJ183LAhUJqB4KHcpzAdkQ6AEILTAD#v=onepage&q&f=false

Wilson, Lawrence. *Itinerary of the Seventh Ohio Volunteer Infantry, 1861-1864, with Roster, Portraits and Biographies.* New York and Washington: The Neale Publishing Company, 1907. Google e-book. https://books.google.com/books?id=tBJCAAAAIAAJ&printsec=frontcover&dq=Itinerary+of+the+Seventh+Ohio+Volunteer+Infantry&hl=en&sa=X&ved=0ahUKEwif34OMwIHeAhUao4MKHccMBqgQ6AEIKTAA#v=onepage&q=Itinerary%20of%20the%20Seventh%20Ohio%20Volunteer%20Infantry&f=false

Wittenmyer, Annie. *Collection of Recipes for the Use of Special Diet Kitchens in Military Hospitals.* St. Louis, Missouri: R.P. Studley and Co., Printers and Binders, 1864. Digitized book found at Internet Archive: https://archive.org/details/63850820R.nlm.nih.gov/page/n3

Wittenmyer, Annie. *Under the Guns: A Woman's Reminiscences of the Civil War.* Boston, Massachusetts: E.B. Stillings & Co, 1895. Digitized book found at Internet Archive: https://archive.org/stream/undergunswomansr00witt#page/n7/mode/2up/search/special+diet

Wood, Major George L. *The Seventh Regiment: A Record.* New York: James Miller, 1865. Digitized book found at Internet Archive: https://archive.org/details/seventhregimentr00woodgeo/page/n5

Wright, G. Frederick, D.D., LL.D., F.G.S.A. *Story of My Life and Work.* Oberlin, Ohio: Bibliotecha Sacra, 1916. Google e-book: https://books.google.com/books?id=cr8EAAAAYAAJ&printsec=frontcover&dq=George+Wright+Story+of+My+Life+and+Works&hl=en&ei=TqnXTsLWLMf50gGHw9mYBA&sa=X&oi=book_result&ct=result&resnum=1&ved=0CDIQ6AEwAA#v=onepage&q&f=false

Catalogs

Centennial Catalogue Company. *International Exhibition 1876 Official Catalogue, Philadelphia, Pennsylvania.* Cambridge, Massachusetts: John R. Nagle and Company, 1876. Digitized book found at Internet Archive: https://archive.org/details/officialcatalogu00cent/page/n9

Woodhull, Alfred A., Assistant Surgeon and Brevet Major, U.S. Army. *Catalogue of the Surgical Section of the United States Army Museum.* Washington, D.C.: Government Printing Office, 1866. Google e-book: https://books.google.com/books?id=GPpAAQAAMAAJ&pg=RA1-PA93&lpg=RA1-PA93&dq=Assistant+Surgeon+Cuyler+Hospital+Germantown+Pa&source=bl&ots=FISPnH0zVV&sig=MwdaB8ZnfLw1rsEFtZ9zdPcSvEM&hl=en&sa=X&ved=0ahUKEwjOyJmq1M_VAhWD3SYKHWHVDKYQ6AEIMDAC#v=onepage&q=James%20R.%20Bell&f=false

Church records

Able, Augustus H., III. The Christian Recorder: The Holdings of Mother Bethel African Methodist Episcopal Church Historical Museum in Manuscript and Print. Mother Bethel African Methodist Church, Philadelphia, Pennsylvania, publishing date unknown. Digitized documents found at Internet Archive: https://archive.org/details/christianrecordephil_7a/page/n3

Databases

Civil War Genealogy Database, found online at MilitaryHistoryOnline.com: https://www.militaryhistoryonline.com/genealogy/ancestorcomments.aspx?id =6170&state=Virginia&type=4&rid=2659#a

Pierpont Civil War Telegram Series, 1861-1865. Digital collection, West Virginia University, found online at: https://civilwarwv.lib.wvu.edu/?utf8=&search_field=all_fields&q=

War of the Rebellion: A compilation of the official records of the Union and Confederate Armies. Series II, Volume II. Washington, D.C.: Government Printing Office, 1897. Found online in Cornell University's Making of America   Collection   at: https://babel.hathitrust.org/cgi/pt?id=coo.31924079570242;view=1up;seq=3

U.S. National Library of Medicine Digital Collections: https://collections.nlm.nih.gov/catalog/nlm:nlmuid-14121350R-mvset

Diaries

Daniel, Judson S., Private, Company C, Seventh OVI. 1861-1862. Oberlin Heritage Center Library, Oberlin, Ohio.

Dean, Otis, Company E, 56th Massachusetts Infantry. 1864-1865 (Ms2008-010). Blacksburg, Virginia: Special Collections, Virginia Polytechnic Institute and State University. Digitized diary found online at Virginia Tech Special Collections Online: http://digitalsc.lib.vt.edu/CivilWar/Ms2008-010

Warren, Leroy, Private, Company C, 7th Regiment, Ohio Volunteer Infantry. 1861-1862. Oberlin, Ohio: Oberlin and the Civil War Collection, Oberlin College Archives Online: http://dcollections.oberlin.edu/cdm/ref/collection/civilwar/id/78

Family Bible Records

Goshorn Family Bible Records, submitted by Rose Peterson, Bible Records
A-J, Vital Records, *Kanawha County, WV*, WVGenWeb and USGenWeb
page, found online at:
http://www.usgenwebsites.org/WVKanawha/bibleaj.html

Histories

Condit, Jotham H. and Condit, Eben. *Genealogical Record of the Condit
Family, Descendants of John Cunditt, 1678-1885.* Newark, New Jersey:
Ward and Tichenor, 1885. Digitized book, PDF format, found at Library of
Congress American Memory Collections Online:
http://memory.loc.gov/master/gdc/scdser01/200401/books_on_film_project/l
oc06/nov13batchofPDFs/20060927013ge.pdf

Journals: Medical

Abbott, W.C., et al, Editorial Staff. *The American Journal of Clinical
Medicine: A Monthly Journal Devoted to Accuracy, Dependability and
Honesty in Every Department and to the Safeguarding of the Doctor,
Volume 19.* Chicago, Illinois: The American Journal of Clinical Medicine,
Inc., 1906. Google e-book:
https://books.google.com/books?id=7JxEAAAAYAAJ&pg=PA943&lpg=PA94
3&dq=Oil+of+Turpentine+typhoid+fever&source=bl&ots=tSIF4UFB4A&sig=
bo3npdF3jaG3H-
MJpU9Z3_qD7EY&hl=en&sa=X&ved=0ahUKEwiKl5CW56TKAhXJFx4KHQ
ArC4EQ6AEINzAJ#v=onepage&q=Oil%20of%20Turpentine%20typhoid%20
fever&f=false

Ayeres, E.W., Publisher and Proprietor. *Confederate States Medical and
Surgical Journal.* Richmond, Virginia: Confederate States of America
Surgeon General's Office, January 1865. Digitized journal found at Internet
Archive: https://archive.org/details/confederatestate12conf/page/n5

Butler, S.W., M.D. *Medical and Surgical Reporter, Volume XI.* Philadelphia,
Pennsylvania: King & Baird, Printers, 1863. Google e-book:
https://books.google.com/books?id=zjegAAAAMAAJ&pg=PA77&lpg=PA77&
dq=U+S+Army+General+Hospital+Gallipolis&source=bl&ots=1qY-
BJ32_a&sig=4BPh0wzMGojax0v03a3xVaOrnxg&hl=en&sa=X&ved=0ahUK
EwjzitGD0q3ZAhWOu1MKHUb_DYwQ6AEIVzAH#v=onepage&q=U%20S%
20Army%20General%20Hospital%20Gallipolis&f=false

Edwards, Landon B., M.D., Editor and Proprietor, and Edwards, Charles M.,
M.D., Associate Editor. *Virginia Medical Semi-Monthly, Volume IX.*
Richmond, Virginia: The Williams Printing Co., 1905.

Fairbanks, A.W., Chairman, Printing Committee. *Sanitary Fair Gazette.* Cleveland, Ohio: United States Sanitary Commission, Cleveland Branch, 1864. Digitized journal found at Internet Archive: https://archive.org/details/sanitaryfairgaze11864unit/page/n5

Hare, H.A., M.D., Editor: *The Therapeutic Gazette, A Monthly Journal of General, Special and Physiological Therapeutics. Third Series, Vol. VIII, No. 1.* Detroit, Michigan and Philadelphia, Pennsylvania: George S. Davis, 1892. Google e-book: https://books.google.com/books?id=TFU9AQAAMAAJ&pg=PA368&lpg=PA368&dq=Oil+of+Turpentine+typhoid+fever&source=bl&ots=NRqTJ7h9CR&sig=SU3MlzWA58OU5HRpoqMf4XxHFhl&hl=en&sa=X&ved=0ahUKEwiKl5CW56TKAhXJFx4KHQArC4EQ6AEIJjAC#v=onepage&q&f=false

Smith, Stephen, M.D., Editor and Shrady, Geo. F., M.D. *American Medical Times: A Weekly Series of the New York Journal of Medicine, Vol. VI.* New York: Bailliere Brothers, January to July, 1863. Google e-book: https://books.google.com/books?id=K6hCAQAAMAAJ&pg=PA107&lpg=PA107&dq=%22Management+of+Military+Hospitals,%22+American+Medical+Times&source=bl&ots=83FT6D0w62&sig=IRuddKEu3fSOx0iderLwnJri6N8&hl=en&sa=X&ved=0ahUKEwiV0LDOy6fVAhXIWz4KHcN2A3UQ6AEINDAC#v=onepage&q=%22Management%20of%20Military%20Hospitals%2C%22%20American%20Medical%20Times&f=false

Surgeon General's Office. *The Medical and Surgical History of the War of the Rebellion, 1861-1865.* Washington, D.C.: U.S. Government Printing Office, 1883. Google e-book: https://books.google.com/books?id=3do5AQAAMAAJ&printsec=frontcover&source=gbs_ge_summary_r&cad=0#v=onepage&q&f=false

West Virginia Medical Society journals, 1900-1920, found at Internet Archive: https://archive.org/details/statemedicalsocietyjournals?and%5B%5D=%22west+virginia%22&sort=-date

Journals: Religious

Minutes of the Annual Conferences of the Methodist Episcopal Church, 1860-1862. New York: Carlton & Porter, 1860. Google e-book: https://books.google.com/books?id=iV7UAAAAMAAJ&pg=RA1-PA21&lpg=RA1-PA21&dq=Benjamin+Darlington+Methodist&source=bl&ots=xAYxOghwJy&sig=EifVUUEDdNkXjSFZAggkFYH3nMU&hl=en&sa=X&ved=0ahUKEwjbjPXAncvLAhXFSiYKHXXjB0QQ6AEILzAD#v=snippet&q=1863&f=false

Journals: State Government

Annual Report of the Adjutant General of the State of West Virginia for the Year Ending December 31, 1865. Wheeling, West Virginia: John Frew, 1866. Google e-book:
https://books.google.com/books?id=GghAAAAAYAAJ&pg=PA139&lpg=PA139&dq=west+virginia+deaths+typhoid+18**&source=bl&ots=wAEFDI0Wzq&sig=xdprFPvqiLAIfVMa_u0Fgbv3jyw&hl=en&sa=X&ved=0ahUKEwiYs8Kqp-bLAhVGKiYKHeRVC0kQ6AEIKzAD#v=onepage&q&f=false

Letters and Official Correspondence

Aleshire Family Letters, 1865-1883. Ms 4, Catherine Bliss Enslow Papers, Huntington, West Virginia: Marshall University Special Collections.

Carter, Charles B., POW, Letter to his wife Eliza Carter, April 26, 1862 written from Camp Chase, Columbus, Ohio. Found online at Valley Personal Papers digital collection, University of Virginia Library and Virginia Center for Digital History: http://valley.lib.virginia.edu/papers/A0100

Carter, Charles B., POW, Letter to his brother James H. Carter, April 26, 1862. Found online at Valley Personal Papers digital collection, University of Virginia Library and Virginia Center for Digital History:
http://valley.lib.virginia.edu/papers/A0101

Grabill, Elliott F., Captain, 5th US Colored Troops, letter to his fiancée Anna S. Jenney, November 28, 1864. Found online in the Oberlin and the Civil War Collection, Oberlin College Archives:
http://dcollections.oberlin.edu/cdm/compoundobject/collection/civilwar/id/136/rec/37

Grabill, Elliott F., Captain, 5th US Colored Troops. Letters, 1863-1865. Found online at Oberlin College Digital Archives: http://www2.oberlin.edu/archive/oresources/civilwar/grabill/album/indexGL.html

Jenney, Anna S., Letter to her friend Charles Bowler, May 24th, 1862. Found online in the Oberlin and the Civil War Collection, Oberlin College Archives: http://dcollections.oberlin.edu/cdm/compoundobject/collection/civilwar/id/143/rec/28

Moses, Charles, POW. Letter to his father, April 21, 1862 written from Camp Chase Prison, Columbus, Ohio. Found online at Valley Personal Papers digital collection, University of Virginia Library and Virginia Center for Digital History: http://valley.lib.virginia.edu/papers/A0102

Overall Family Civil War Letters, 1862-1866. Camp Summersville, Virginia; Camp Meadow Bluffs, Virginia; Christiansburg, Ohio; Camp Potomac, Maryland; Gauley Bridge, Virginia; Camp Crook, Charleston, Virginia; Carthage, Tennessee; Murfreesboro, Tennessee; Addison, Ohio; Columbia Furnace, Virginia; North Hamilton, Ohio. Found online at Overall Family Civil War Letters blog: https://goverall.wordpress.com/

Patterson, William T. Quarter Master Sergeant, 116th Regiment, Ohio Volunteer Infantry. Diary, April 2-9, 1865. Found online at University of Washington Digital Collections, https://digitalcollections.lib.washington.edu/digital/collection/civilwar/id/743

Shurtleff, Giles Waldo, Lt. Col., 5th US Colored Troops. Letters, 1863-1865. Found online at Oberlin College Digital Archives: http://www2.oberlin.edu/archive/oresources/civilwar/grabill/album/indexGL.html

Shurtleff, Mary E. Burton. Letter to her husband Giles Waldo Shurtleff, April 22, 1865. Found online in the Oberlin and the Civil War Collection, Oberlin College Archives: http://dcollections.oberlin.edu/cdm/compoundobject/collection/civilwar/id/197/rec/31

Stone, Lincoln S., M.D., Assistant Surgeon, 2nd Massachusetts Volunteers, POW, et al. Letter to Hunter McGuire, Medical Director, Army of the Valley, Confederate States of America, written from Winchester, Virginia May 31, 1862, where Stone and 6 other US Army Surgeons were held captive by the CSA. Found online at Ohio State University Department of History eHistory online collection: https://ehistory.osu.edu/exhibitions/cwsurgeon/cwsurgeon/release

United States. Army General Hospital, Gallipolis, Ohio. 1864-65. Correspondence, orders, rules and regulations. 1864-65. National Library of Medicine, National Institutes of Health, Bethesda, Maryland.

Van Derveer, Ferdinand. Correspondence, 1861-1870. Oxford, Ohio: Smith Library of Regional History, found online at National Union Catalog of Manuscript Collections: http://www.loc.gov/coll/nucmc/2014CivilWar/11_VanDerveer.html

Military Records

The War of the Rebellion: A Compilation of the Official Records of the Union and Confederate Armies (alternate title: *Official Records of the Union and Confederate Armies*). Washington, D.C.: Government Printing Office, 1880-

1901. Making of America digital archive, Cornell University Library. http://collections.library.cornell.edu/moa_new/waro.html

Newspaper articles

Huffman, Carrie Jo. "Nicholas County History Lesson". Transcribed from article published in The Nicholas County News Leader. Richwood, West Virginia: Jim Comstock and Bronson McClung, Publishers, 1957. Found online at The History of Mt. Outlook, WV blog: http://mymtlookoutheritage.blogspot.com/

Ruane, Michael E. "Rare Walt Whitman letter, written for a dying soldier, found in National Archives." March 9, 2016. *The Washington Post.* Washington, D.C.: Graham Holdings. Article online at: https://www.washingtonpost.com/local/rare-walt-whitman-letter-written-for-a-dying-soldier-found-in-national-archives/2016/03/09/6b172142-e228-11e5-8d98-4b3d9215ade1_story.html?utm_term=.e86ba1722b27

Special Correspondent to *The New York Times.* "From the Kanawha Valley; Advance of Gen. Cox's Brigade Precipitate Flight of the Rebels Burning of the Steamer Julia Maffitt Rebel Intrenchments Our Entrance into Charleston, &c." August 2, 1861. Up the Kanawha, Fifteen Miles from Gauley Bridge: *The New York Times.* Article online at: https://www.nytimes.com/1861/08/02/archives/from-the-kanawha-valley-advance-of-gen-coxs-brigade-precipitate.html

Pension Records

Auditor of Public Accounts, Confederate States of America. *1919 Roster of Confederate Pensioners of Virginia.* Richmond, Virginia: Davis Bottom, Superintendent, Public Printing, 1919. Digitized Roster found online at: http://sites.rootsweb.com/~vacfrede/rosterofconfede191921virg.pdf

Periodicals

Bailey, Kenneth R. *Anthony L. Rader and the Test Oath: A Nicholas County Tale.* West Virginia Historical Society Magazine, Volume XXVI, No. 2, Fall 2012. Found online at: http://www.wvculture.org/history/wvhs/wvhs2602.pdf

Cook, Roy Bird. "The Civil War Comes to Charleston." *West Virginia History Journal,* Volume 23, Number 2 (January 1962), pp. 153-167. Charleston, West Virginia: West Virginia Division of Culture and History, 1962.

Lady, Claudia Lynn. "Five Tri-State Women During the Civil War: Day-to-Day Life." *West Virginia History Journal*, Volume 43, Number 3 (Spring

1982) and Volume 43, Number 4 (Summer 1982), pp. 303-321. Charleston, West Virginia: West Virginia Division of Culture and History, 1982.

Howison, Robert R. "History of the War, Chapter IX." *The Southern Literary Messenger*. Richmond, Virginia: Macfarlane & Fergusson, 1863.

Stutler, Boyd B. "The Confederate Postal Service in West Virginia." *West Virginia History Journal*, Volume 24, Number 1 (October 1962), pp 32-41. Charleston, West Virginia: West Virginia Division of Culture and History, 1962.

West Virginia State Gazetteer and Business Directory, 1882-3, Volume II. R.L. Polk & Co., Detroit, MI and Phildelphia, PA, found on Internet Archive: https://archive.org/stream/westvirginiastat18821883rlpo#page/n3/mode/2up

Poems

Dickinson, Emily. "A not admitting of the wound." Amherst Manuscript #105, *A great hope fell.* Emily Dickinson Archive, Amherst College, Amherst, MA. Found at http://www.edickinson.org/editions/1/image_sets/240281

Rossetti, Christina. "Remember." *Goblin Market and Other Poems*. London and Cambridge: Macmillan and Co., 1865. Digitized book found at Internet Archive: https://archive.org/details/goblinmarketand01rossgoog/page/n74

Whitman, Walt. "Beat! Beat! Drums!" 28 September 1861. Ed. Susan Belasco, assisted by Elizabeth Lorang. *The Walt Whitman Archive*. Gen. ed. Ed Folsom and Kenneth M. Price. Accessed 4 October 2018. https://whitmanarchive.org/published/periodical/poems/per.00055

Whitman, Walt. "Oh Captain, My Captain." *New-York Saturday Press. Remembering Lincoln*. Web. Accessed October 21, 2018. http://rememberinglincoln.fords.org/node/517

Repositories

Hardman, Larry. *Home Camp of the Seventh Regiment, Ohio Volunteer Infantry.* Ohio State University History Department, Columbus, Ohio, 1999. Found online at eHistory: https://ehistory.osu.edu/exhibitions/Regimental/ohio/union/7thOhio/index

Songs

Hopkinson, Joseph. "Hail Columbia." The American National Song-Book, Songs, Odes, and Other Poems, on National Subjects; Compiled from Various Sources by Wm. McCarty. Philadelphia: Wm. McCarty, 1842. Found online at: https://www.bartleby.com/338/31.html

Speeches

Cross, Judson N., Captain, Company C, 7TH Regiment, Ohio Volunteer Infantry. "The Campaign of West Virginia of 1861," delivered to the Minnesota Commandery of the Military Order of the Loyal Legion of the United States, published in *Glimpses of the Nation's Struggle, Volume 2*. St. Paul, Minnesota: St. Paul Book and Stationery Company, 1890. Google e-book: https://books.google.com/books?id=cs8NAQAAMAAJ&pg=PA146&lpg=PA1 46&dq=JN+Cross+the+campaigns+of+west+virginia&source=bl&ots=ia60sU 0Dax&sig=qleATsvJBZfQxhWLqVqAmO1Bhcl&hl=en&ei=bKHXTuS0G6nV0 QHNruD4DQ&sa=X&oi=book_result&ct=result&resnum=4&ved=0CDIQ6AE wAw#v=onepage&q&f=false

Sherman, John. Speech on reconstruction and voter's rights. Circleville, Ohio, 1865. Reprinted in *The New York Times*, June 15, 1865. Found online at: https://www.nytimes.com/1865/06/15/archives/national-affairs-burdens-and-responsibilities-of-the-war-the-issues.html

Websites

New River Gorge National River, West Virginia. *African Americans and the Railroad: Gauley Bridge Depot, Gauley Bridge, WV*. National Park Service website, found online at: https://www.nps.gov/neri/planyourvisit/african-americans-and-the-railroad-gauley-bridge-depot-gauley-bridge-wv.htm

Ohio Civil War Central. "David Tod" (2019) Retrieved March 25, 2019, from Ohio Civil War Central: http://www.www.ohiocivilwarcentral.com/entry.php?rec=927

CHRISTY PERRY TUOHEY is an author and freelance writer. She was born and raised in West Virginia and her historical fiction books, Panther Mountain: Caroline's Story and Panther Mountain: Lydia's Story are based on real events in her ancestors' lives in 19th Century Virginia/West Virginia.

Christy is a 30+ year veteran of newsrooms and classrooms. She was a TV news reporter and anchor in markets including Charleston/Huntington, WV; Charlotte, NC; and Columbus and Cleveland, OH. Her writing has been published in multiple print and online newspapers and magazines including the Cleveland Plain Dealer, Pillars Magazine, Family Times Magazine and the Charleston (WV) Gazette.

Perry Tuohey taught broadcast journalism and was also the web content manager for the S.I. Newhouse School of Public Communications at Syracuse University.

www.ingramcontent.com/pod-product-compliance
Lightning Source LLC
Chambersburg PA
CBHW031106260626
47172CB00001B/238